HEADLINE MURDER

Superbly crafted and breezy as a stroll along the pier, this Brighton-based murder mystery is a delight. Headline Murder is the real deal, giving a wonderful insight into local journalism and capturing the swinging sixties to perfection. Bring on the next Crampton Chronicle.
Peter Lovesey, award-winning crime mystery writer

They say that if you remember the Sixties you weren't there. So if you fancy taking a trip down someone else's memory lane, you can't do better than Colin Crampton, crime reporter extraordinaire in Headline Murder. The clipped noir style of Peter Bartram's prose fits both the man and the times to perfection. The story is a real 'whodunit' in the classic mould. The characters and the city of Brighton leap off the page newly minted but feeling like old friends. And don't worry if you don't remember the sixties because you weren't even born then. There is none of the clunky scene-setting that so many writers find so necessary. Crampton takes you back effortlessly.
M. J. Trow, acclaimed author of 40 crime mystery novels

Headline Murder

A Crampton of The Chronicle Mystery

Headline Murder

A Crampton of The Chronicle Mystery

Peter Bartram

ROUNDFIRE
BOOKS

Winchester, UK
Washington, USA

First published by Roundfire Books, 2015
Roundfire Books is an imprint of John Hunt Publishing Ltd., Laurel House, Station Approach,
Alresford, Hants, SO24 9JH, UK
office1@jhpbooks.net
www.johnhuntpublishing.com
www.roundfire-books.com

For distributor details and how to order please visit the 'Ordering' section on our website.

ISBN: 978 1 78535 072 6
Library of Congress Control Number: 2015933326

A CIP catalogue record for this book is available from the British Library.

Design: Stuart Davies

Printed in the USA by Edwards Brothers Malloy

We operate a distinctive and ethical publishing philosophy in all
areas of our business, from our global network of authors to
production and worldwide distribution.

Chapter 1

The phone call that set me on the trail of the disappeared golf man who left his balls behind came one scorching Saturday afternoon in August.

I was sitting at my desk in the newsroom of the Brighton *Evening Chronicle* feeling like a barbecued steak that'd just been flipped on the griddle. The window was open and the high summer's heat oozed into the newsroom like boiled treacle.

I could hear a saxophonist playing a jazz riff in the Royal Pavilion gardens. Something slow and sultry in a minor key.

Even the long plangent notes seemed to be dripping with sweat.

I leant back in my chair, loosened my collar and tried to imagine I was Nanook of the North huddled in an igloo. But after a hard day, my brain was too tired to make the leap. The last edition – the Night Final – was on the streets and the newsroom was deserted. The other reporters had left for the beach. Or, more likely, the pubs. I should've joined them. I could almost taste the fizz in the gin and tonic. Hear the tinkle of the ice cubes. Smell the zest of the lemon.

But I had to work late. And the heat was doing nothing for my scratchy mood. My byline – Colin Crampton, crime correspondent – hadn't been on the front page for more than two weeks. Worst of all, Frank Figgis, the news editor, had started to hassle me about the dearth of hard crime news in the paper. As if he thought I was Mr Big of the Brighton underworld. What did he expect me to do? Stage a payroll snatch? Mastermind a bank heist? Order up a body thoughtfully bludgeoned with a blunt instrument?

I picked up the Night Final from my desk, turned to page fourteen. The best I'd come up with for this evening's paper was a vicar fined five pounds for cycling without lights. I was frustrated. Brighton's more imaginative criminals seemed to have taken a vacation along with everyone else. Except me. I badly needed a holiday.

But I needed a front-page headline – a splash – even more.

I put down the *Chronicle* and reached for my notebook. I flipped through the pages. Stared at my Pitman's shorthand. I willed the strokes and logograms, the dots and dashes to give up a story. Any story. But it looked as though the only way I was going to get a splash was to jump off the end of Palace Pier.

The saxophonist reached his crescendo. The last notes faded in the heat.

I tossed my notebook back on the desk, stood up, walked over to the window and looked out.

The saxophonist was putting his instrument back into its case. He took out a spotted handkerchief and wiped his brow.

Behind me a voice said: "'What is this life, if full of care, we have no time to stand and stare.'"

I turned. The poet was Frank Figgis who had materialised in the newsroom. He was a small man with a craggy face and skin creased with fine lines like worn leather. He had hard brown eyes and a prominent nose. He carved his shiny black hair into a strict centre parting with a tram line of bald pate down the middle. He had his jacket slung over his shoulder. His red braces hitched his trousers up so tight he always looked as though he was walking on tip-toe to avoid a painful injury. He smelt of Brylcreem.

I gestured at the empty room. "Let's forget about the staring and just call me the last man standing."

I crossed to my desk and sat down. "Or, in this heat, sitting."

Figgis perched on the edge of my desk looking like an emaciated vulture in search of a snack. He shook the last Woodbine out of his packet and lit up.

"I've got nothing to lead with in Monday's paper," he said.

"August is always a slow news month," I said. "The silly season."

"Don't I know it." He took a long drag on his cigarette. "Anything at this morning's magistrates' court?"

"Saturdays are always quiet," I said. "We were supposed to have gross indecency under the West Pier but the lawyer didn't turn up."

"Under the pier?"

"At the court. To defend the accused."

"Who was the dirty dog?"

"A beach-front photographer. Looks like he'd got the wrong idea about close-ups."

Figgis took another drag on his cigarette. "Might make a down-page par with a teaser headline."

Figgis had a penchant for headlines with dreadful puns. I could usually second guess what they'd be.

"Over exposed?" I said.

"No. Sign of the times," he said.

"As a headline on that story, it makes no sense."

"No, I mean the story is a sign of the times."

"Get with it," I said. "This is nineteen sixty-two, the swinging sixties."

"Doesn't mean you have to swing it under the pier," Figgis said. He rubbed his forehead as though he had a headache. The lines on his face looked deeper than usual.

Figgis was one of the old-school journalists. I suspected he still yearned for the days when respectable spinsters sent their maids out the room, drew their curtains, dipped a digestive into their Earl Grey, then drooled over a column of court reporting in which "intimacy" took place, preferably with the lights on.

He stubbed out his fag between his fingers and tossed the dog-end into my waste bin.

"Swinging or not, we need some hard crime news to boost circulation," he said. "Find something for Monday's paper. And make it a stronger story than a dirty old man with his trousers round his ankles."

He slid off the edge of my desk and headed back to his office swinging his jacket behind him.

"And, by the way, the headline on that West Pier story," he said over his shoulder. "Beach bum."

Figgis disappeared into his office. I thumped my desk with frustration.

And it was at that moment that my telephone rang.

I lifted the receiver.

A voice said: "Got a minute?"

It was a deep confident voice with a hint of rural Sussex in the vowels. It belonged to Ted Wilson. He was a detective inspector in Brighton's police force.

I said: "What's wrong with this town? It seems to have gone all law abiding."

"Yes. Great isn't it?"

"Not from where I'm sitting. Figgis and I have just been scratching around for a front-page story for Monday's paper."

"As it happens, I could have something that might make a column or two for your rag."

"I'm listening."

He said: "The owner of the miniature golf course on the seafront has disappeared."

"So call the Salvation Army. They deal in missing persons. I deal in hard news. When I can get it."

"So you don't want to hear what I've got to tell you?"

"There are only two types of missing persons," I said. "Those that are never seen again because they don't want to be found. And those that turn up of their own free will because they do."

He said: "You've forgotten the third category."

"You mean the ones that turn up again dead?"

"Yes."

"Is that likely with the disappeared golf man?"

"I'm not saying that."

"Has a crime been committed?"

"Not as far as we know. But we don't think he planned to leave."

"Why?"

"He left his equipment behind."

"Equipment?"

"His golf clubs. And his balls."

"That could be embarrassing."

Wilson said: "Are you looking for a laugh or a story?"

I said: "What makes you think this is worth even a column inch?"

"Because there's a backstory to it."

"Tell me."

There was a pause. I imagined Ted scratching his beard as he decided how to play it.

He said: "Perhaps we could talk about it over a drink. Let's meet later."

I said: "Not too much later. I've got a date this evening."

"Anyone I know?"

"Fortunately not," I said.

"How about seven o'clock?" Wilson said.

"Fine, as long as we don't take more than twenty minutes."

"Seven it is, then. The usual place."

"Discreet, as always. I'll be there."

The line went dead.

I sat there for a minute thinking that a disappeared golf man who'd left his balls behind would barely make a ripple let alone a splash for the front page.

Then I remembered what Figgis had said about finding a story by Monday, shrugged into my jacket and went out.

Chapter 2

Prinny's Pleasure was the ideal rendezvous for a clandestine meeting.

It was a run-down boozer in a modest street of terraced cottages in the North Laine part of town. The place had frosted glass windows and a door with peeling brown paint. A pub sign board hung from a rusting bracket above the door. The board featured a portrait of Mrs Fitzherbert wearing a bouffant wig. Or it could have been her own hair with a following wind.

More to the point, the place had hardly any customers, which suited Ted and me just fine. I pushed through the door into the bar. The room was an old-fashioned snug once patronised by Victorian gentry who thought themselves too posh to drink with workers in the public bar. Green flock wallpaper had turned grey. The place smelt of stale beer.

Jeff, the landlord, perched on a stool behind the bar. He was a thin man wearing a blue shirt at least one size too big. He had two-days of face fuzz on his chin and dirt under his fingernails. He was lighting a Capstan Full Strength.

I walked over to the bar. It was empty except for an ashtray of Jeff's dog-ends and a glass cabinet containing two cheese sandwiches and a dead fly.

I said: "Give me a large gin, small tonic, one ice cube and two slices of lemon."

He said: "Bleedin' hell. What do you think this is? A cocktail lounge?"

"I took it for a slop house that had gone down in the world but I thought I'd try and get a drink anyway. Still, I can always take my raging thirst elsewhere."

"Journalists! Full of backchat and bullshit."

Jeff grumbled something else in the same vein and slid off his stool. He grabbed a glass from under the bar and turned towards the optics.

The pub's door creaked. I looked round. Ted Wilson stood framed in the opening. He glanced back furtively, then hurried inside.

"Better add a large scotch to the order," I said to Jeff. "No ice. And don't be too quick on the draw with those optics."

Ted and I took our drinks to the corner table at the back of the bar.

Ted was a heavyset man with the weary expression of somebody who'd seen too many nasty things in dark corners. He was wearing a crumpled blue suit. He had a couple of Bics and a blunt pencil stuffed in the breast pocket.

He took a swig of his whisky and said: "That hit the spot."

I'd first met Ted shortly after I'd joined the *Chronicle* a year ago. He was a cautious copper who made sure of his facts. No shooting star, but he'd climbed through the ranks which can't have been easy in Brighton's police where funny handshakes often determined who got on and who didn't.

I swallowed a good slug of the G&T and said: "So what's the story with the vanishing golf impresario?"

Ted took another pull at his scotch. "You'll have seen the Krazy Kat miniature golf course?" he said.

I nodded. It occupied a hundred-yard stretch of the beach close to the Esplanade. I'd seen trippers tapping golf balls round the concrete fairways. It was the sort of thing holidaymakers do when they're bored or desperate.

Ted said: "Thursday evening, the desk sergeant took a call from the young lad who runs the ticket kiosk."

He flipped open a notebook. "Robert Barnet. Apparently, he's a student from London who's been hired for the summer season. Anyway, he was calling to report the Krazy Kat's proprietor missing. One Arnold Trumper. Hadn't been near the place for two days. Barnet says until then Trumper had been there every day, regular as a high tide. Barnet was calling because he was worried that if Trumper didn't put in an appearance on Friday he wouldn't get his week's wages. Which, as Trumper is still absent without leave, I'm assuming he hasn't."

"So why the teasing telephone call this afternoon?"

Ted took another gulp of whisky. "Two reasons. First, although we've noted the details, this isn't something we're taking too seriously at the moment. Trumper is an adult and he's only been gone four days. And there's no evidence of a crime. So the report is just a piece of paper in an in-tray."

"And the second?"

"That's where I come to the backstory. You see, Trumper has been involved in a police investigation before. His wife – Mildred, I recall – was murdered."

Ted picked up his glass and drained it. He put the glass back on the table with a flourish. Like a conjuror who's just pulled off a trick. Which I suppose, in a way, he had. He'd certainly surprised me.

I finished my own drink slowly. I needed time to think about what he'd told me. I signalled to Jeff to bring refills.

Then I asked: "When was Mildred murdered?"

"Shortly after war broke out. In early 1940, I believe."

"And you're suggesting there might be a connection between this murdered woman and Trumper's disappearance now – if he has vanished – twenty-two years later?"

"Not necessarily. It's just that Trumper is a man with an interesting past."

"But not a criminal record?"

"A man of good character, as far as we know."

Jeff shuffled over and thumped our drinks on the table. I handed him a fistful of coins.

I turned back to Ted: "So who murdered Trumper's wife?"

"That's where it becomes more complicated. You see, Mildred had been having an affair with a Reginald Farnsworth. He owned a small building firm – nothing fancy, more of a man-and-boy operation. Back in early 1940, Trumper had hired him to make some alterations to his golf course. One day Trumper found Reggie and Mildred in the little room at the back of the ticket office. You can guess what they'd been doing."

"Scoring a hole in one."

"If you're going to be crude about it. Anyway, Trumper threw Mildred out on the spot. He made it clear he'd finished with her for ever. At first, Mildred wasn't bothered. It seems she and Trumper had occupied opposite ends of the fairway for years."

"A loveless marriage?" I asked.

Ted nodded. "Mildred assumed she'd move in with Reggie. But there was a complication. It turned out that Reggie hadn't been entirely straight with her. He was already married with a young daughter. He'd been spreading his cement on both sides of the wall."

"So she was out in the cold."

"Not exactly. Farnsworth told Mildred that he'd leave his wife and find somewhere to live with her. So she found cheap lodgings in a B&B while she waited for Farnsworth to break the good news to his missus. But by the spring of 1940 the 'phoney war' as they'd been calling it became all too real. The Germans invaded Belgium. Farnsworth was in the Territorial Army and was called up for active service. It seems that what with going away to fight and the uncertainty of war, he couldn't bring himself to leave his wife and kid."

"So Mildred had burned her boats," I said. "No Reggie and no Trumper."

"Precisely. Mildred threatened to tell Farnsworth's wife everything unless he moved in with her – she sent him a letter saying as much. She obviously wasn't going to let her Reggie go without a fight. But Farnsworth's regiment was due to leave from Brighton station the day after he received the letter. In the letter, Mildred had threatened to come and wave him off and tell his wife about their affair at the same time."

"Vindictive," I said.

"A woman scorned," he said. "When the train pulled out, Mrs F and the kid were at the station waving flags. But there was no sign of Mildred."

"She was dead by then?"

"The investigating officers believed so."

"And where did they find her body?"

"That's it. They never have. There was a theory at the time that Farnsworth had buried Mildred's body on the Downs. A shepherd told the police he'd seen a van similar to Farnsworth's parked in a lane off the Fulking Road. But you don't need a body to prove murder. There was a search – as much as there could be in wartime – and the evidence pointed clearly to Farnsworth. He'd decided to stick with his wife through troubled times – and Mildred was threatening to scupper that for him. He had to silence her."

"So you arrested him?"

"No. Trouble was, by the time all this had been uncovered, Farnsworth was just outside Dunkirk. Part of the rear forces fighting off the German advance. He was killed in action – a hero by all accounts."

"But he never faced a court of law?" I asked.

"No. Nor the hangman's noose. But as far as the investigating officers were concerned, it was case closed. The war was piling up deaths by the thousands. They weren't going to spend time on one more."

"I guess he received his justice the hard way on the battle-field," I said.

I picked up my glass and swirled the drink round. The ice had melted.

"I'm not sure whether there's a story in it for us," I said. "Especially as we can't be certain that Trumper is the victim of a crime. But I suppose I could have a word with this Robert Barnet at the Krazy Kat. See whether there's anything he remembers which might give a clue as to why Trumper has gone AWOL. And where he is. If there is anything in it, the backstory certainly adds colour."

We drained our glasses. I glanced at my watch. I'd stayed longer than planned. And I didn't want to be late for my date.

"I'll let you know if I turn up anything," I said.

Ted said: "As it's Saturday, I think I'll stay and have another. And I feel a bit peckish." He nodded towards the bar. "I might have one of those sandwiches."

I said goodbye and headed for the door.

Wilson walked up to the bar and peered at the sandwiches.

As I went through the door, I could hear Jeff saying: "The fly? I wouldn't worry about that. It's only visiting."

"This Trumper guy sounds about as fragrant as a wallaby's bum."

Shirley Goldsmith came from Adelaide and didn't care who knew it. When she was roused, she had a voice that circled a room like a boomerang in the outback.

We were at a window table in the Starlit Room at the top of the Metropole Hotel. We could see the summer illuminations flashing their gaudy colours along the seafront as far as the Palace Pier. We'd eaten smoked mackerel, tournedos Rossini and Black Forest gateau. We'd drunk *Chateau Cantemerle*. We were lingering over the coffee and old Armagnac.

I said, *sotto voce*: "That's a sweeping judgement. You can't be sure."

Shirley turned up the volume: "Sure I can be sure. Stands out like a dog's balls. Didn't pay his worker's wages. That makes him as yucky as a dunny can."

A waitress at the serving station giggled and dropped a handful of knives and forks. On the next table, a fat bloke with side whiskers and a wine stain on his dress shirt chuckled. A dowager type across the room took out a compact and powdered her nose. It had to be at its best if she was going to look down it at a rough colonial.

I said: "I expect they can hear you at Ayres Rock."

"What do I care?" Shirley said.

She grinned and it was like the sun coming out from behind a storm cloud. Shirley looked like a model and spoke like a trucker. She had short blonde hair that curled round a face as perfect as a china doll's. She had blue eyes and wild lips and a lithe figure. She was one of those women who look beautiful but don't realise it. She was wearing a sleeveless black dress with a tiny silver broach in the shape of a koala bear.

Shirley was taking a year out to travel the world. She'd turned up in Brighton two months ago and was working as a waitress to finance the next stage of her trip. We'd been dating for six weeks and I hoped she wouldn't save the money for her next air ticket too soon.

I took a sip of my Armagnac. "Chances are Trumper will turn up somewhere, sometime with a perfectly ordinary explanation for his absence. Which won't suit me. Journalists aren't looking for the perfectly ordinary."

"I suppose you'd rather have him croaked and his body thrown down a mineshaft," Shirley said.

"There aren't any mineshafts in Sussex."

"Somewhere else then."

"Weakens the story. Dilutes the local interest."

Shirley spooned sugar into her coffee and stirred. "You journos are cynical bastards. Always looking for the angle. Never thinking about what it means for the poor mug on the other end of the story. How'd you get mixed up in a shonky game like that?"

"I put it down to a misspent youth," I said.

"Running wild in the streets? Like a dingo."

"No. Watching too many old films."

"How do you mean?"

I took a sip from my glass. "I think it was when I was about fourteen. I remember it was a wet Saturday night. We – that's Mum, Dad and me – were sitting round watching TV. There was some ancient movie playing. Made back in the 'thirties. I think it was one of the early talkies. It was called *The Front Page*."

"Not seen that on the square screen. Don't believe it's played in Oz."

"I don't think Mum and Dad were paying much attention. Mum was knitting and Dad was checking his pools. But I was riveted by the story."

"Plenty of sex and violence?" Shirley asked loudly.

The dowager type spluttered into her coffee.

I smiled. "Very little of either. It's a story about a journalist who's planning to quit the muck-raking newspaper he works for. He wants to get a respectable job and marry his fiancée. But he stumbles across a big story and it takes over his life. He can't resist it. And, of course, he has a crafty old editor who exploits his dedication."

"So he doesn't get the dinkum job? Or marry the girl?"

"That's right. But he does something that's more important to him. He writes a big story for his newspaper – a story that rights a wrong. That saves an innocent man's life. I can remember sitting on our old horsehair sofa and thinking 'I want to be like that'."

"Righting wrongs?"

I smiled and took another sip of Armagnac. "Why not? If there's the chance to do it. Trouble is, the only stories I seem to get these days are about dirty old men under the West Pier who can't keep their trousers buttoned or disappeared golf men who've left their balls behind."

"Sex and mystery – that's what interests the public," Shirley said. "Don't knock it."

"Sure. But what interests the public is not always what's in the public interest. There is a difference. If I'm to make a name on this paper, what I need is a story which makes a mark because it stirs up the town and gets under the skin of important people. Reveals their dirty little secrets."

"Makes a nuisance of yourself, in other words."

"You can't be a good journalist if you're afraid of being a nuisance. And, anyway, journalism should throw light onto the rich and powerful – especially those who like to lurk in the shadows."

"And that's important to you?"

"I guess so. A campaigning newspaper should seek justice for those who can't get it themselves. Does no harm to circulation either."

"More important than finding your vanished golf man?"

"Yes."

"Or wedding bells?"

"Hey, it's the journalists who are supposed to ask the questions." I picked up my Armagnac. "Shall we finish these and go on?"

Shirley looked hard at me. Her pupils dilated when she was suspicious. "When you say 'go on' do you mean 'on' as in your place or 'on' as in my place?" she said.

I grinned. "I was thinking your place. But I've got a golf-course assistant to interview in the morning. So there won't be time for you to bring me breakfast in bed."

Shirley finished her Armagnac. She put down the glass with exaggerated care.

"Do you know the big difference between Australia and England?" she said.

"No."

"In Australia, the sharks are all in the sea."

Chapter 3

The following morning, I battled along the seafront towards the Krazy Kat in a force-seven gale.

The weather had changed as swiftly as one of those new reversible raincoats I'd thought of buying in Hannington's. The thunderstorm had broken during the night. Now heavy grey clouds, like soggy wet blankets, raced through the sky. Summer bunting snapped in the wind. Last night's chip wrappings rustled along the gutters. Waves crashed and roared over the shingle. The air smelt like a fishmonger's slab.

But I was feeling good. So good, I'd even brought Shirley the full English in bed. With two eggs. She'd eaten the lot, then turned over and gone back to sleep. After a busy night, a girl needs nourishment and rest.

I trudged round the corner by the Aquarium and crossed the road to the Krazy Kat. It was closed. A blind drawn down over the ticket-office window announced the Sunday opening hours as ten o'clock to six o'clock. I glanced at my watch. Ten past ten. Not a good omen. Perhaps Barnet had done a runner as well as Trumper. The Krazy Kat was going to the dogs.

I decided to do a bit of reconnaissance. On the front of the building was a large painted signboard, faded with age, featuring a cartoon cat that looked like the character from George Herriman's comics that I used to enjoy as a kid. It was standing on two legs and holding a golf club. It was dressed in plus fours and a checked sweater. It had a baggy cap on its head. This was presumably the moggy that gave the Krazy Kat its name. I couldn't spot the logic of a cat playing golf. But then I'd never been able to understand the point of golf anyway. Who was it said the only trouble with golf is that it spoils a perfectly good walk? I couldn't remember.

I strolled round the ticket office to see whether the sides and back revealed anything. The place was larger than I'd expected – big enough to serve as a staff room and general store as well as selling tickets. It was built out of red bricks that had mildewed with age. There was one door secured with a heavy padlock. There were a couple of windows on the seaward side. The windows had crusted with salt and been targeted by seagulls. I peered through them. Inside, heavy net curtains hung with cobwebs. I couldn't see much beyond.

Beside the ticket office was a little wicker gate that opened on to what I suppose you'd call the golf course. I pushed it open and walked through. There were no fairways, sandy bunkers or well-tended greens. This wasn't the sort of course where you'd turn up with a mashie niblick over your shoulder. There were eighteen miniature fairways covered in some kind of green felt material that simulated grass. Each fairway was surrounded by a little brick wall. Some of the fairways had little hills, others sharp corners, one had a tunnel, another a bridge. The only thing the place had in common with a real golf course was the frustrating need to get a small ball into an inconveniently located hole.

I was thinking about whether to wait around to see whether Barnet turned up or slope off for a coffee when a voice behind me said: "Can I help you?"

I turned. The voice came from a short youth with a prominent nose, thin lips and zits on his chin. He was wearing a green windcheater and jeans.

He said: "Customers are not permitted to enter the playing area until the course is officially open." He had a high-pitched voice which couldn't quite pull off the commanding-presence bit.

I said: "I'm not a customer." I walked over to him, flashed a smile and added: "You're Robert Barnet."

He looked worried and said: "You're not from the police?"

I fished in my pocket, took out a card and handed it to him.

He took it as though I were serving him a writ, looked at it and relaxed a little. He said: "*Evening Chronicle*. The local rag. I suppose you want to talk about Mr Trumper."

I ignored the "rag" bit and said: "If you can spare a few minutes."

"I'm very busy," he said.

I looked up and down the deserted seafront. In the distance, a couple of figures in pac-a-macs huddled in a shelter.

"I can see you're rushed off your feet," I said.

He frowned. The zits on his chin jiggled into a surly arrangement.

"I suppose I could spare you a minute," he said.

We moved round to the ticket-office door. Barnet pulled a small bunch of keys out of his pocket, unlocked the padlock and we went inside. The room was small and smelt of dust. There was a door leading somewhere else – probably to the storage accommodation at the back.

Barnet said: "I considered becoming a journalist once, but there's no money in it." He started fiddling with a ticket machine and cash box, getting ready to open.

"But you decided to become a crazy-golf ticket man and get rich."

"Only for the summer. I'm at London University studying law. Plan to become a barrister. That's where you can make the big money. Especially company law. When large firms start suing one another you can really cash in."

"Very public spirited of you," I said.

"What's the money like at the *Chronicle*?" Barnet asked.

"Same as here," I said. "Mostly round. The bigger denominations are printed on paper."

He looked puzzled. Then he laughed, a kind of high-pitched croak. He sounded like an angry crow.

He said: "I get it. Mostly round. It's a sort of joke."

"Yes, a sort of joke. And this is a sort of golf course. Did Mr Trumper give you any indication that he planned to take a few days off?"

My sudden change of topic threw him off balance. The zits took on a worried formation. "I don't have to answer your questions," he said.

"Of course not. I could simply write, 'Mr Robert Barnet, a law student at London University, who is employed at the Krazy Kat golf course, was not willing to answer questions about Mr Trumper's disappearance.'"

"But that makes it look as though I've got something to hide."

"It's a factual statement which accurately reflects what you've just told me."

"I could sue you for libel."

"No you couldn't. You wouldn't have a case. And, even if you did, you wouldn't be able to afford the barrister. As you say, they make big money. Unlike golf-course ticket attendants."

Barnet slumped on the stool by the ticket window. The zits took on a defeated look.

"It's true this doesn't pay much," he said.

"Downtrodden workers, eh?" It was time to pick him up again and make him receptive to the serious questions.

"I need the money."

"Don't we all."

"My grant is very small. It doesn't cover my living expenses. Then there are the textbooks to buy. Law books cost a small fortune."

"So it's a costly course."

"I don't even think my earnings this summer will cover next year's expenses."

We fell silent. He seemed to be thinking about his money problems. I let him ponder that for a moment. He did something with the ticket machine. He was thinking about his next move.

Then the zits tried a smile and he said: "Have we got off on the wrong foot? Could we start again?"

"Let's do that."

Barnet said: "In fact, I've got an excellent idea. Let's talk over a round of golf."

The last thing I needed was a round of golf. In a force-seven gale. But, perhaps, Barnet would open up as we strolled round the course.

The wind had stiffened by the time we stepped on to the first tee. I put down my ball, took a generous swing with the putter and whacked it along the fairway. It bounced off the back wall and plopped into the hole.

"Hole in one," said Barnet.

"Pure luck," I said. "Tell me about Mr Trumper. Was he a good employer?"

Barnet put his ball down. "Don't have much experience of employers. But, yes, I suppose he was – is."

"And he had a regular routine?"

"Sure. Arrived every day before we opened. Stayed behind to count the takings after we closed."

"What are you doing about the takings now?"

"I count them and lock them in a strong box in the back room."

Barnet gave his ball a clinical tap. It rolled up the fairway, teetered on the lip of the hole and dropped in.

He grinned: "When we're not busy, Mr Trumper lets me practise."

We moved to another hole.

"Did Mr Trumper appear to have any financial worries?" I asked.

"I know he didn't."

"How can you be sure?"

"In the few weeks I've been here, I've become quite a confidante. I've been able to put him straight on a few legal points."

"I'm sure he appreciated that."

I stooped to retrieve my ball from a hole. It came out covered in green slime. I showed Barnet.

"Advise him to clean out these holes did you?" I said.

"Well, yes, as a matter of fact I did. They're supposed to drain away when it rains but they haven't been cleaned out for years."

"But he's not taken your advice."

"No, he said it wasn't worth the trouble."

We ploughed on grimly round the course.

"Could Mr Trumper be at his home?" I asked.

"I've called his home number twice every day. There's no answer."

"Where does he live?"

Barnet gave me an address in Woodingdean, on the outskirts of Brighton.

"Have you been there?" I asked.

"No. It seemed pointless as nobody answered the phone. Besides, I didn't want to waste money on the bus fare."

I scored another hole in one. Then said: "Got any theories why Mr Trumper has disappeared?"

"None. Especially now."

"Why especially now?"

"A buyer has made an offer for the Krazy Kat."

"And Mr Trumper is going to accept?"

"That's it. I don't think he is."

Barnet put his ball on the tee and did the Arnold Palmer bit. The ball rolled over a hillock and down a hole. I skirted a puddle and moved to the next tee.

"How can you be sure?" I asked.

"He asked me some general questions about selling property."

"But not specifically about selling the Krazy Kat?"

"No. You see, I don't think he knows I know he's had an offer."

"And how do you know?"

"A man who I think might be the prospective buyer came to see Mr Trumper a few days ago."

"Just before he disappeared?"

"Yes. They went into the back room and closed the door. I

think they thought they couldn't be heard but the walls in that ticket office aren't that thick."

"And you couldn't help overhearing the conversation?"

"Not all of it. But I did hear the man say, 'This is the best offer you'll ever get for this dump. Don't make the mistake of turning it down. Mistakes can be dangerous in your business.'"

"That sounds more like a threat than an offer," I said. "Did you hear what Mr Trumper replied?"

"No, he was speaking quite softly. I think he felt a bit – how shall I put it? – cowed by the other man."

I thought about that as we moved on to hole eighteen, the last one.

"How long were the two in the back room together?" I asked.

"About ten minutes. Perhaps fifteen."

"Did you hear them say anything when they came out?"

"The visitor just said, 'I'll be calling again.' Mr Trumper didn't seem that he was looking forward to it. In fact, he became quite jumpy after the visit."

I holed my ball. It splashed as it went in. The hole was full of water. I plunged my hand in and pulled out a snail. Barnet smiled sheepishly. Even the zits looked embarrassed.

"Sorry about that," he said. "That last hole seems to collect the water from the others."

He stuck his hand down and pulled out the ball.

"Who was this mystery man?" I said.

"I did ask Mr Trumper who he was."

"And what did he say?"

"Someone you don't want to know."

"So you don't know who he is?"

"Oh, I know who he is."

"How's that?"

"I was talking to Rocky Roxbury in the Fancy Rock Bazaar next door. He'd seen him come out of the ticket office and told me."

We struggled back towards the ticket office.

"Who was it?" I said.

"Apparently, his name is Septimus Darke. Never heard of him. Have you?"

"Yes," I said. "I've heard of him."

In my book, Septimus Darke was the most dangerous man in Brighton.

Chapter 4

I sat in Marcello's Coffee Bar sipping a cappuccino and nibbling an Amaretto biscuit.

I'd left Barnet fussing about whether he should stay open or close up – and whether he'd be paid if he did. Or whether he'd be paid at all now that Trumper had disappeared.

Marcello's hummed with the disgruntled muttering of day-trippers who'd taken refuge from the south-westerly. They stared at empty cups and bickered with each other about how long they could sit it out before they had to pay their bill and brave the seafront. Behind the counter, Marcello clattered about cheerfully with cups and saucers. The espresso machine hissed and bubbled.

I stirred another sugar cube into my coffee and wondered what a man like Septimus Darke would want with a run-down place like the Krazy Kat. I had good reason to believe Darke was the most dangerous man in Brighton. Trumper had been right to fear his return. The words on Darke's business card said "property developer". It was as though Hitler had handed out cards describing himself as a "painter and decorator". The real story was much more sinister.

Darke had arrived in Brighton ten years earlier, apparently with very little. He bought a run-down boarding house in an otherwise respectable part of Kemp Town; word had it for a fraction of its true value. At first, it looked like the sort of move a property developer would make. Neighbours expected that he would renovate the property and sell it on.

But instead of doing up the place, Darke allowed it to become even shabbier. In fact, he turned it into a slum. He moved in a host of misfits and undesirables – career burglars between sentences; terminal drunks gasping for neat meths; assorted ne'er-do-wells with time on their hands to make mischief. A couple of Alsatians were allowed to run wild in the street. Windows broke and were boarded up. Tiles slid off the roof. One night, the front gate caught fire. The garden became a car breaker's yard.

The place turned into a clearing house for most of the petty – and sometimes not so petty – crime in Kemp Town. Neighbours who complained were reminded by large men with tattoos on their arms that the Royal Sussex County hospital was located conveniently nearby. The police took an interest – but then lost interest. Local residents muttered about them being paid to keep out of the way. More likely, they'd worked out that a truncheon is not much defence against a couple of hungry Alsatians.

Soon nearby houses were up for sale as neighbours clamoured to sell up and move out. Except that, by now, the place had such a reputation that no one was eager to move in. So neighbours cut their selling prices. Then cut them again. And again. And there were still no buyers. Except one. Septimus Darke. When Darke had bought enough properties in the street at knock-down prices, the burglars, drunks and ne-er-do-wells suddenly disappeared. The street became respectable again. Even, as Darke at last renovated the houses, highly desirable. Darke sold out – and pocketed a large profit.

It was a scam he'd repeated in different parts of Brighton and Hove during the past ten years. Residents lived in fear that Darke or one of his front companies would buy a nearby house and install the neighbours from hell. In the process, Darke had acquired wealth which he wasn't shy to flash about town. He'd become rich – and untouchable.

But why did he want the Krazy Kat? Why had Trumper turned down a generous offer? And had his refusal something to do with his disappearance?

I pondered the answers to those questions as I spooned the

last froth from the cappuccino out of my cup. Barnet hadn't known who Darke was but, I remembered, he'd said that Rocky Roxbury had. The Fancy Rock Bazaar was next door to the Krazy Kat. I wondered whether Darke could have made an offer to Roxbury as well.

There was only one way to find out. I left Marcello's and hurried across the road.

An old-fashioned bell tinkled as I opened the door and went in. The cloying aroma of boiled sugar wrapped me in its sickly embrace. The place was painted in pink and white stripes. Shelves were stacked with sticks of peppermint rock in cross-hatch arrangements.

At the far end of the room, a polished counter topped a long glass cabinet packed with gaudy boiled sweets.

Behind the counter was a middle-aged man with thinning fair hair and a matinee-idol moustache. He wore a pink and white striped apron and a straw boater. A large badge pinned to his apron read: "Rocky".

I ambled up to the glass cabinet looking, I hoped, like a tourist with time on his hands. I peered in wondering whether anybody actually bought any of the products on display. There was some rock shaped to look like a fried egg, and a rock rasher of bacon to go with it. A rock baby's dummy. Bizarrely, sets of rock false teeth. Presumably to replace the ones that had rotted after scoffing this stuff.

"Our speciality products," Rocky said. "Each a testament to the confectioner's art." He reached into the cabinet.

"Here is our *pièce de résistance*, new this season. A miniature lady's leg. Made entirely from peppermint rock. Perfect in every detail, right down to the little pinkie on the foot. Tasteful," he said.

"In more ways than one," I said.

He giggled in a girlish sort of way.

"They say," – his voice dropped to a conspiratorial whisper –

"the leg is modelled on one of Brigitte Bardot's."

He handed the leg to me. I looked at it. It seemed hard to imagine the French sex kitten taking time out from filming *And God Created Woman* to model for an anatomical sweetmeat.

"Is there much demand for confectionery body parts?" I asked.

"Oh, very popular. We've sold hundreds of them this season already."

"Given your sales a leg up, then."

He trilled a little laugh. "Leg up. Oh, leg up. I must remember to tell that one to my friend Stanley when he comes in. Stanley loves a joke."

"So which new body part will you introduce next season?" I asked. "A hand? Perhaps the whole arm? Or maybe a torso?"

Rocky's face fell. He leaned heavily on the counter.

"There's not going to be another season," he said. "At least, not here. We've had an offer to buy the shop."

"Good offer?"

"The money is certainly fair. More than fair. It's just…" His voice trailed off.

"Is the offer from another rock company?" I said. "If you don't mind me asking."

"Not at all," he said. "The offer comes from a property developer."

I decided to push my luck. "Anyone local?"

Rocky shifted uneasily. "I believe so. At least, he's been responsible for quite a number of local, er, developments."

"So you're selling out?"

"I think there comes a time when it's wise to move on," he said. "Particularly in the present circumstances."

"What circumstances would they be?"

"The developer seems anxious to acquire the property. Very anxious. He's been quite, er, pressing about it."

I decided I'd pushed my luck as far as it would go.

"So you'll leave the rock business?"

"No. Definitely not. Stanley and I are thinking of opening a new rock shop next year. Perhaps somewhere classy. Like Margate."

"A change might do you good," I said.

"Yes, I suppose it might." He didn't sound convinced.

"I suppose I better buy something," I said. I was still holding the lady's leg. "How much is this?"

Rocky cheered up a bit at the prospect of a sale. "That'll be two and sixpence."

I handed over half a crown.

"I'll eat it later," I said. "I'll start with the foot and work my way up. You never know what it might lead to."

Rocky trilled another of his little laughs. "Oh, you are naughty," he said. "Never know what it might lead to! Stanley will love that."

I left him chortling about what Stanley would think. I made sure I was out of sight before I threw the leg in a bin.

After I'd discreetly disposed of the leg, I started to think about my next move.

My meeting with Rocky had convinced me that I was on to a story with strong legs. And I wasn't thinking of Brigitte's rock substitute.

Rocky hadn't mentioned Darke by name, but I had little doubt that he was behind the offer the confectioner had felt obliged to accept. Yet he was still trading, if only to the end of the season. Trumper had apparently rejected Darke's offer and had disappeared. I wondered whether that was cause and effect. And, anyway, I couldn't understand what a big-league deal-broker like Darke would want with small-time businesses such as Trumper's and Rocky's.

The only man who would know the answer to that question was Darke. I couldn't expect to get a straight answer from him.

But it might be worth asking him just to see his reaction.

In the meantime, I needed to get Trumper's side of the story. But I couldn't ask him any questions until I found him. That, I guessed, would come down to some serious door-stepping work in Trumper's neighbourhood of Woodingdean. It would mean a drive – so I bent into the wind and headed along the seafront to collect my car from the mews behind my flat.

Beatrice Gribble was known as Beattie to her friends and the Widow Gribble to her tenants. I fell firmly into the latter category.

The Widow owned a five-storey house in Regency Square, just off the seafront, an address that wasn't as posh as it sounded. The house was full of small rooms, dark corridors and creaking stairs. There was lots of embossed wallpaper and brown paint. A faded print of Holman Hunt's *Light of the World* hung in the hallway but failed to relieve the gloom. At night, the house sounded to the dyspeptic gurgles of temperamental plumbing.

After her husband Hector had gasped his last breath, the Widow had retreated to the ground floor and turned the rest of the place into apartments. I rented the one on the top floor. It suited me fine. It was about as far away from the Widow as I could get in the same house.

I reached the house, inserted my key quietly into the lock, went in and closed the door silently behind me. Moving like a wraith, I avoided the hall table with the glass ornaments that tinkled when you knocked against them. I stepped over the first stair to avoid the creaking tread. I crept upwards stepping only on the threadbare carpet to muffle the sound of my footsteps. I retrieved my car keys from my flat and crept back down the stairs.

The Widow's door opened ajar as I passed and two dark eyes peering over horn-rimmed glasses appeared at the crack.

"And a very good afternoon to you, Mrs Gribble," I said. "You want to take care you don't catch your nose when you shut the door. You might chip the nice brown wood."

I heard her door slam behind me as I went out.

I hurried round to the mews where I kept my car, an MGB: white coachwork with black trim, leather upholstery, walnut dashboard. Worth every penny of the two thousand pounds I'd paid for it. A favourite uncle had left me a legacy and I'd blown the lot on the car. I hadn't regretted it for one minute. I climbed in and revved the engine. It growled low and gently like a tigress warning her cubs. I pushed down on the accelerator, drove out of the mews, swung on to the seafront and headed towards Woodingdean.

The wind had dropped by the time I pulled the MGB into the kerb outside Trumper's bungalow in Woodingdean.

I climbed out of the car and glanced up and down the street. Nobody's head popped out from behind a hedge. No net curtains twitched. No dog-walkers gave me sideways looks as their pooches watered the lampposts.

Trumper's bungalow was a modest affair – probably just a couple of bedrooms and a living room – but it looked well kept. The fascias had been recently painted and the windows were clean. A privet hedge which marked the boundary of his property was growing a bit wild. But that's what hedges do.

There was a wooden gate. The hinges squealed as I opened it. A brick path led up to a small porch. I walked up the path to the front door. Weeds were growing in the gaps between the bricks. The lawn needed mowing.

I rang the doorbell. Chimes ding-donged the opening bars of *Greensleeves*. Nobody came. I hadn't expected Trumper to appear, but I had to be certain there was no one at home.

I peered through the window in the top of the door. There was a pile of letters on the hall floor. More, I thought, than he'd be likely to receive in one day. I walked round and looked through the other windows. The rooms seemed clean and well kept. There was an Agatha Christie, bookmarked with an old envelope, on the bedside table in Trumper's bedroom and a large pile of wilting vegetables in the rack in the kitchen. It looked as though Trumper hadn't been at the house for several days – all consistent with Barnet's story. But there were no clues as to why he had left.

Or whether he had been prevented from returning.

I decided I'd learnt everything I could from the Trumper residence. I walked back round to the front of the house, down the path and out through the gate. I closed it carefully behind me.

I strolled up the street examining the other properties. The bungalow to the right of Trumper's had an overgrown garden. A child's tricycle had been abandoned on the front path. I stood at the garden gate and listened. Inside the house I could hear a small girl screaming and a woman shouting. Not a good time to call.

I walked back down the street and looked at the bungalow on the other side of Trumper's. The windows were hung with heavy net curtains. A pull-along shopping bag had been left neatly in the porch. I strode up the path and listened. Inside a radio was playing the opening music of *Down Your Way*. I rang the doorbell and waited. Nobody came.

I waited a minute then rang the doorbell again. Twice. This time there was a shuffling sound in the hall and the front door opened.

An elderly lady with silver grey hair tied back in a bun said: "Did you ring the bell before?"

She was small and slender with a kindly face which had lots of smile lines around her mouth. She was wearing a grey dress in some kind of heavy woollen material. She had tartan slippers on her feet and wrinkles in her stockings.

She said: "I can't always hear the bell when the radio's on."

I said: "And why should you?"

"I wasn't really listening to it anyway."

"Who does these days?"

"I just have the radio for company."

"The best kind. There when you want it. Turned off when you don't."

She said: "It's a point of view."

I said: "My name's Colin Crampton. I'm from the *Evening Chronicle*. I'm a reporter. I was wondering whether you could help me. It's about a story I'm working on. Mrs..."

"Sturgess. But everyone calls me Harriet. A story, you say? How interesting."

Her eyes narrowed as she looked at me. It was a natural reaction when people were deciding whether they should ask a journalist into their homes. The eyes widened again. She'd taken her decision.

"Perhaps you'd better come in."

She led me up a dark hall and into a small sitting room. It had regency stripe wallpaper and a worn red carpet. Knitting – something in dark blue wool – rested on the arm of an easy chair by the fireplace. On the radio, Franklin Englemann had reached a pottery factory in Stoke-on-Trent. He was asking a worker how to put the spout on a teapot. "And the way to stop the spout dripping is to..."

Harriet turned off the radio. She had probably consigned me to a lifetime of dripping teapots.

She gestured me to a chair on the other side of the fireplace, picked up her knitting and sat down.

"You don't mind if I carry on with this while we talk?"

"Not at all."

The knitting needles started.

Clackety-clack.

"I wanted to ask you about your neighbour, Arnold Trumper," I said.

"More questions about poor Arnold."

"Someone's already been here asking questions?"

"Yes."

Clackety-clack.

"Recently?"

"Good gracious, no. In nineteen forty. I won't ever forget. It was the year my Charlie went away to France."

"Charlie being your husband?"

"Yes."

Clackety-clack.

"And he left to fight?"

"Yes." She stopped knitting. Her gaze strayed to a photo in a frame on a side table. It showed a handsome young man in uniform. "And he never came back," she said.

I stayed quiet for a moment while she remembered her Charlie who never came back. Then I said: "I'm sorry."

"It was a long time ago."

She started knitting again.

Clackety-clack.

"So you were questioned about the murder of Arnold's wife? About Mildred?" I said.

"A police officer asked me what I knew about her."

Clackety-clack.

"What did you tell him?"

"That I never got on with the woman. You could tell what she was like. Flighty. Chased after anything in trousers."

Clackety-clack.

"What did Arnold think of that?"

"I don't think he knew. He was so wrapped up in setting up his business. It wasn't easy at the start of the war."

She finished a row of her knitting and rummaged in a bag at the side of the chair. She pulled out a skein of wool.

"I need to wind another ball. Would you?"

I looped the wool over my hands and held them apart as she started to wind.

"How did Arnold take Mildred's killing?" I asked.

"Badly at first. It was the second blow he'd had in a few days."

"The first being his discovery that Mildred had been having an affair?"

"Yes."

"Not a marriage made in heaven, then?"

"They'd never really got on. Lived separate lives. Simply different temperaments. She was all for fun. He was all for work. Oil and water. Didn't mix," she said.

The wool winding flagged.

"Keep your arms apart, please, Colin."

"Sorry."

The winding restarted, even faster. The strand on the skein raced from one hand to another.

"Did you see much of Arnold in those days?"

"A little. But I had my own troubles when my Charlie went missing."

"Of course."

"Arnold had a sister," she said. "Dorothy, I believe. She came to see him quite a bit in those days. Cooked the odd meal. Did a bit of housework. That sort of thing. But then she got married and the visits dwindled."

"When did she marry?"

"I'm not sure. It was either in the closing months of the war or in the four or five years immediately after the war."

"Who did Dorothy marry?" I asked.

"I don't know. As I say, I had my own troubles."

"You can't remember his name?"

"No."

"When did you last see Dorothy?"

"I've not seen her for two years – since her husband died. I had thought about going to the funeral, but didn't in the end. We were never close friends. Little more than acquaintances. You know how it is?"

"I do," I said.

Harriet finished winding the wool.

"Was Arnold friendly with any of his other neighbours?" I asked.

"He kept himself to himself most of the time. For the past few years, we've only been on nodding terms. Not more."

"One last question," I said. "Have you any idea why Arnold should suddenly disappear?"

She stuffed the ball of wool into her bag. Followed it with the needles and knitting. Looked at me over the top of her half-moon glasses with those intelligent grey eyes.

"I don't think Arnold has been a contented man ever since the unhappy events with Mildred," she said. "To find his wife was unfaithful and then that she'd been murdered by her lover must have been a shattering blow for him. He seemed haunted by it. He never spoke to me much afterwards."

I thought about that for a moment, then said: "Thank you. You've been most helpful."

I put my notebook back in my pocket and stood up.

She said: "I have to disagree with you on one point."

"What's that?"

"I don't think the radio is the best company there is."

"You don't?"

"I find yours much more congenial."

"Too kind."

She grinned at me and there was a crafty look in her eye that made me sense what was coming next.

She said: "I made a fresh cherry cake today. You'll have a cup of tea with your slice?"

I sat down again. "Milk and one sugar," I said.

Chapter 5

An hour later, I left Harriet Sturgess's house awash with tea and stuffed with cherry cake.

I levered myself into the MGB and drove back into town. I had a lot to think about. From what I'd seen, it was clear that Trumper had left his house suddenly. He surely would have taken his Agatha Christie bedtime reading if he'd been planning to leave on an extended trip. And why should he order so many vegetables that were now rotting in his kitchen if he knew he was going away? But it was impossible to say whether he'd gone for good or was coming back. I'd picked up some useful backstory from Harriet. But, on a newspaper, a backstory is only useful when you have a peg to hang it on. And I had nothing that would stand any kind of scrutiny.

In the morning, I'd hoped to present Figgis with the first instalment of a running story that we could develop in the days ahead. He'd been adamant he wanted a splash. But I needed hard facts. I needed that peg. And there was one man who might provide it.

Septimus Darke.

The Golden Kiss nightclub was exclusive in much the same way as Lewes Prison. Not many people got in there and those who did were mostly crooks.

The place was one of Septimus Darke's business ventures. It was supposed to show that he wasn't just a property racketeer, but a businessman who could mingle at ease in respectable company.

But there were two groups he definitely didn't want sitting on his *faux* leopard skin-covered stools at his purple-velvet fascia bar – police and journalists. He employed a small group of muscled thugs with short tempers and small IQs to act as doormen. So if I wanted to get into the place, I would need to employ some of those journalist skills that have served the profession so well down the years – deceit and subterfuge.

I swung the MGB through the traffic lights at the Old Steine and drove past the Golden Kiss for a quick reconnaissance. The door was being patrolled by Fat Arthur. He looked like a man with a barrel for a body and a pumpkin for a head. I already knew him. He'd entertained the readers of the *Chronicle* when his career as a heavyweight boxer came to an abrupt close. The dolt had stepped into the ring and whacked the ref by mistake.

I accelerated past the club and drove towards Kemp Town. I was heading for a late-night shop which sold one or two items I needed for the evening's assignment.

Twenty minutes later I was back in the mews behind the club with my purchases in a cardboard box.

There were several doors leading from the mews into buildings. It wasn't difficult to tell which belonged to the Golden Kiss. There was a sign on the door which read: *Strictly no admittance except to accredited tradesmen.*

I hefted the box out of the car and walked over to the door. I used my back to push my way in. There was a short corridor lit by a bare light bulb. I walked down the corridor and entered the club's kitchen through double swing doors.

I took in the room in a moment. A chef held a spoon to his lips, tasting a sauce from a pan on a stove. A sous-chef chopped carrots. A kitchen porter at a sink, up to his elbows in greasy water, was working his way through a pile of dirty dishes. Their eyes swivelled towards me. At first, curious. Then hostile.

I marched across to a low deal table on the other side of the room and plonked the box down on it.

"There's the special order," I said. "As required – onions, green beans, and two extra caulis."

The chef looked surprised, then angry. He put down the

spoon. Took the pan off the stove. Advanced on the box. Peered in it. I expected him to speak with a French accent. Instead, it was straight off the Mile End Road.

"What the effing blazes is this? I didn't order no more veggies."

"Order came in from the office," I said.

"But they don't effing place orders for my effing kitchen."

"And I don't normally have to deliver them. Extra delivery, at Mr Darke's very special request."

The mention of the feared name calmed tempers.

"He don't effing tell me nothing."

"Bosses, eh? Same the world over," I said.

I waved a piece of paper from my notebook.

"I'll just pop through to the office and get the paperwork signed off."

Without waiting for a reply, I pushed through the nearest door, hoping it was the right one.

I found myself in another corridor, this one better lit and with a thick red carpet.

Music was coming from the far end of the corridor. Somebody was doing an impression of Frankie Vaughan singing *Something's Gotta Give*. It sounded as though it might be the singer's vocal cords. I walked towards the music, opened the door and entered what was clearly the club restaurant.

The room was lit by a couple of chandeliers that would have looked extravagant at Versailles. There was a small dance floor in the middle of the room with tables arranged around it. A short man with a bald head and stomach the size of Beachy Head manoeuvred a young woman with bleach blonde hair and a look of professional boredom on her face around the dance floor. I couldn't tell whether they were dancing the foxtrot or the rumba. He looked as though he was pushing a wheelbarrow to music.

The singer was strutting his stuff on a small stage at the far end of the room. He was backed by a four-man combo. Three were routine session musicians but the double bass player plucked a mean string.

I walked up to the bar, sat on one of the leopard skin-covered stools and ordered a large gin, small tonic, one ice cube and two slices of lemon. It came just as I wanted, served on a little paper doily with a bowl of peanuts on the side.

I looked round the room. There was no sign of Darke. I'd heard there were few evenings when he didn't visit the place. I took a swig of my drink and decided to sit it out.

I didn't have to wait long. I was scarcely halfway into the G&T when Darke walked in. He was a good couple of inches over six feet with broad shoulders and a muscular body. He had a full head of thick black hair. He had high cheekbones and a Roman nose. His eyes were too close together. He was wearing a grey mohair suit that must have left a herd of angora goats with a few chilly nights. He moved with the confidence of a man used to getting his own way.

Darke had a girl on each arm.

On his right, a tall blonde had corn-coloured hair cascading over bare shoulders. On his left, a short brunette had curly hair, a tough little face and a voluptuous figure that looked as though it had been especially inflated for the evening.

A waiter bustled up to Darke and showed him to a table near the band. A bottle of Krug and a tray of canapés appeared. The waiter poured the drinks. Darke took a good pull at his champagne and joked with the girls.

I finished my G&T, ordered another and considered how to approach the situation. The barman brought the fresh drink. The singer had started on Frankie Vaughan's *Green Door*. It was hanging by a hinge. I took a bracing swig of G&T, slid off the stool and walked across to Darke's table.

I said: "Mind if I join you, Mr Darke?" and sat down before he could say "no". He looked surprised more than angry.

So I said: "Why are you buying properties on the seafront?"

"Who the hell are you to be asking questions about my private business?" he said. He had a cold voice which rasped when he got angry.

I pulled out a card and flicked it across the table.

"Crampton. Colin Crampton. *Evening Chronicle*."

He looked at the card without picking it up. "And who invited you in?"

"I came uninvited. But I thought you'd want to talk to me."

"Why should I want to talk to you?"

"So I can print your side of the story."

"What story?"

"The story I'm writing about the mystery."

"What mystery?"

"Why you're buying up seafront properties."

Darke leaned forward in his chair. He reached for his glass and drained it. A waiter hurried forward to pour a refill. The temperature in the room seemed to have dropped.

"Give me one reason why I shouldn't have you thrown out," he said. "The hard way."

"Because it wouldn't look good in the *Chronicle*," I said. "Local businessman on assault charge."

He laughed. Reached for his glass. Drained it again. The waiter did the honours a second time.

I said: "I already have a story that you're buying seafront properties."

"You know nothing."

"And I know why."

"Don't bluff me. You said it was a mystery."

"Just a turn of phrase," I said. "There's no mystery about the fact that you're planning a seafront development. All I want to know is what it is." I leaned forward. "Why are you trying to buy the Krazy Kat?"

"That's my business."

"Have you met Arnold Trumper?"

"Go to blazes."

"Do you know where he is?"

"I've warned you, newspaperman."

"Getting under your skin am I, Septimus?"

Darke's fist crashed down on the table. Heads turned. Fat Arthur materialised in the room. The band's number ended in a discord of bum notes. The blonde twisted her hair. The brunette looked as though she'd sprung a puncture. The temperature in the room headed towards freezing point.

"Only my...only certain people call me that," Darke said.

"Call you, what? Septimus. It's your name, isn't it?"

"It's my name," he said.

"Because you were your mother's seventh child."

"As I said, you know nothing."

I was curious. Why was Darke so touchy about his name?

"Runt of the litter, were you? Got an inferiority complex as a result?"

"Fat Arthur." Darke summoned his heavy. "Mr Crampton, is leaving. By the back door. Be a shame if he tripped over the step and broke his leg on the way out."

"I understand, boss. Could be he also breaks an arm in his fall."

Darke laughed. "Excellent thinking."

Fat Arthur preened himself. I gave him a withering look. I hate a crawler.

"Don't hurt him. Not tonight." It was the blonde. She'd grabbed Darke's arm and was looking into his eyes.

"What's it to you?" Darke asked.

"Nothing. Really, nothing. It's just that he's kind of cute," she said. "Not as cute as you, Septimussy Pussy," she added hastily.

Darke lounged back in his chair thinking. I could see the clockwork ticking over in his brain.

"But this man has insulted me, Myrtle," he said finally.

"Please, Pussy," she said. "It's just that I don't want to be thinking about it later when we're...you know."

The clockwork ticked some more.

"So I'll give him a chance."

"Thank you, Pussy." She planted a red lipstick kiss on his cheek.

Darke turned back to me. "Sporting man are you?"

"I played a bit of cricket at school. Useful middle-order batsman and occasional leg spinner."

Darke laughed. "Not the kind of sport I had in mind."

"So what were you thinking of?"

"You think I was called Septimus because I was my mother's seventh son."

"Seems I was wrong."

"So I give you three chances to guess why I was called Septimus."

"Surely in view of your name, I should have seven chances."

"Seven, then."

"And why should I want to play this game?"

"You win and you get to walk out of the front door."

"And if I lose?"

"You leave by the back door. With Fat Arthur."

Darke had relaxed again. He was enjoying this. He meant it, too. I didn't like it one little bit. Despite his size, Fat Arthur still looked as though he could handle himself. It seemed as though I had no choice but to play Darke's game.

"Very well," I said.

"So your first guess."

"You were born on the seventh of the month," I said.

"Not quite right."

"In July, the seventh month."

"Getting warmer."

"In a year with a seven in it."

Darke said: "All wrong. I'm beginning to enjoy this."

He drank more champagne.

Darke had tricked me. It had nothing to do with dates at all. I'd wasted three of my seven guesses. I thought again.

"You were born under Libra, the seventh sign of the Zodiac."

"No."

"It was you father's lucky number."

"No."

"Your father was a seventh son. So you're the seventh son of a seventh son."

Darke said: "My old man would have enjoyed that one. Not sure about my old lady, though."

I had one guess left. One chance to avoid a trip through the back door with Fat Arthur.

I thought about what Darke had just said.

"My old man would have enjoyed that one. Not sure about my old lady."

There was something about the name which made it congenial to his father but not his mother. I forced ideas round my brain. I thought I knew the reason why Darke's father had liked the name. It was like a trophy name. It marked the fact that he had done something seven times. Something that involved the baby Septimus. A name which Darke's father was proud of. But it was a trophy name which the mother hated. Every time she called Darke by his given name she'd remember something she'd prefer to forget. But which Darke's father wanted her to remember – perhaps to control her, to keep her in her place. Septimus. What seven would a father like Darke's want to remember but the mother want to forget?

My brain felt like a furnace running out of fuel.

"Come on," Darke said. "You're keeping Fat Arthur waiting."

Darke laughed. Fat Arthur laughed. The brunette laughed. The band laughed. Everyone in the room laughed. Even Myrtle, my newfound ally, laughed. I didn't laugh.

I said: "Because you were your father's seventh son by seven different women."

Darke stopped laughing.

"Shall I take him out the back now?" Fat Arthur said.

"He's right." Darke's voice sounded like an iceberg cracking.

The laughter died away. Myrtle chewed a fingernail. The brunette crumpled liked a deflated balloon. The band looked as though they didn't know whether to strike up *"For He's a Jolly Good Fellow"* or play Mendelssohn's *Funeral March*.

I got up and sauntered over to the bar. Took a few peanuts from the bowl. Walked towards the door. Turned to face Darke.

"It's been an interesting evening, Septimus," I said. "I'll have some more questions for you soon."

I tossed a peanut in the air, caught it in my mouth and went through the door.

The air seemed very cold when I stepped into the street.

I had to get back to my car in the mews, so I walked down the street to the turning that would take me round to the back of the block. When I reached the corner, I looked back. A cab had drawn up outside the Golden Kiss. A man dressed in a dinner jacket got out and slipped quickly into the club. He was carrying an expensive-looking leather briefcase.

He didn't look as though he was on his way for a big night out. Not with a briefcase. He had business with Darke. It would be dirty business. But I couldn't go back to ask him what it was.

Instead, I walked round to collect my MGB from the mews. In the morning, I would have to discover who Darke's mystery visitor was. And I'd already had an idea about how to do it.

Chapter 6

The following morning, I walked into the newsroom at five past eight. I had a busy day ahead of me.

The newsroom was gearing up for the midday edition. There was already a deadline buzz in the air – the kind of creative tension which gets newspapers out on time. Reporters hollered down telephones at contacts they should have called earlier or cursed as the keys on their antique typewriters jammed. The cigarette fug under the fluorescent lights was thicker. I nodded to a few colleagues, checked the messages on my desk, then headed for the telephone booths at the side of the newsroom.

The idea of the booths was to provide some privacy for calls to special contacts. In practice, they were usually used by reporters for placing bets with bookies or arranging dates they didn't want their colleagues to know about.

I normally called my contacts from the telephone on my desk. But I had a special reason for keeping the call I was about to make confidential. Every newsroom has a snitch – someone not averse to picking up some pocket money by passing details of exclusives to rival papers. I didn't want colleagues earwigging this call. No rivals were going to chase after this story if I could help it.

I opened the door of the quietest booth, kicked some scrunched-up copy paper from the floor into the newsroom, brushed some dog-ends off the phone shelf and picked up a phone handset that smelt of stale sweat.

The number I dialled was Devil's Dyke Taxis, Brighton's largest cab firm. The cab delivering the briefcase-carrying figure to the Golden Kiss the previous evening had been a Devil's Dyke car.

The phone rang eight times before it was answered and a cigarette-stained voice croaked: "Scroggins. What do you want at this time of the morning?"

"And a very good morning to you, too, Harry," I said. "Colin Crampton."

"Oh, you. You're not calling me for a cab, surely? Ring the despatcher."

"I don't want a cab, Harry. I want information. One of your cabs dropped off a punter at the Golden Kiss around ninety-thirty yesterday evening. I'd like you to find out where the pick-up came from."

"We drop off scores of punters at that rip-off joint."

"I only want to know about one," I said.

"We can't remember individual punters."

"Your driver wouldn't forget this one. Middle-aged bloke. Late thirties. Dressed in a DJ. Carrying a briefcase."

"Most of the punters we drop there wear DJs."

"But they don't carry briefcases. So it shouldn't be difficult to put out a general call to your drivers asking them which one handled the fare?"

"If he was driving last night, chances are he's tucked up in noddy land having a kip."

"Then put out the call again later."

I was puzzled. Harry had helped me before on stories. Now he was playing hard to get.

"This shouldn't be difficult, Harry," I said.

"I don't know." He coughed. He fell silent. I waited. He was probably lighting another fag.

"What's the problem?" I asked.

"Customer confidentiality," he said.

"What? It's never bothered you before."

"This time is different."

I knew why. Had I been asking about a cab drop at the Metropole or the Grand Hotel, Harry would have had the information for me by now. He was worried because it was the Golden Kiss. Owned by Septimus Darke.

"I give you my personal guarantee that there'll be no

comeback on this," I said.

"That won't mean much if I suddenly find you-know-who on my arse."

"You won't. Nobody else will know."

"Sorry. I can't do it. Now, can I finish my breakfast? I've still got half a packet of Weights to smoke." He gave a throaty cough.

"That's a pity, Harry."

"Sure. Perhaps another time."

"There may not be another time after I've run the other story," I said.

"Other story? What other story? You're talking in riddles."

"Well, if you're going to close off one story I'll have to write another. We've got to fill up those empty columns with something. Perhaps it's just as well. I've been meaning to run that story about the cab firm which has a contract to deliver Madame Blenkinsop's girls to punters at certain seafront hotels."

There was a wheezing sound at the other end of the phone.

"Special rate, I understand, at twice the money on the clock," I said. "Sounds like profitable business."

More wheezing plus a kind of strangled cough.

"I'd even heard that the cab firm's owner occasionally got a freebie – courtesy of Madame – for transport services rendered," I said.

The guttural sounds of Harry having a hawk and a spit came down the line. It sounded like a rat swimming through treacle. I held the phone away from me. Then I heard a more chastened voice. I put the receiver to my ear.

"You wouldn't run that story…would you?" he said.

"Personally, I'd rather it remained a little secret between old friends," I said.

"And are we old friends?"

"I'd like to think so," I said. "And I'd hope we remain that way."

"I suppose I hope so, too." He didn't sound enthusiastic.

"So I can rely on you to put out the call?"

"I'll put out the call. Can't promise that it'll produce what you want."

"I know you'll do your best."

I put down the phone and left the booth. As I got back to my desk, Frank Figgis walked into the newsroom. He came over towards me and said: "I want to have a word with you."

"It's mutual," I said. "But I've got the police briefing in ten minutes. Can we speak when I get back from the cop shop?"

"I'll be in my office."

Figgis wandered off to hassle someone else.

I picked up my notebook and went out.

The briefing took place at Brighton Police Station in Eastern Avenue every morning except Sunday, at nine o'clock.

The occasion was intended as an opportunity for the cops to tell journalists about anything interesting they'd been dealing with in the past twenty-four hours. It was supposed to be a shining example of the officers of the law aiding the gentlemen of the press. It rarely turned out like that. The gentlemen of the press normally meant me from the *Chronicle* and Jim Houghton, my opposite number on the *Evening Argus*, the town's other daily paper.

The briefing took place in a room furnished with cheap plastic tables and hard chairs. The cells downstairs were probably better equipped. I suppose it reflected the relative respect Brighton's top coppers had for the criminal classes and the press.

Jim was already in the briefing room when I arrived. He was nursing a plastic cup of weak tea. I generally avoided the cop-shop cuppa. Like most of Brighton's police, it smelt a bit off.

I walked in and said: "What's news, Jim?"

He said: "If you read the *Argus* today you'll find out."

Jim was a veteran newsman. He was pushing sixty and looked it. He had a lined face and thinning dark hair which covered a large head. He walked with a slight limp. He looked a bit past it. Except when you tried to beat him to a story. Then you realised there was still power in those old legs and a bushel of brainpower in that oversized head. He'd scooped me on several stories since I'd become the *Chronicle*'s crime correspondent – and I respected him for that. But I was damned if he was going to scoop me on the Trumper disappearance.

I grinned: "Read it in the *Argus*. I guess I opened myself for that one."

Jim smiled. He was wearing the same threadbare brown suit that he sported every day.

"Know who's giving the briefing this morning?" I asked.

"Sergeant Fairbrother, I think."

"So probably nothing worth writing about."

"Guess so."

Fairbrother handled the meeting when there was no serious crime to talk about. If anything big happened a more senior officer stepped in.

I was about to ask Jim whether he was working on anything interesting, on the long-shot chance that he might let something slip, when Fairbrother walked in.

He was a big man who'd run to fat since he'd been taken off the beat to handle admin at the main police station. He was carrying a small sheaf of papers. He sat down opposite us.

"What's doing?" Jim asked.

Fairbrother shuffled through his papers.

"Yesterday was a quiet day," he said.

"So bad news," I said.

"Not for us," Fairbrother said.

He extracted a sheet of paper and started to read. "A bicycle stolen from a house in Maldon Road, a minor motor accident at Five Ways – nobody hurt – and a dog lost in Stanmer Park."

"What breed?" Jim asked.

"King Charles spaniel."

"Any pictures?" I said.

"No."

We put down our pencils. Animal stories without a picture are a non-starter.

Fairbrother frowned. "There's nothing else, so if you've got no further questions." He stood up and left the room.

"I don't know why we bother about these meetings," I said to Jim.

"I do," he said. "It's the only way I can keep an eye on what you're doing. Same for you in my respect, I guess."

"You've discovered my little secret," I said.

"Not yet," Jim said. "But I have a feeling you're working on a big story you're not telling me about."

"What makes you think that?" I asked.

"Instinct," he said.

He tapped the side of his nose and left.

I worried about what Jim had said on my way back to the office.

I had two concerns. The first was whether Jim had got a whiff of the Trumper story through his own contacts. He'd been covering crime much longer than I had and his contacts went right up to the most senior levels in Brighton's police. My only reliable contact was Ted Wilson. The second was whether I should mention what Jim had said to Frank when I got back to the office. If Figgis thought the *Argus* could scoop us, he might force me to run the story before I'd covered all the angles.

I still didn't have answers to either question when I walked into Figgis's office fifteen minutes later. He was sitting behind his desk and lighting a cigarette. He'd hung his jacket over the back of his chair. He'd loosened his tie and undone the top button of his shirt. Rolled up his sleeves. He was settling in for a hard session.

"Anything from the rozzers this morning?" he asked.

"Bicycle theft in Maldon Road. Might make a nib," I said.

"So the front-page splash I asked you for becomes a news in brief." He waved me to a chair. "Circulation has dropped this month," he said.

"Always happens in August."

"More than usual this year. His Holiness is getting twitchy."

Gerald Pope – His Holiness behind his back – was the *Evening Chronicle*'s editor. He exuded an Olympian detachment from the grubby business of news gathering. He had a plummy voice – "off" came out as "orf" – which must have impressed the paper's proprietor but didn't do a lot for the rest of the staff. He came into the newsroom on rare occasions, usually by mistake.

I said: "As you know better than anyone, it's hard news that sells newspapers."

"Yes," Figgis said. "But it's the big running stories that get people buying papers every day."

"I might have something," I said. "I've got a feeling that it could be big but at the moment it doesn't amount to much."

I recounted what Wilson had told me in Prinny's Pleasure and summarised my visits to the Krazy Kat, Woodingdean and the Golden Kiss.

Figgis smiled when I told him about Darke. "Sort of scam I might have got up to twenty years ago. But you'll need to watch your back with Darke."

"I intend to."

"I agree you've not got enough at the moment," Figgis said. "But I think it's worth taking it further. What's your next move?"

I told him about my call to Scroggins.

"Seems a long shot," Figgis said. "But see what you can do?"

I got up and moved towards the door, then turned back. Figgis was stubbing out his ciggie on the edge of his desk.

"There's something else I ought to tell you," I said. "At the police briefing this morning, Jim Houghton mentioned he thought I was working on a big story. I'm wondering whether he's got wind of it."

Figgis opened his cigarette packet slowly. He took out a fag and rolled it between his fingers.

"Jim's a crafty operator. I think he was probably on a fishing expedition. Sort of trick he'd try to pull. Even so, let's be careful. Don't make any calls about the story from your desk if you can help it. And keep me informed."

Figgis had lit the fag and was staring out of the window in thought as I left.

Twenty minutes later, I was sitting at my desk batting out two pars about the stolen bicycle on my Remington when the phone rang.

I lifted the receiver and a tar-encrusted voice said: "It's your lucky day, sunshine."

"And yours, too, Harry," I said.

"Let's not go into that. That drop-off at the Golden Kiss. I've spoken to the driver. He picked up the punter from an address in Westdean."

He gave me the street and house number.

"No need for me to tell you who lives there. I expect you'll find out anyway. Tat-ta." The line went dead.

I got up and went over to the bookcase on the other side of the room. I pulled down a bulky file containing the electoral register for Westdean. I turned to the street and ran my finger down the page until I reached the house number Harry had given me.

"Well, well," I murmured to myself.

The visitor to the Golden Kiss had been Derek Cross. He featured regularly in the *Chronicle*'s columns. He was a leading member of Brighton Council and tipped as next year's mayor.

So what business did this prominent citizen have late at night with Septimus Darke?

Ten minutes later I was in the *Evening Chronicle*'s morgue with a large bag of jam doughnuts.

I needed Henrietta Houndstooth's help – and the doughnuts would be the perfect bribe. Henrietta ran the *Chronicle*'s morgue as punctiliously as a Victorian undertaker. But she watched over no dead bodies. Instead, she kept one and a half million press clippings from back issues of the *Chronicle* meticulously filed away for future reference. The morgue was where old copies of the paper went to rest in peace.

Or, as they were in clippings, that should be in pieces.

Henrietta was a small bird-like woman with a petite intelligent face and a pointy nose. To help her, Henrietta had three sturdy matrons – Elsie, Mabel and Freda. They were known around the paper as the Clipping Cousins, although they weren't related to one another as far as anyone knew.

When I walked in, Henrietta was sitting at her desk. She was wearing the kind of tweed suit that would be perfect for stalking deer and which made her look like a domineering duchess. I imagined it was part of her armoury for intimidating reporters with unreasonable demands. Like me.

The Clipping Cousins sat round a large table that was piled with wire baskets overflowing with clippings and heaps of newspapers that spilled over the table like snowdrifts. They'd taken a break from snipping yesterday's paper and were passing round a bag of sweets. The room smelt of sherbet lemons.

I dropped my bag of doughnuts on Henrietta's desk and said to nobody in particular: "Elevenses, with my compliments."

Henrietta picked up the bag and peered inside it.

"Doughnuts, ladies," she said.

"Goody," Elsie said.

"Yummy yummy, says my tummy," Mabel said.

"My tummy usually keeps its opinions to itself," Freda said.

Mabel frowned.

Henrietta quickly said: "He wants something special."

"Just a little token of appreciation for all the work you do to help the hacks in the newsroom," I said.

Henrietta gave me a look that would fell a stag at a hundred yards and said: "Cut the flannel and tell me what you want."

I said: "Cross. Do we have anything on him?"

Henrietta said: "Which Cross? We've got at least thirty."

Hastily, I said: "Derek Cross. Member of Brighton Council."

"Oh, him. We've got a fat file on him. Anything in particular you want to know?"

"Just general background."

"Let's start you on the file, then."

She stood up and said: "Follow me."

We disappeared into the warren of wooden floor-to-ceiling filing cabinets behind Henrietta's desk. It was a strange twilight world of narrow corridors flanked with cabinets on either side. The corridors were lit by dim bulbs. There was cheap linoleum on the floor, cracked in places. The air smelt musty. The sounds of the real world seemed to fade away as we walked further into the maze of corridors. It felt like being in a strange world of the living dead.

We turned a corner and stopped. Henrietta pulled a stepladder on wheels towards her, climbed up the first two steps and pulled out a drawer. She handed me down a thick buff manila file.

"That's it," she said. "Everything we know about Derek Cross."

We retraced our steps out of the filing-cabinet maze. As we emerged, Elsie said: "These doughnuts are scrummy."

"Delicious, if I can express an opinion" Mabel said.

"Since when have I tried to stifle free speech?" Freda said.

Mabel frowned.

I walked over to a desk reporters used when they didn't want the bother of taking a file back to the newsroom. I sat down and opened the file. There must have been more than a hundred cuttings, arranged in reverse date order. I started to flip through them.

Derek Cross, it appeared, was a local lad made good. He was the son of a bus driver and hospital cleaner who'd lived in Coldean, a valley filled with soulless housing developments on the outskirts of town. He was evidently a bright lad. He'd passed the eleven plus and won a place at Varndean Grammar School. He'd left school at eighteen and gone to work as a negotiator at a local firm of estate agents.

He'd started his own estate-agency business when he was in his early twenties. The business thrived as the town boomed during the nineteen fifties and after three years, Cross & Pringle – he'd taken on a junior partner – had two branches in Brighton and one in Hove.

Cross had become a Brighton councillor eleven years ago when he was twenty-eight. He'd been the "baby" of the council when elected, which hadn't prevented him pushing his way up through the ranks in the following years. He'd got himself onto a couple of sub-committees, one dealing with allotments, the other with parks and gardens. He'd made a few speeches in the council chamber on planning matters. I formed the impression he wanted to make a mark in the council chamber without upsetting his party leaders.

His big break had come six years ago when he'd been appointed to the Planning Committee. In another three years, he'd been made chairman. Now in a seat of power, he'd pushed for more commercial developments of factories and offices on the outskirts of town. The cuttings showed this hadn't made him popular with residents near the new developments or country types who liked bracing walks over the Downs.

But he'd become the darling of the town's business community. There was a cutting which described a Chamber of Commerce dinner. The chairman had lauded him as a "great business ambassador for Brighton". Cross had replied to the speech by saying that he stood for "prosperity and principle".

Piffle and poppycock, more like.

I flipped over to the last cutting. It was one of those awful group photographs which the paper sometimes felt obliged to publish. This one showed Cross and sundry other dignitaries at the new casino which had opened earlier in the year at the Metropole Hotel. The headline ran:

BRIGHTON HOSTS BRITAIN'S FIRST CASINO

Needless to say, Cross had made another of his speeches. This time he'd said that the government's new laws on gambling meant that Brighton could become a "punters' paradise".

I closed the file and thought about what I'd learnt.

Over at the table, Elsie said: "My fingers are all sticky."

Mabel said: "I've got sugar all round my mouth."

Freda said: "I've got jam on my jumper."

Mabel smiled.

It was clear that Cross was a man on the make. Estate agent. Councillor. Planning Committee chairman. Future mayor. But selfless public servant? I didn't think so. Not from what I'd read. His career smelt of man getting into a position where he could do himself a bit of good. He wouldn't be the first man to enter public life with his eyes on a personal pay-off.

But it didn't answer the two key questions. What was Cross's connection with Darke? And did that connection have anything to do with Arnold Trumper's disappearance?

I stood up, picked up the file and walked over to the table.

Elsie said: "We've eaten the doughnuts."

Mabel said: "All of them."

Freda said: "Hope you don't think we're greedy."

"Not at all," I said. "With all these newspapers to clip, you need to keep your energy up."

They giggled in a sturdy matronly sort of way. I handed the file to Henrietta.

She looked up at me. "Did it tell you what you wanted to know?"

"Up to a point," I said.

"And what point is that?"

"The point where I feel I understand the man, but I'm not sure what he's intending to do next."

"Perhaps we have the detail you need in other files," she said.

"You've got more files on Cross?" I said.

"Not specifically. But there may be passing references to him in other files. We'd only put a clipping in his own file if it was wholly or substantially about him."

I thought about that for a moment.

I said: "The last cutting had Cross attending the opening of the new Metropole casino. Do you have a file on casinos?"

Henrietta considered that. She rested her head to one side when she was thinking, like a sparrow having a kip.

"I think we started one when the Metropole casino opened, but there's probably only one or two cuttings in it. I think we do have a file on gambling, though," she said. "Wait here."

She disappeared into the filing-cabinet warren and emerged a minute later carrying a buff file. She sat down, opened it and flipped through the cuttings.

"Not a lot here," she said. "Clipping about one of the local MPs having a moan about the Betting and Gaming Bill which went through Parliament last year. Small item about a petition from the Mother's Union opposing the Metropole casino. Item that looks as though it comes from the business diary column about a group of local businessmen on a trade mission to the United States. It's in this file because it mentions that they visited Las Vegas to study the gambling industry. That's all, I'm afraid."

"Could I look at that last clipping?" I said.

She handed it to me.

It was a standard diary item. Soft news of no particular interest except to the people mentioned. Fodder for their scrap-books. I let my eye wander down the column. Several names I didn't recognise. One or two vaguely familiar. One that jumped out like a firecracker at a funeral. Septimus Darke.

"Can I keep this cutting for a bit?" I said.

Henrietta nodded.

I moved towards the door. Turned back to the table. The Clipping Cousins were scissoring their way through newspapers.

"Thanks for all the work you do, ladies" I said. "I wouldn't be able to write half my stories without it."

Elsie said: "We've enjoyed your visit very much."

Mabel said: "It's been ever so lovely."

Freda said: "Do come again any time you like."

I stepped swiftly through the door before one of them offered me her hand in marriage.

I walked round to Frank Figgis's office, knocked on the door and went in before he could growl "enter".

Figgis was putting down the phone. He said: "That was His Holiness wanting to know the top line on today's news. I've had to wing it again. When are we going to get a story worthy of a splash?"

I said: "I think we may have something but it's not ready to roll yet."

Figgis reached for a mug of coffee on his desk, took a swig and said: "Tell me."

I gave him a summarised version of my visit to the morgue.

I said: "You know the government changed the law on gambling last year with the Betting and Gaming Act."

"Of course. It's now legal for the first time in Britain to open member-only casinos. But word on the street is that some dubious characters are moving in on the business."

"There's been some talk about the Mafia taking an interest."

"The home-grown hoodlums are quite enough," Figgis said. "I hear there are a couple of brothers in London – the Krays I think their name is – who've muscled in on the business. By all accounts, they're not the sort of people you want to mess with."

"I think we may be getting a similar problem in Brighton," I said. "My theory is that Septimus Darke is planning to open a casino."

"That figures. Darke has been racketeering in this town for too many years for my liking."

I said: "He's trying to buy the Krazy Kat and, incidentally, the Fancy Rock Bazaar next door. I think he wants the two as the site for his casino."

"Makes sense. A casino right on the seafront would be a big draw."

"But it only happens if Arnold Trumper wants to sell. And, if he doesn't, Darke might start to think of some unorthodox ways to make him."

"You think Darke has got to Trumper in some way?"

"He's got to other people in this town. When Darke wants something, 'no' is not a word he understands."

Figgis nodded. "Of course, even if Trumper agreed to sell, Darke would need planning permission," he said.

"That's where Cross fits into the picture as chairman of the Planning Committee. At the very least, Darke would want to get an idea what line the council would take if he submitted a formal planning application."

"And you think that's why Cross was at the Golden Kiss?"

"Could be. But now I know more about Cross, I'm wondering whether there's more to their relationship."

"You mean he's on the receiving end of a backhander?"

"Yes."

"We can't print that. We've no evidence. The lawyers would have our balls on toast and His Holiness would add the sprig of parsley."

"But we do know that Darke has made an offer for the Krazy Kat, which Trumper has turned down."

"And has now disappeared." Figgis drank some more of his

coffee, then said: "What we've got here is too much suspicion and not enough genuine evidence. We need some hard facts. How are you going to get them?"

"I plan to see Cross. If I show him that I know about Darke's casino plans I may be able to shake him into an indiscretion or two."

"It's worth a try," Figgis said. "But watch your back. If you're right and Darke finds out you're asking around about his deals, you could find yourself taking an unscheduled swim off the end of Palace Pier."

Chapter 7

I walked back to my desk in the newsroom and pulled the telephone directory from the shelf beside my desk.

I thumbed through the pages looking for Cross, D. He wasn't there. He had to be ex-directory. So I had to charm the number out of directory enquiries. And when it came to ex-directory numbers, that was about as easy as extracting a winkle from its shell without the aid of a pin.

I walked over to one of the booths, picked up the phone and dialled.

A bored voice said: "Directory enquiries. How may I help you?"

I said: "This is Inspector Wilson from Brighton Police Station. Our lost-property section has just received some confidential papers that were left in the back of a taxi by Councillor Derek Cross of Brighton. We need to contact Councillor Cross immediately on his ex-directory number to arrange return of the papers. I know that you can only provide an ex-directory number after proper verification. So as a security check, will you please call back to Brighton Police Station lost-property section and ask for me by name? That's Inspector Wilson."

I gave her the number of the booth phone.

"In that case, there shouldn't be a problem."

"Thank you. Please ring back right away. We believe Councillor Cross urgently needs these papers for a meeting."

I put down the phone. I didn't think she'd make an independent check of the phone number for the police's lost-property section. She was probably being harassed by other callers. But I couldn't be sure.

I opened the door of the booth. Sally Martin, who wrote for the woman's page, was walking by. She had bobbed blonde hair, and the kind of teasing expression which made her look as though she was always about to say something cheeky.

I said to her: "In a moment, this phone will ring and the caller will ask for Inspector Wilson. Please answer the phone as Brighton Police Station, hold the caller for a moment or two, then hand the phone to me."

Sally grinned. "Beats writing a piece on baking the perfect scone," she said.

We waited for the phone to ring and chatted about life on the paper.

The phone didn't ring.

We talked about writing for the woman's page.

The phone didn't ring.

I started to think of the excuse I'd make for impersonating the police.

The phone didn't ring.

After a couple of minutes I was drumming my fingers on the side of the booth.

I said to Sally: "If this doesn't come off, I may join you writing about scones."

She said: "If this doesn't come off, you'll be lucky to be eating them."

The phone rang.

Sally lifted the receiver and said: "Brighton Police Station." I picked up the sound of a distorted voice at the other end.

Sally said: "Hold the line please, caller, while I put you through to Inspector Wilson."

She tapped the mouthpiece a few times with her fingernails to simulate a number being transferred to an extension. She handed me the phone.

I put my hand over the mouthpiece and said to her: "You've done this before."

"We don't only bake scones," she said. She swung her hips with extra confidence as she headed back to her desk.

I said: "Inspector Wilson. Is that directory enquiries? I believe you have Councillor Cross's phone number for me."

I noted down the number and said with a suitably official voice: "Brighton Police thank you for your help."

I put down the phone, picked it up again, checked there was a tone and dialled the number. It rang three times and then a woman's voice said: "Geraldine Cross."

I said: "Could I speak to Derek, please?"

She said: "Who are you?"

"Colin Crampton."

"Do you know Derek?"

"I saw him last night at the Golden Kiss."

"Derek was at the Golden Kiss?"

Genuine surprise. She hadn't known. I decided to surprise her some more: "I believe he had a meeting with Septimus Darke."

"That dreadful man. I do wish he'd have nothing to do with him."

"No doubt it was business."

"No doubt. Anyway, he's not here."

"Do you know where I can find him?"

"Why do you want to know?"

"I need to check one or two facts with him. I'm a reporter with the *Evening Chronicle*."

"Something to do with the Planning Committee, is it?"

"Along those lines."

"Well, this morning he's at the Town Hall. But he'll probably be in meetings. He usually is."

She sounded as though she preferred it that way.

"Thank you for your help," I said. I rang off.

It was clear from my call to Geraldine that I needed to interview Cross as soon as possible. But when I got back to my desk, I found a message that Shirley had called my desk phone while I'd been in the booth. She was at her flat. I picked up the phone and dialled her number.

"Hi, Bozo. Didn't hear from you yesterday?" she said.

"I brought you breakfast in bed. Remember?" I said.

"I meant after that. After you'd had your wicked way with the simple colonial girl."

"I was working on a story until late."

"Yeah. How about seeing me tonight?"

"I thought you were working."

"Got the night off. Marco says we're not likely to be busy in the restaurant."

"What would you like to do?"

"Thought we might see that new movie – *To Kill a Mockingbird*. It's on at the Duke of York's."

"That's the Gregory Peck picture."

"Yes. I thought it might appeal to the great journalist and righter of wrongs."

I laughed. "I suppose I'll never live down that little heart-to-heart we had in the Starlit Room."

"You betcha."

"Anyway, I've read the book and I've heard the film is just as good," I said. "When does it start?"

"Seven forty-five."

"Let's do it. I should be finished by then. I'll meet you in the foyer."

"See you then," Shirley said. The line went dead.

I picked up my notebook and went out. I was heading for the Town Hall. I had my own mockingbird to confront.

When I arrived at Brighton Town Hall, I still had no firm idea about how to tackle the interview with Cross.

Everything I'd learnt about him suggested he wouldn't give away information readily. I'd need to manoeuvre him into a position where he had no choice but to answer my questions.

Brighton Town Hall was a large solid building fronted by a row of columns which looked as though they'd been borrowed from the front of a Greek temple. There were wide steps up to massive wooden double doors. The doors were open when I arrived. So I bounded up the steps between the columns and went in.

In the lobby, a commissionaire with a peaked cap, toothbrush moustache and sergeant's stripes on his arm barred my way. He demanded to know my business.

I flashed my press card and said: "Interview with Councillor Cross."

He nodded and reluctantly moved aside.

I clumped down the corridor which led to the committee rooms. It had a polished parquet floor and tiled walls. It was hung with a rogues' gallery of photographs of previous mayors. There was one with a rubicund face and a belly that bulged like the dome on the top of the Royal Pavilion. A thin one with wire-framed spectacles and an apologetic expression. One with bushy eyebrows and a thin moustache – the town's first woman mayor. One dressed in red robes and tricorn hat, like Alderman Fitzwarren out of Dick Whittington. And one, with pointy ears and dark eyes, who looked like Dick's cat.

A noticeboard at the end of the corridor listed which meetings were taking place in which rooms. The Planning Committee was in room six. The meeting was scheduled to finish at twelve-thirty. I glanced at my watch. Ten past twelve.

I hurried along to the room, opened the door and went in.

There were about fifteen people sitting around a large boardroom table. To the side was a smaller table for the press. An old guy with straggly hair and a bored expression was sitting there. He was wearing a worn grey suit that looked as though it might have become a haven for wild life. I recognised him as a reporter from the *Evening Argus*. He was freewheeling the last few months of life as a journalist before retiring. His news editor would have sent him to this news-free meeting to get him out of the way. I think he was called Mick. Or it may have been Nick.

He could be a nuisance if he hung around after the meeting

when I was trying to get Cross on his own. I didn't want him getting wind of the fact that I needed to interview Cross. For a moment, I considered ducking out of the meeting and bearding Cross elsewhere in the Town Hall. But heads had swivelled when I entered the room, including Mick's. Or Nick's. Going out now would look odd if not downright suspicious. But I'd have to find a way to shake off Mick at the end of the meeting. So I smiled sheepishly at the swivelled heads and mock tip-toed across the room to the reporters' table.

I sat down beside Mick and whispered: "Good to see you again, Mick."

He whispered: "It's Nick."

I whispered: "Of course. Can't think why I said Mick. Must be going senile."

I took out my notebook and pretended to be absorbed in the fascinating proceedings. Cross was seated at the head of the table. He was a tall man with broad shoulders and long arms. He had bushy black eyebrows and thin lips. He was wearing a well-cut chalk-stripe suit that didn't look as though it had come off the bargain rail at Burton's. He spoke with the kind of studied precision that people use when they want to make an impression but which comes over as self-importance.

He said: "Have we fully ventilated the subject of new railings around the children's paddling pool?"

There were murmurings round the table and an outbreak of nodding heads. Apparently, the paddling pool railings had been fully ventilated.

Cross said: "Then we shall move to next business."

I ignored next business and wrote something in my notebook, tore out the page and slipped it across to Nick. My note said: *Feel like meeting for a drink after this?*

He wrote on the bottom: *Great.* He pushed the note back to me.

I wrote: *How about The Cricketers? Might have a ploughman's too.*

On me. I pushed the paper back to him.

He wrote: *Be delighted. Thanks.*

The meeting wound on. Cross was saying something he thought important because he kept repeating himself.

I ignored him and wrote on my note: *After the meeting, could you go and grab a table before the lunchtime rush? I need to get some money from the bank.*

He wrote: *No trouble.*

I wrote: *Could you get the first round in?* I took out a ten-shilling note and pushed it across to him with the paper.

He wrote: *Thanks. No problem.*

I turned the paper over to the other side and wrote: *Mine's a G&T.*

I didn't bother to specify one ice cube and two slices of lemon. I didn't expect to be there to drink it.

When the meeting ended, Nick obediently trotted off to reserve our table at The Cricketers.

I didn't feel too bad about it. He had my ten bob to spend on drinks and lunch. I made an excuse to stay in the committee room by telling him I wanted to write out a cheque before I went to the bank. In reality, I was waiting for an opportunity to pounce on Cross. After the meeting, he went into a little huddle with a couple of officials. I worried they'd all leave the room together and I wouldn't be able to get Cross on his own. But after three or four minutes, the officials collected up their files and left the room. Cross ignored me and began shuffling his papers together. I walked over to him.

I said: "Colin Crampton, *Evening Chronicle.* Could you spare me a minute, Councillor Cross?"

Cross looked up from his papers and frowned. "Have we met before?" he said.

"I don't think so."

"But I recognise your name. You're the *Chronicle*'s crime correspondent."

"That's right."

"So what brings you to the Planning Committee? Not a sudden interest in the railings round the children's paddling pool, surely?"

"No. I want to talk to you about the plans for the new casino on the seafront."

He stopped gathering together his papers. I'd surprised him, but he recovered his composure. He picked up his brown leather briefcase from beside the chair and opened it.

"I think you must be mistaken," he said. "The council has not received any planning application for a casino on the seafront."

He started to put his papers in the briefcase.

I said: "I know that there's no formal application. But I also know that a property developer is seeking to acquire land as a site for a seafront casino."

"Property developer? Which property developer?"

"Septimus Darke."

"We've had no planning application from Mr Darke."

"You know Mr Darke?"

"I know that he's a property developer in Brighton."

"That's not quite what I asked. Do you know him?"

"I have met him once or twice."

"Your wife seems to think you know him quite well."

Cross stopped fiddling with the papers in his briefcase. Those thin eyebrows were drawn together. He didn't look friendly.

"You've spoken to Gerry."

"Yes. What were you doing at the Golden Kiss nightclub last night?" I asked.

Now there was a flash of genuine worry behind his eyes.

"Where?"

He'd recovered but not quite quickly enough.

"The Golden Kiss, the nightclub on the seafront," I said.

"I don't think…"

"I saw you there."

"I didn't see you."

"The Invisible Man," I said.

"I've had enough of this," Cross said. "You're treating me like one of those criminals you seem to enjoy spending your time with."

He slammed the lid on his briefcase, picked it up and marched from the room. I tagged along beside. We trooped down the corridor like a pair of guardsmen going on parade. We passed the mayor who looked like the cat and the one like Alderman Fitzwarren.

"I'm just trying to get some answers to questions that interest our readers, Councillor," I said.

"My visit to the Golden Kiss was on council affairs," Cross said.

"On a Sunday evening? In a nightclub?"

"Mr Darke is a very busy man. So am I. It was the only time we could manage for a brief meeting."

"Business or pleasure?"

"Strictly business," Cross said. "I have never met Mr Darke on a social occasion."

"Never?"

"I must stress never," he said.

"And last night's business meeting was about the casino plans?" I asked.

We'd reached the lady mayor who needed a shave. Cross stopped. I stopped. We faced each other.

"Yes," he said. "Mr Darke wanted to consult me informally about whether the Planning Committee would consider an application positively."

Cross went into his pompous chairman act. "Of course, I cannot prejudge any decision my fellow committee members may take but I told Mr Darke that I thought we would give the application favourable examination."

He grabbed my arm. There was the kind of desperate light in his eyes that I associated with street-corner preachers and people trying to borrow money.

"This could bring thousands of new visitors into Brighton," he said. "Millions of pounds. Scores of new jobs for local people. It's just what the town needs to drag it into the nineteen sixties, Colin. I may call you Colin, mayn't I?"

So it was best-friend time.

"Of course, Derek. You don't mind me calling you Derek?"

He nodded, a touch reluctantly. He let go my arm. We continued our march down the corridor. We passed the thin mayor with the apologetic expression and the fat one with the rotund belly.

"The casino project is something everyone in Brighton will benefit from one way or another," Cross said.

"Arnold Trumper doesn't think he's going to benefit from it."

"Arnold Trumper?"

"The owner of the Krazy Kat miniature golf course."

"Of course. I'm afraid I haven't yet been able to ask Mr Trumper for his views."

We reached the foyer. It was crowded with staff scurrying about making the best of their lunch hour. Suited management types strolled out to restaurants. Secretaries tucked their bags of sandwiches under their arms and headed to the seafront.

Cross looked relieved by the general bustle. I didn't think there was much more I could get from him in the crowd.

He said: "I'm going to have to say goodbye now, Colin. It's been a pleasure."

"I expect we'll talk again soon, Derek," I said.

We shook hands. Cross turned to leave. He stepped backwards. Two secretaries running for the door cannoned into him. The lid of his briefcase flew open. His papers crashed on to the parquet and skittered across the floor in all directions.

When they realised whom they'd jostled, the two secretaries

looked as though they'd been convicted of multiple murder. They crouched to gather up papers. Cross bent to pick them up. Everyone stooped to help. The lobby was filled with prostrate bodies bumping into one another grasping at papers.

I retrieved a bundle that had slid towards the door. I patted them together – and stared at the letter on top. In the background, I sensed a dozen people milling around Cross helping him put papers back in his briefcase.

I sensed the secretaries sniggering. A couple of copies of *Health & Efficiency*, the nudists' monthly magazine, had fallen out of one of his files. I sensed Cross, red as a radish, stammering that they were evidence for the chairman of the Watch Committee. That this kind of filth must be driven out of a pure and innocent town like Brighton. I sensed a young lad opening one of the magazines, nudging his mate and saying, "Hey, bet you don't get many of them to the pound." I sensed Cross snatching the magazines back.

And I only sensed it because my attention was riveted on the letter on top of the pile I was holding – the carbon copy of a letter from Councillor Derek Cross to Mr Arnold Trumper. What had Cross just told me?

"I'm afraid I haven't yet been able to ask Mr Trumper for his views."

I'd caught him out in a lie. And I realised that Cross and I had something more to talk about. But not now.

My eye raced down the page, absorbing the text, striving to memorise the key phrases. My mind whirled. There would be only seconds before Cross had disposed of the secretaries and started looking for his other papers. Could I pocket the copy letter? Should I? No. Cross would miss it and he'd know I'd taken it. I thrust the letter back among the other papers. I walked over to Cross.

"You dropped these, Derek," I said.

"That's very kind of you, Colin. Very kind indeed."

We were still best friends. He bustled off through a door into another part of the Town Hall. He couldn't get through the door fast enough.

Somehow I didn't think we were going to be best friends much longer.

Chapter 8

I skipped lunch and went straight back to the *Chronicle*.

I wanted to discuss what I'd discovered with Figgis as soon as possible. When I walked in, I found that he'd left for lunch half an hour earlier. I thought about trawling round the pubs that were his usual watering holes but decided to wait until he returned. Besides, I'd found a message on my desk marked "confidential and urgent". I was to telephone a William Shakespeare on a London number. I didn't recognise the number.

I was tempted to dismiss it as the kind of spoof journalists play on one another. After a couple of pints, it was hilarious to leave a fake message to call R. Hugh-Leakey – or some other invented name – on a colleague's desk. When the mug called the number, he'd find himself asking the baffled person on the other end of the line: "R Hugh-Leakey?" It would be one of the town's plumbers. As the realisation that he'd been duped appeared on the sucker's face, the newsroom would burst into uproarious laughter.

But I didn't think this was a joke. Most of the wheezes involved Brighton phone numbers. And never the Bard of Avon. So I headed into one of the booths and dialled the number.

A throaty voice with a touch of London's East End answered: "Hallo."

I took a deep breath and said: "I'd like to speak to William Shakespeare, please."

The voice said: "Forsooth, it's Colin Crampton. Hail, fellow, and well met. This is Albert Petrie."

I stepped back in shock and banged my elbow into the booth's door.

"The news editor of the *Daily Mirror*?" I asked.

"The very same."

Petrie had become a legend among national newspaper news

editors. He was one of the journalists, alongside Hugh Cudlipp, the paper's editor, who'd made the *Mirror* the country's biggest-selling national newspaper with a circulation of more than five million copies a day.

"I expect you're wondering why I've asked you to call me with this elaborate deception."

"It had crossed my mind, Mr Petrie."

"Call me Albert. Fact is that Jonnie Slingsby, our crime correspondent, is retiring in a couple of months. We're looking for a replacement and I was wondering whether you might be interested."

I found myself gripping the receiver as though it were a lifebelt. I forced myself to relax.

"Of course. Most certainly. Thank you."

"Well, don't thank me just yet, young Colin. You don't get on the *Mirror* that easily. We're going to interview three likely lads for the post so you'll have a bit of competition."

"I'd still like to be considered."

"We'll certainly do that."

"When are you making your decision?"

"That's the reason for the sudden call. Jonnie's retiring a bit earlier than we'd expected. Bought himself a place down in Spain, lucky bugger. So we're doing the interviews on Thursday. We'll make the decision the same day. Can you be here?"

"Well, Thursday is a working day and I'm expected…"

Petrie cut me off.

"Know what you're going to say. Don't want any suspicious absences from the office at edition time."

"Could be awkward," I said.

"That's why we've scheduled the interviews for early evening. Could you get to Fetter Lane by six o'clock?"

"That should be no trouble," I said.

Petrie told me who to ask for when I arrived at the *Mirror* offices.

He said: "One last thing. I'm not pre-judging the issue but we would certainly like to have your name on the short-list. If you take my drift."

"I do."

"Good. Any questions?"

"Only one. When I called and asked for William Shakespeare how did you know it was me and not one of the other two candidates for the job?"

"Good question," Petrie said. "I gave each candidate a different code name. The other two are Geoffrey Chaucer and John Milton. Answer your question?"

"Yes. Look forward to meeting you on Thursday."

"And you."

I replaced the receiver. Stood for a minute absorbing the implications of the call. Looked at myself in the mirror at the back of the booth. Decided I looked a bit flushed. Pushed my way out of the booth. And ran straight into Frank Figgis returning from lunch.

"Watch where you're going," he said. "Hey, you look like you've just stepped out of a Turkish bath."

"That booth feels like one," I said.

I wondered whether he'd heard any of my conversation. I didn't think so, but I couldn't be sure.

I said: "There are developments on the Trumper story. Can I speak to you in your office?"

"Come in now."

We walked round to his room and went in.

"Well, is it good news?" he asked when we'd sat down. He reached for his cigarettes.

"It's certainly progress," I said. "I've seen a letter Councillor Cross has sent to Trumper."

I told Figgis how I'd come to see the carbon copy and how Cross had lied to me about not being in contact with Trumper.

"I only had about five or ten seconds to scan the black, but, as far as I could see, Cross was telling Trumper that if he continued to hold out, the council could consider issuing a compulsory purchase order to make him sell the Krazy Kat."

"This was a formal notification?"

"No. Nothing like that. The letter was cleverly drafted with lots of 'ifs' and 'buts' and 'maybes'. I remember one sentence began, 'The theoretical position in certain circumstances could be…' and so on."

"So Cross was covering his back," Figgis said.

"Certainly. But also firing a warning shot across Trumper's bows. Letting him know that if he didn't voluntarily sell to Darke, the council could get involved and make him."

"So what does this mean?"

I leaned back in my chair. Figgis sat with his cigarette between his lips. The smoke curled round his face making him look like the Guy on a November the fifth bonfire.

"I think it shows that there must be some kind of arrangement between Cross and Darke over the casino plan. Otherwise, why would Cross be writing an unofficial letter before the committee has even considered the plan? I suspect money has changed hands. Of course, we can't prove it for one very obvious reason."

"We haven't got the letter." Figgis had his displeased frown on. "So how are you going to get it?" he asked.

"I've only seen the carbon copy of the letter," I said. "The original went to Trumper. He may still have it."

"But we don't know where he is."

"True, but I think there's a chance the letter could be at the Krazy Kat, perhaps unopened."

"So that's your next step?"

"I'm going back to the Krazy Kat to see if the letter is there. If you agree."

"Sure. This is your story. For the moment."

I left the newsroom with a couple of worries on my mind.

The first was that Figgis seemed to be getting twitchy about my handling of the story. He hadn't seemed happy about the way I'd dealt with the business of Cross's letter. But, then, he hadn't been there.

The second was the effect the story might have on my chances of getting the *Mirror* job. If I could land the story by Thursday, I would be able to go into the interview room trailing clouds of glory. But the problem was that Jim Houghton of the *Argus* had picked up vibes that I was working on something big.

My harmless deception of Mick (or, rather, Nick) at The Cricketers would have fuelled Houghton's suspicions further. Nick would have staggered back to the office after spending my ten bob and moaned about my no-show to his fellow hacks. I didn't think Nick had the gumption to impute a nefarious motive to my absence. He may simply have concluded that I'd got caught up in something more urgent. But the ever-suspicious Houghton would have done.

So as I stepped into the street, I stooped to re-tie my shoe lace and had a quick shufty at who was about. I wouldn't put it past Houghton to put a tail on me. The street was busy with shoppers. A couple of middle-aged matrons pushed passed me laden with shopping bags from Hannington's. An old gent with a bowler hat and striped trousers ambled along smoking a pipe. A fancy piece wearing stilettos like daggers tottered by with a poodle on a leash.

Shoppers don't spend much time standing in the same place. So it wasn't difficult for me to spot Houghton's nark. He was a young lad lounging beside the phone box on the other side of the road. He was reading the midday edition of the *Chronicle*. A nice touch to read the *Chronicle* rather than the *Argus*, his own paper. But not nice enough. He wasn't waiting to make a call because the phone box was vacant. He'd have done better to stand inside and pretend to be on the phone. If you have to stand still when you're on the *qui vive*, go somewhere where your target expects to see standing people – such as a bus queue.

I recognised the lad as a trainee reporter who'd joined the *Argus* a couple of months earlier. He was the nephew of one of the paper's directors and there were mutterings that better-qualified but less well-connected candidates had been overlooked for the coveted post. His name was Peregrine Foulkes-Hartington-Smythe, which was going to give the subs a problem when he got to earn his first byline. He was wearing grey flannel trousers and a check sports jacket that probably cost more than my entire wardrobe. I'd have to shake him off before I could go to the Krazy Kat.

So after I'd re-tied my shoe, I headed towards The Lanes, the maze of eighteenth-century passages in the centre of the town. As I sauntered into Meeting House Lane I caught a glimpse of his reflection in a shop window. Peregrine was doing well but he wouldn't be ready for what I had in mind.

I hurried through The Lanes, turned right on to the seafront and walked towards the Old Ship Hotel. I slowed down and gave my tail a chance to come round the corner so that he could see me step into the hotel.

Peregrine didn't disappoint. He still had his copy of the *Chronicle* under his arm as he bustled round the corner. I slipped in the door and made my way through the foyer to the restaurant. I entered the restaurant which was empty – the lunch service had long finished.

On the far side of the room were two service doors used by waiters to get between the kitchen and restaurant. I hurried over to one of them. Looked quickly behind to make sure my tail was out of sight. Slipped through the door.

In the kitchen Antoine, the head chef, was in the middle of berating a sous chef about some canapés. I caught a few choice words that hadn't been in my school French dictionary. Antoine was everything you'd expect of a French chef – fat, quixotic, temperamental. He had a handlebar moustache and a goatee beard. He'd taken off his toque and was mopping his high forehead with a red polka-dot handkerchief. When he saw me, he turned from the hapless sous chef.

"Colin, I am working with idiots. But you have come to speak with me. No?"

"No. I'm just passing through, Antoine. You haven't seen me."

"I get it." He tapped the side of his large Gallic nose. "You are on one of your *histoires, n'est ce pas*?"

"*D'accord*. Just need to avoid someone."

"Antoine's kitchen is the gateway to freedom. No?"

"Yes," I said.

"And the temple of the *gastronomie magnifique*. No?"

"Yes."

"But you must try one of these caviar canapés before your – how you say? – *disparition*. No?"

"Yes."

He grabbed the platter from the sous chef and shoved it towards me. The canapés looked good. I took one and bit into it.

"*Délicieux*," I said. "But I must go. If anyone comes after me, see what you can do to hold them up."

"Leave it to me," Antoine said. "I give him caviar canapés sprinkled with – what you call? – Kruschen Salts."

"That should slow him down a bit," I said.

"The caviar hides the taste of the salts. No?"

"Yes."

"He makes very loud – how you say? – *framboises*."

"Raspberries."

"*Ici*." He pointed to his ample rump.

"Don't give him too large a dose," I said. "He moves in elevated company."

I crossed the kitchen and went out through the back door.

When I reached the Krazy Kat, there was no sign of Barnet at the ticket window.

I walked round to the side of the building. A couple of elderly women, one tall, one short, were just coming off the course.

I gave them my brightest smile and said: "Did you enjoy your golf today?"

"We couldn't think of anything else to do," the tall one said.

"We're making the best of a bad job," the short one said.

It didn't sound like a ringing endorsement.

"Shall I take your clubs and balls and return them to the office?"

They handed them over, then wandered off down Madeira Drive bickering about what to do next.

I went over to the side door, knocked lightly and went in without waiting for an invitation. There was no sign of Barnet in the ticket-office room but the door to the storeroom at the back was ajar. I pushed the door open. Barnet was there with his head in a large cardboard box. As I came round the door, he jumped up.

"Oh, it's you. What are you doing in here?"

He didn't sound pleased to see me. He hurriedly closed the lid on the box.

"Two of your customers left these," I said. I handed over the clubs and balls.

"That's my job," he said.

"Just trying to be helpful. Can't be easy running the place by yourself," I said.

He relaxed a bit. Tried a smile. The zits were still in action but they didn't look happy.

"Why have you come?" he asked. "It's not, presumably, to help me."

"No. I was hoping you might've had word from Mr Trumper."

Barnet turned away from me and tightened the lid on the box he'd had his head in. He lifted the box over to the far side of the room. The box had a label on the side printed in an old-fashioned typeface. It read: *Ministry of Food: National Dried Milk.* I made a mental note.

"I've not heard from him," Barnet said. He shoved the box into a corner and lifted another on top of it.

"No letter, no phone call?" I said.

"Nothing."

I had a good look round the room. It was packed with old cardboard boxes. In places they piled from floor to ceiling. Most were covered in years of dust. But on others the dust had been recently disturbed. Barnet had been moving them about. There was no sign of any recent letters. Certainly nothing official bearing Brighton County Borough Council's crest.

"So you're soldiering on?" I said.

"Trying to," he said.

We fell silent. I watched Barnet's face. He was trying to decide whether to tell me something. He reached a decision.

"I suppose you're wondering what I'm doing in here," he said.

"It had occurred to me."

"Mr Trumper asked me to throw all this lot out."

"How?"

"A council garbage-truck visits the seafront traders every day. I was told to arrange it with them."

"But you've not done so?"

"Not yet."

"Why's that?"

"I thought I better sort through them first to see whether there was anything that Mr Trumper might want to save."

"Did he ask you to do that?"

"No. But he's had a lot on his mind."

"I see."

I looked round the room. Some of the boxes looked as though they dated back years. They were a mixed collection which had started life containing branded products. Lifebuoy soap. Colman's mustard. Cadbury's drinking chocolate. EasyGo laxatives.

"What's in all these boxes?" I asked.

"Just rubbish, mostly," Barnet said. "Old newspapers, broken golfing equipment, files of papers, old unused tickets for the golf course. Just rubbish."

"What's the point of keeping it?"

"I think Mr Trumper must be one of these people who hoards things."

"Have you found anything worth keeping?"

"Not really."

Barnet edged towards the door. "I don't want to keep you. And I really ought to get back to the ticket kiosk."

I stood in his way. He couldn't get round me. There were too many boxes.

"I'd be very grateful for anything you could show me that might give me an idea of the kind of man Mr Trumper is," I said. "I'm looking for local colour."

The zits on Barnet's chin oscillated uncertainly.

Then he said: "You might be interested in this."

He pulled out a large roll of paper from between two of the boxes and started to unroll it.

"Just hold that end," he said.

The paper had been tightly rolled for so long, it wanted to roll itself up. The paper was foxed at the edges and there were mildew patches over it, but the drawing was still clear. It was a surveyor's plan for the golf course. I looked at the details in the bottom right-hand corner. Stannard & Partners, 1940.

"This is a plan of the Krazy Kat," I said.

"Yes."

I thought back to the conversation I'd had with Ted Wilson in Prinny's Pleasure. He'd mentioned that Trumper had been having the course remodelled at the time Mildred was having her affair with the builder Reginald Farnsworth. These looked like the plans Farnsworth must have been working to. I studied them for a minute or two while Barnet hovered at my shoulder. The architect had used the narrow site cleverly to position all eighteen holes so that players could walk round the course without crossing one another's path.

But the course had been built – it was all out there in concrete and imitation felt grass – and I couldn't really see the point of keeping the plans. I would have thought that Trumper would have wanted to forget the Farnsworth and Mildred episode. But people react to personal tragedy in strange ways. And, perhaps, keeping all this old stuff was his way of coming to terms with it. I wondered whether the thought of having to get rid of it all had unhinged him. Perhaps led to his disappearance.

I let go my end of the plan and it rolled itself up. Barnet stuffed it back between the boxes.

"Did Mr Trumper ask you to throw this stuff out long before he left?" I asked.

"Only three days before," Barnet said.

"How can you be sure?"

"He'd received a letter that morning. I couldn't help noticing it came in an official Brighton County Borough Council envelope."

"Of course you couldn't."

So Trumper had received Cross's letter.

"He seemed worried about the letter," Barnet said. "In fact, he went back into the storeroom and stayed there most of the morning."

"Did you ask him what was in the letter?" I said.

"I asked him whether he was worried about anything. He said he wasn't. But later that morning he asked me whether I'd studied property law yet on my course."

"Have you?"

"As it happens, we did a module on it last year. Mr Trumper asked me if I knew anything about compulsory purchase orders."

"Do you?"

"I told him I didn't as that was a bit specialised. But if he wanted I could go to Brighton reference library and look up the subject for him."

"Did he ask you to do that?" I said.

"No. He said there was no point."

"What did he do with the letter?"

"I don't know. I think he stuffed it in his pocket."

As I thought, Trumper had the original of the Cross letter. To find the letter, I had to find Trumper. And my visit hadn't revealed any clues about where he might be.

I looked out of the window at the golf course. It was empty. In the enclosure an old ice-cream wrapper was blowing about. A couple of seagulls descended and squabbled over it.

"What will you do now?"

"I thought I would stay here until the end of the week, get rid of the rubbish boxes, then lock the place up."

"What about the pay Mr Trumper owes you?" I asked.

Barnet frowned. He looked away. Shifted from one foot to another. Fiddled with a book of tickets.

"There's a little money in the cashbox. I thought I'd take what I'm owed out of there. In fact, I don't even think there'll be enough to cover it. Do you think that's all right?"

"I don't see how Mr Trumper can object," I said.

I moved towards the door.

"I suppose I won't see you again," he said.

"Maybe not. But let me know where you're staying in case I get any news."

He gave me the address of a flat in Kemp Town. I scribbled it in my notebook.

"You'll let me know if you hear from Mr Trumper?" I said.

"Somehow I don't think I will," he said.

Chapter 9

On the way back to the office, I called at the bakers and bought a bag of custard tarts.

I needed to make a fresh visit to the morgue. This time I'd be asking Henrietta and the Clipping Cousins for help way above and beyond the call of duty. I knew that Frank Figgis wouldn't be pleased that I'd failed to track down the letter Cross had sent Trumper. So I'd decided to have another try at establishing a documented link between Cross and Septimus Darke. Cross had been adamant that he had never met Darke socially. I suspected that he'd lied about that just as he'd lied about not being in touch with Trumper. If I could prove Cross did know Darke socially – and not just through business – it would make his dealings over the casino project look bad. It could make Cross look as though he was doing a favour for a friend – rather than acting in an impartial manner as chairman of the Planning Committee. With that information, I would be able to pressure him to answer other questions. And the secrets of the morgue offered my best hope of establishing that link between Cross and Darke.

Buying the tarts reminded me that I hadn't had any lunch, so I sat on a bench in the Old Steine and ate one of them. While I wrestled with the crumbly pastry, I thought about my visit to Barnet. True, I hadn't got a sight of Cross's letter, but I had learnt something useful. Barnet had confirmed that Trumper had received the letter and that it had worried him. In fact, it seemed to have sent him into a panic, because he'd ordered Barnet to throw away the old boxes that he'd been hoarding for years. And then promptly disappeared.

Then there was Barnet's behaviour. Why was he sorting through all the old boxes Trumper had asked him to dump on the garbage truck? The lad clearly had a passion for other people's business that would ensure he went far as a lawyer. Perhaps he was just bored and was looking for something to do. Maybe he simply wanted to keep occupied. But I didn't think so. Barnet wasn't the helpful type. So I decided that my visit to the Krazy Kat hadn't been wasted and that I'd picked up some useful information.

I'd also picked up a blob of custard on my tie. I wiped it off as best I could with my handkerchief. I didn't think it showed. Then I stood up and hurried back to the office.

When I arrived back at the *Chronicle*, I avoided the newsroom, where I might run into Figgis, and went straight to the morgue. I walked in and Elsie said: "You've got a stain on your tie."

Mabel said: "It looks like custard."

Freda said: "Would you like us to sponge it off for you?"

I said: "No thank you, ladies."

I waved the bag in the air and said: "I've got something for you. Custard tarts."

Henrietta said: "You want something. What is it this time?"

I said: "When I was here this morning, you mentioned that there were sometimes passing references to people that weren't specifically catalogued."

"That's right," Henrietta said.

"So there could be lots of passing references to Cross in the cuttings that we don't know about," I said.

"That's almost certainly correct," Henrietta said.

"And the same would apply to Septimus Darke?"

"To a lesser extent. He hasn't been a public figure so he hasn't sought as much publicity as Cross."

I sat on the corner of her desk. She swivelled her chair to face me.

"I want to find out if Cross and Darke have ever attended the same social events. Is there any way that information could be somewhere in the cuttings?" I asked.

Henrietta chewed on the end of a pencil. A single wrinkle in her forehead furrowed in thought.

"It's possible," she said. "But, then, possibly not. The only way you'd find out would be by looking at every cutting."

"And that would be the work of a lifetime?"

"Certainly mine, possibly even yours."

I eased to a more comfortable position on the edge of Henrietta's desk while I thought about that.

"Presumably you keep files on the kind of organisations that hold social events – dinners, cocktail parties, dances and the like."

"What kind of organisations?" Henrietta asked.

"I'm thinking of groups such as the Chamber of Commerce, Rotary Club, Masons, Brighton Festival and so on. Could I work through them systematically?"

"You could still be talking about hundreds of files with thousands of cuttings," Henrietta said. "It would take you several days."

I got off her desk and stood up.

"I haven't got several days."

"Of course, it would be quicker if several people were looking," Henrietta said.

"I don't have several people," I said.

"I do," Henrietta said.

She turned to the Cousins. Elsie was licking the custard out of the centre of her tart. Mabel was nibbling the edge of the pastry. Freda was cutting dainty slices of her tart with a knife.

"Would you be able to help Mr Crampton by looking up some cuttings? It will mean unpaid overtime," Henrietta said.

Elsie said: "How exciting. I'd love to help."

Mabel said: "Thrilling. Count me in."

Freda said: "My George expects me to have his supper on the table by seven o'clock every evening."

She stood up and crossed the room. She turned at the door and said: "But I'm going to phone him and tell him that tonight he has to bring in some fish and chips."

It took me ten minutes to brief the Cousins on what we were looking for. I wanted to see any cutting about a social event which mentioned both Septimus Darke and Derek Cross.

Henrietta and I began on a list of organisations which held events the *Chronicle* had covered. We started at A. The Accountants' Association (wine and cheese party). Animal Welfare Trust (dog show). Alcoholics Anonymous (temperance tea).

Elsie, Mabel and Freda scurried off into the maze of filing-cabinet corridors and came back with their arms laden with folders. They started to skim through the files. Running fingers down columns. Eager to read quickly. Anxious to miss nothing.

It took us forty minutes to reach the Bs. Bridge Club (happy families snap contest), Bakers' Guild (sandwich lunch), Bus Drivers' Union (coach outing).

Nothing.

Even with all five of us working on the files, it was going to be a long job. By half past five, we'd only reached G. Golf club (match play tournament). Gun club (murder mystery evening). Gymnastics Association (fun run).

Nothing.

Seven o'clock came and went. Preston Park Residents' Association (whist drive). Publicans' Ladies Night (shove ha'penny tournament). Pensioners' Club (olde time dancing).

Nothing.

By half past eight, we were near the end. Yacht Club (seafood soiree). Young Conservatives (pyjama party). Zoological Association (beetle drive). Nothing. And no more files to search.

The table was piled high with the files we'd scanned. We all slumped on our chairs exhausted. The heavy smell of failure hung over the room.

Henrietta had kicked off her shoes. Elsie had slung her

cardigan over the back of her chair. Mabel had taken off her surgical stocking. Freda had loosened her stays.

I slumped on the desk feeling deflated. And defeated.

Henrietta said: "Well, that's that."

I ran my hands over my face. My shoulders ached.

"I'm sorry that I've wasted all of your time," I said.

Elsie said: "We had to try."

Mabel said: "It was the only thing we could do."

Freda said: "And to think we came so close."

She retightened her stays. They zinged and pinged as super-strength elastic and formidable fastenings clicked back into position.

"I don't think we came at all close," I said. "I'm sorry."

"But I did find a picture of Mr Darke," Freda said.

"How did you know it was Darke?" I asked.

"His name was captioned."

"But not Cross's?"

"I'm sure it wasn't. I'll just double check. I think it was in the Rotary Club file."

Freda rummaged among the mountain of files on the table. "Here it is," she said. "Caption reads: 'Septimus Darke entertains guests at his table at the Rotary Club's annual dinner'. The cutting's dated to March this year."

She handed me the flimsy piece of newsprint. I looked at the picture. It was Darke all right. Black tie and black heart. The centre of attention.

My hand tensed. The man sitting to Darke's right was pictured only in profile. But it was a profile I'd recognise anywhere. Councillor Derek Cross had told me twice that he had never socialised with Darke. But he was sitting at Darke's table next to the man himself. It got better. The pair were having a toast. Clinking champagne flutes. Smiling. And no doubt plotting.

I looked up. "Thank you," I said.

"You mean..." Henrietta started.

"Yes. This cutting provides the evidence I need to ask Councillor Cross some very awkward questions."

Around the table, bodies straightened in chairs. Lips turned upwards in smiles. Eyes lit up with delight.

"And tomorrow morning, ladies, it'll be chocolate éclairs all round."

I hurried back to the newsroom.

It was late, just after half past nine. A couple of colleagues were still batting out copy on their typewriters for tomorrow's midday edition. Maisie, the cleaner, was sweeping piles of screwed-up copy paper into a sack. Nobody took any notice of me so I decided to make a call from my desk rather than one of the booths.

I put the cutting in the middle of my blotter where I could see it and dialled Cross's number. It was answered after five rings by Geraldine Cross.

I said: "Sorry to trouble you twice in one day, Mrs Cross, but could I please speak to your husband?"

She said: "He's not here." She sounded a little drunk.

I said: "Do you know where I can reach him? I need to speak to him about an urgent item of council business."

"I think he's at the Town Hall. A reception for the town twinning association. It might be true. Sometimes it is."

I said: "Thank you very much."

She said: "You seem to be seeing more of him than me."

"Do I?"

"Suits me fine," she said and rang off.

I picked the cutting off the blotter and headed for the Town Hall.

At the Town Hall the same commissionaire with the peaked cap, toothbrush moustache and sergeant's stripes that I'd seen that morning was still on duty. I gave him a friendly nod.

I hurried round to the room with the reception. The town twinners had clearly had a convivial evening. The bar was loaded with empty wine bottles. The buffet table was stripped bare except for a plate with a lonely *vol-au-vent*.

Cross was at the far end of the room schmoozing a tall blonde with long legs and a haughty expression. She was wearing a figure-hugging red dress and pearl drop earrings. From the way she kept taking a step back, I guessed she wanted to shake Cross off.

I walked up to them, handed her my card and said: "Sorry to bust in on your cosy *tête-à-tête* but I wonder if you'd mind if I took Derek away to ask him a couple of questions."

I caught a flash of relief – even salvation – in her eyes.

She said: "Don't mind me. I have to be going anyway."

She turned to Cross, shook his hand, headed across the room to the exit. It looked to me as if it was all she could do to stop herself breaking into a run.

Cross simmered with subdued fury. "What's the meaning of this, Mr Crampton?"

So we were no longer best friends.

I said: "This morning you told me that you'd only held business meetings with Septimus Darke. That you'd never socialised with him. Do you still stand by that statement?"

"Of course. My word is a legend in this council."

"Is it really?" I produced the cutting and showed Cross.

"That figure sitting next to Darke is you."

He looked at the cutting.

"I don't think so."

"I do. And so will anyone else who sees it. Your wife, for example."

"Keep Geraldine out of this."

"I hope to do so. But this is you?"

"Yesh. I mean yes." His speech was slurring.

"Drinking champagne with Mr Darke. At his expense"

"I'm not standing here to listen to your jibes."

He moved off at a trot. I followed. We weaved between the tables like a couple of runners on an obstacle course.

"Why did you tell me you'd never socialised with Darke?"

"I forgot about the Rotary dinner."

"But it was only held in March."

"I'm a busy man. I attend many functions. I can't be expected to remember all of them."

We'd reached the Town Hall foyer. It was deserted except for the commissionaire.

"Was that the only social event you've been to with Darke?"

Cross turned and faced me. His face was flushed.

"I can't see what business it is of yours anyway," he said.

"Let me explain. Darke wants to build a casino on the seafront. You're the man who can decide whether the plan gets the go-ahead or not. If Darke is entertaining you with lavish hospitality, people might think he's buying you off."

"That's an outrage." Cross was shouting now. The cool councillor act had vanished.

"Is it?"

"And let me tell you, if you persist with these slanders, you better look for another job. If you can get one. By the time I've finished with you, they won't even let you write the gardening notes on the *Isle of Arran Sporran*."

He turned on his heels and stormed out. I watched him go. Sauntered over to the door.

"His nibs doesn't seem happy," the commissionaire said.

"When they start making idle threats you know you're winning," I said.

"It was the same with the Gerries," he said.

I nodded at him and said: "Goodnight".

Bong.

As I stepped out into the street the Town Hall clock was

striking ten.

Bong.

I came up hard as though my feet had just been bolted to the pavement.

Bong.

An invisible hand closed round my heart and made it beat faster.

Bong.

A black thought chased through my mind.

Bong.

I'd missed my date with Shirley.

Bong.

I was supposed to meet her at the Duke of York's cinema at seven forty-five.

Bong.

We were going to see *To Kill a Mockingbird*.

Bong.

By now the poor creature would be long dead.

Bong.

So would my relationship with Shirley if I couldn't find her and explain why I hadn't been there.

Bong.

I wondered what she'd done when she'd realised I wasn't turning up. Would she have stormed off or seen the flick by herself? She'd've been as angry as a dingo denied its dinner. But, being Shirley, she'd have also been practical. She'd've seen the film on her tod. I was certain of it. I didn't know how long the film lasted but I thought if I could get to the cinema in the next few minutes I'd stand a good chance of meeting her coming out. Trouble was, the Duke of York's was a good mile from the Town Hall.

So I got my feet moving and ran down the road towards the East Street cab rank. The street was crowded. I sashayed around strolling lovers and stumbling drunks. I leapt over a stray dog. I darted between late-evening traffic.

I raced into East Street. And came face to face with a taxi queue that snaked down the street as far as I could see. I hurried to the head of the queue, barged ahead of a middle-aged couple and shouted: "Emergency. Someone's dying."

They stepped back. I glimpsed the shock on their faces as I wrenched open the cab door and threw myself in beside the driver.

He was an old bloke with a whiskery chin and a beer belly.

I slammed the cab door behind me.

He said: "Hospital?"

I said: "Duke of York's cinema."

He said: "I thought someone was dying."

"I meant to say something."

"What kind of something?"

"I believe it's a mockingbird," I said.

"Bloody joker," he said.

He put the car into gear and we took off.

The lights were still on in the foyer of the Duke of York's when I arrived.

I paid off the cabbie, jumped out and raced into the deserted foyer. I could hear the film still playing. A commissionaire slouched by the ticket kiosk. He was wearing a scarlet uniform with lots of gold braid. He looked like a general in a Ruritanian army. He was picking his nose while eating a box of popcorn.

I walked up to him and said: "What time does the film end?"

He stuffed a handful of popcorn in his mouth and said: "Finishes in ten minutes." Bits of popcorn sprayed out of the sides of his mouth. His index finger disappeared up his right nostril.

I moved swiftly to the other side of the foyer to wait.

I paced up and down looking at the posters previewing forth-coming attractions. If Shirley wanted to see another film with me

– and that was looking like a big "if" – we could choose from *That Touch of Mink* or *Carry on Cruising*. It didn't seem much of a selection.

At last, the doors to the auditorium banged open and people streamed out. There were lots of thoughtful faces. They were still digesting the film's messages. It hadn't been a comfortable evening's entertainment. The stream had slowed to a trickle when Shirley walked through the door.

She was with a man.

He was about twenty-five. He was tall and slim. He had an intelligent face with a strong chin. He was wearing a red sloppy-joe sweater and jeans. He was talking in an animated way to Shirley, using his hands a lot to emphasise points.

She was engrossed in what he was saying. They crossed the foyer. Neither of them noticed me. They were wrapped up their conversation. They pushed through the doors into the street. They stopped walking and faced one another. He said something. She said something. He extended his hand. She took it. She moved closer and kissed him on the cheek. He smiled, turned, walked off.

I hurried out of the cinema. I came up behind Shirley and said: "I've been looking for you."

She turned. She frowned. She said: "Oh, it's you. What are you doing here?"

I said: "We had a date."

"We had a date three hours ago."

"I'm very sorry. I was held up on a job."

"Were you?"

"It was important. I want to tell you about it."

She stomped off towards the town centre. I tagged along beside. We jostled through crowds on the pavement.

I said: "It's not only the story we need to talk about. There's something else. It could be big for both of us."

"Could it?"

I said: "This is not the best place to talk. Could we go for some supper somewhere?"

"I don't know that I want to eat with somebody who's just stood me up."

"At least, you found a friend to watch the film with," I said.

She looked sideways at me and grinned.

"Jealous?"

"Curious," I said. "An old friend?"

"He's a bonzer guy. A real brainbox. Student at Cambridge. Reading natural sciences."

"I didn't know you'd been to Cambridge."

"I haven't. He comes from round here. He's got a summer job working in the same restaurant as me."

"And he just happened to be going to the film?"

"He was behind me in the ticket queue. Coincidence, eh?"

"Happens all the time," I said.

She looked at me and smiled. "You going to keep up this third-degree stuff or take me to eat. I'm starving."

I said: "I'm famished, too. Let's treat ourselves and go to the Four Aces."

I looked back up the road. A cab was heading towards us. I put two fingers into my mouth and whistled it up. It pulled into the kerb. We both bundled into the back seat. It was the same driver that had delivered me to the Duke of York's.

He looked over his shoulder. "You, again," he said. "Did you see the deceased?"

I said: "It turns out there is life after death."

We had the alcove in the first-floor dining room at the Four Aces.

Depending on your point of view, it was either a cosy or poky room in a narrow bow-fronted house in Meeting House Lane. The room was decorated with scarlet flock wallpaper.

I ordered dressed crab and *wiener schnitzel*. Shirley ordered melon cocktail and *coq au vin*. We drank a bottle of Medoc.

Over the first course, I told Shirley what I'd been doing on the Trumper story. She ate her melon and listened quietly.

"Sounds to me like you've got yourself more tangled than a spider's web," she said. "And that guy Darke sounds like the funnel web in the centre."

"Funnel web?" I asked.

"Aussie spider. Poisonous. Aggressive. Dangerous."

I drank some wine. "I guess all three could apply to Darke."

"Watch your arse with that guy on your case," she said.

"I intend to."

A waitress came and cleared our plates. I refilled our wine glasses.

"There's something else," I said. "It's possible that I may get a new job."

"On the *Chronicle*? I thought you liked the crime beat."

"I do. This would be on a national paper. The *Daily Mirror*."

"Gee," Shirley said. "The big time." She picked up her glass. "I guess we better drink to that."

"Let's not tempt fate," I said. "There's competition – two other applicants."

"You'll walk it. You may be a cocky bastard but I can tell that you're a bloody good journalist."

"Thanks for the vote of confidence."

"When does this all kick off?"

"The interviews are on Thursday."

The waiter brought my *wiener schnitzel* and Shirley's *coq au vin*.

"If I get the job, it will mean moving to London," I said.

Shirley speared a mushroom with her fork. "Big city boy, eh?" She popped the mushroom into her mouth.

"The thing is, if I move up there, will you come with me?"

Shirley stopped chewing and looked at me. "You mean to live together?"

"That's what I had in mind."

Shirley turned back to her plate and cut into a piece of chicken. "I don't know whether I want to settle in one place. Not yet."

"You've been in Brighton for two months."

"Yes, but two months is nothing. One day I'll move on."

"Do you always have to move on?"

"I'm going walkabout," she said.

"I thought walkabouts were for aborigines," I said.

"Don't knock it," she said. "Walkabout is a journey in more ways than one."

"In what ways?"

"I don't just mean a physical journey. It's not about seeing Brighton Pier and Buckingham Palace or the Eiffel Tower – although I'd love to go up that."

"So what journey?"

"Well, for the aborigines it's a spiritual journey – reconnecting with the stories of their ancestors. Learning about their history so they can pass it on to the next generation. It's about finding out who they are."

"And that's what your travels are for you?"

"I need to know what I want from life," she said.

She picked up her glass and drank some wine.

"What I'm saying is: I guess I don't know whether I'm ready to come to London with you." She put down her glass. "I need to think about it some more."

"So the answer is out there somewhere," I said.

"Yeah, somewhere. I think. I hope."

I arrived back at my flat in Regency Square just before midnight.

The supper with Shirley hadn't been quite the success I'd intended. But after we'd discussed our futures, we ordered another bottle of wine and started talking about the film. Shirley was working tomorrow evening but we'd agreed to meet again in two days. And I'd sworn on the Four Aces menu that I wouldn't stand her up a second time.

I walked up the stairs to the front door and inserted my key silently into the lock, opened the door and crept in. I didn't make it as far as the stairs before the Widow Gribble was out of her room.

She was wearing a dressing gown of floral flannelette that came down to her ankles and fluffy pink slippers. She'd put her hair in curlers.

"Mr Crampton, you're in," she said.

"Keenly observed," I said.

"I've been waiting up for you."

"No need. I've been putting myself to bed for years now."

The Widow came as close as she ever did to looking embarrassed.

"I wasn't planning to put you to bed."

"Then what did you want?"

"I was wondering whether you could spare a minute or two."

"Can't it wait until morning? I'm tired."

"It is very urgent," she said.

"Very well."

She led the way into her parlour, a room stuffed with too much furniture. There were little lace doilies on the table and antimacassars on the backs of the chairs. The place smelt of mothballs.

"I've had some dreadful news," she said.

"I'm sorry."

"It's about the vacant house two doors down."

"The one that belonged to the batty old woman?"

"I believe Mrs Saunders was a trifle eccentric."

"What about it?"

"I was told this afternoon that it's about to be sold."

I felt my heart beat faster. I knew what she was going to say even before she said it.

"It's being bought by that dreadful Septimus Darke. You know what he does, Mr Crampton. He ruins neighbourhoods. This house is the only thing I have. If I'm forced out I don't know what I shall do..."

She slumped into a chair. Her hands were shaking. I'd never noticed before that she had such delicate fingers.

"I don't know where to turn. But you're on the *Chronicle*. Surely you can expose this dreadful man. Drive him out of town. Mr Crampton, somebody must do something. Please, you must try. Say you will."

I'd never seen the Widow in such a state. Tears were streaming down her cheeks. Her nose was running.

Even the Widow didn't deserve what Darke had in store for the square. I felt a slow anger burning inside. This was no coincidence. Darke knew where I lived and this was a deliberate attempt to intimidate me. And others would suffer as a result.

I said: "It's late, Mrs Gribble. Leave it with me and I'll see what I can do about it in the morning. Don't worry. Everything will be all right in the end."

I left the Widow dabbing her eyes with a handkerchief and went upstairs to my room. If Darke was the buyer, I had no doubt who'd be the estate agent arranging the sale. Darke and Cross had decided to play rough.

I'd promised the Widow that everything would be all right. But now I wasn't at all sure that it would be.

Chapter 10

I spent a restless night.

The weather had turned warmer again. My bedroom was hot, and the bed lumpier than ever. I couldn't stop thinking about the Trumper case. About Cross and Darke. And about what Shirley had said in the restaurant. I suppose I'd never really faced up to the fact that one day she'd be moving on. I guess I'd harboured the unspoken hope that she might choose not to continue her round-the-world trip and settle in Brighton. But, from what Shirley had said, that didn't seem likely.

And now I had a hysterical Widow Gribble to deal with.

At around four, I drifted into a light sleep. I dreamt that I'd moved into a new flat with the Widow Gribble and that Shirley was our landlady. A removal van with our furniture arrived outside the flat and the men started to unload – Darke and Cross carrying in tables and chairs. And, finally, an open coffin with Trumper lying dead inside.

I awoke in a sweat. I decided there was no point trying to sleep. I showered and dressed and went for a long hike along the seafront as far as Black Rock. The walk cleared my mind and helped me separate the reality of my investigation from the nightmare of the night.

On the way back, I called into Marcello's for breakfast. I ordered a bacon sandwich with brown sauce and a coffee. The place was empty but Marcello was as cheerful as ever.

"*Dio mio*! You look terrible."

"Bad night," I said.

"Then you must drink the special of Marcello, a *caffè corretto*."

"Why not?" I said.

He reached behind the counter for a bottle of grappa and poured a good slug into my coffee.

I took my coffee and sandwich to the window seat. On the

other side of Madeira Drive I could see the Krazy Kat. Dried seaweed was drifting across the golf course in the breeze. Seagulls had splattered the ticket-kiosk window. The place looked even more desolate than usual. I wondered what had kept Trumper at the place for so many years. No doubt, it was his life.

I wondered whether it had also become the cause of his death.

My first call of the morning was at Brighton Police Station.

The daily press briefing started at nine sharp. I was absorbed in the Trumper case, but I couldn't afford to ignore Brighton's other crime stories. If there were any in the silly season.

I walked through the cop-shop's front door and ran straight into Jim Houghton.

"So, the generous benefactor from the *Chronicle* pays us a visit," he said. "Are you giving more alms to the poor today?"

He was grinning but there was suspicion lurking behind those shrewd eyes.

"Morning, Jim," I said. "You've lost me already."

"Just wondering whether you could spare ten bob for me to have lunch in The Cricketers."

"So Nick told you that I missed my lunch date with him?"

"Reckons you stood him up deliberately."

"Couldn't be helped I'm afraid. Checked in with the office and found they needed me for an urgent rewrite on a story for the mid-afternoon edition."

"Since when were you a rewrite man? Don't you have subs at the *Chronicle*?" Jim said.

"Of course, we have subs. But sometimes a story needs the master's touch."

We headed down the corridor towards the briefing room. Entered the room and sat down. A uniformed copper asked if we'd like tea. We shook our heads. There was only one thing worse than the cop-shop's tea – and that was its coffee.

"What I can't understand is what you were doing at the Planning Committee," said Houghton. "It's not your usual beat."

"I like to see the bigger picture sometimes," I said.

"The only bigger picture you're interested in is a hundred and forty-four point headline instead of seventy-two points."

"It pays to understand all aspects the of the town's life when you're covering crime, Jim. You should try it some time."

"Don't you lecture me on what I should and shouldn't try. I was covering crime in this town when you were still wetting your trousers."

"Well, we all have our own ways of approaching things." I said. "By the way, I thought I caught a glimpse of one of your younger lads yesterday afternoon. Trying to remember his name – something to do with a bird. Peregrine, that's it."

"That'll be young Foulkes-Hartington-Smythe," Houghton said. "What about him?"

"If my nature was as suspicious as yours, I could have thought he was following me."

"You don't say."

"But I must have been imagining it."

"You always did have an overactive imagination," Houghton said.

"I'll have to keep an eye out over the next few days in case any other *Argus* reporters end up on my tail."

"Our hacks have got better things to do that follow you around."

"I certainly hope so, Jim," I said.

We sat in silence for a moment waiting for Sergeant Fairbrother to come in and start the press briefing. Jim opened his notebook and wrote something in Pitman's. I glanced sideways to see if I could read it, but Jim's shorthand outlines had taken on a shape of their own over the years and I couldn't make it out.

He closed his notebook and turned to me. "You may think you're clever, but I've scooped you in the past and I'll scoop you in the future."

"I agree with all three propositions in that sentence," I said.

"Arrogant bastard," he said.

I didn't reply to that because the door opened and Sergeant Fairbrother came in. He didn't look like a man about to impart headline news.

After the press briefing, I headed for the *Chronicle* offices.

On the way, I called at the bakers and bought the box of chocolate éclairs I'd promised the Clipping Cousins the previous evening.

The girl behind the counter had hazel eyes and a lot of mascara. She was wearing a pinafore with blue and white stripes.

I said: "Is the cream in the éclairs real?"

She said: "Of course it's real. What do you think it is? A figment of your imagination."

I said: "I meant is it artificial?"

She said: "That's right, it's artificial."

"It can't be real and artificial."

"Of course, it can. It's real artificial cream."

She handed me the box with the éclairs and I left.

Back at the office, a note on my desk in Figgis's handwriting said: *My office the instant you get in.*

I didn't like the tone of that one little bit. I walked round to his office, knocked on the door and went in before he could shout "enter".

He looked up from some copy he was headlining and said: "It's you."

I said: "You can still see the other side of the room without your glasses then."

He said: "I'm not in the mood for any of your cracks this morning. Sit down."

I sat.

Figgis finished his headline and put his glasses on. He reached for his ciggies and lit up.

He said: "I've had His Holiness down here this morning."

"An actual visitation?"

"Yes, slumming it with the workers. The fact is he's had Councillor Derek Cross bending his ear on the dog and bone."

"That fine servant of the people."

"I don't like him any more than you. But, apparently, His Holiness plays the odd round of golf with him up at the Dyke Golf Club."

"All matey on the nineteenth, are they?"

"Quite possibly. What you need to know is that Cross has complained to Pope that you're harassing him. I'm told you actually gatecrashed a reception at the Town Hall last night."

"Hardly. The event was breaking up. Besides, I had documented evidence that Cross had a long-term social relationship with Septimus Darke. He'd lied to me about that in a previous interview and I needed to get his reaction."

I showed Figgis the cutting I'd unearthed the previous evening in the morgue.

He looked at it and then said: "Anyway, the hard fact is this, His Holiness wants you to close this story down."

"What? He can't be serious. Just as I'm getting close to cracking a major case of council corruption and tracking down a missing man?"

Figgis held up his hand. "Hear me out. I know you've put a lot of effort into this story. And, by the great editor in the sky, we need something to give us a decent splash. But you can't harass so-called respected local councillors."

I shrugged. "Okay. I'll go easy on Cross for the time being."

"Yes, well that brings me to the other point," Figgis said.

"Which is?"

"We can't spend forever on this story. You've produced hardly any copy for the last couple of days..."

"You know a big story like this needs development time."

"I know that. But I also need copy for the paper. And you're not giving me any."

"When I've cracked this story you'll have columns of copy. Pages of it."

"Here's the deal. You have one more day on this story. If you haven't turned up anything by the end of today, that's it. *Finito.* The end."

"Give me until the end of the week."

Figgis stubbed out his cigarette and reached for another. "No. I had to wheedle my way round Pope to get him to agree to that. Your deadline is six o'clock this evening. I want you back in this office with some copy at that hour or you're off the story."

He lit his cigarette and blew a perfect smoke ring. It held its shape and floated upwards towards the nicotine-stained ceiling.

"You have eight hours," he said.

"Eight hours," I said. "By that great editor in the sky, I'm going to need a miracle."

I stomped back to my desk, collected the box of éclairs and headed for the morgue.

There was only one way I could crack this story in eight hours – and even the odds on that were longer than His Holiness being canonised.

I didn't have enough evidence to write a story about the corrupt link between Cross and Darke. I didn't have the evidence to establish a link between Darke and Trumper's disappearance. So I needed to approach the story from the other end. I had to find Trumper and get him to tell me what had been happening. I thought the only way I had a chance of doing that was to track his sister Dorothy, the sister Harriet Sturgess had told me about. Dorothy should know Trumper better than anyone. Surely, she would have a good idea about which bolt-hole he'd scurried to.

Harriet had told me that Dorothy had married but she didn't

know her husband's name. I couldn't wander around aimlessly looking for a Dorothy. There'd be thousands of them. I needed to know her married name. And, now, I'd had an idea about how I might be able to find it. But to do that, I needed more help from Henrietta and the Clipping Cousins.

I marched into the morgue carrying the éclairs. Henrietta and the Cousins were sitting round the main table.

Elsie said: "I bet we know what's in the box."

Mabel said: "Something delicious with chocolate."

Freda said: "And lashings of whipped cream."

I put the box on the table and said: "Actually, it's real artificial cream."

Elsie opened the box. Mabel took out the *éclairs*. Freda put them on a plate.

As always, working as a perfect team.

Henrietta said: "You have the look of a man who's about to ask an enormous favour."

I said: "How do you know that?"

"Because most of the people who come in here do. So how can we help?"

I said: "I need to trace a Dorothy whose maiden name was Trumper. I don't know her married name, but I was wondering whether her wedding might have been advertised in the classified columns."

Around the paper, the births, marriages and deaths columns were known as batches, matches and despatches. I was hoping that Dorothy Trumper's wedding would have been announced in the matches.

I said: "If Dorothy's marriage announcement had appeared in the paper, I'd be able to find her husband's name from it. So I'd then know her married name."

Henrietta frowned. "It's a good idea, but we don't file announcements from the births, marriages and deaths columns in the clippings files."

I said: "I thought that would be the case. But you do have bound copies of all the back issues of the paper in here. We could look through them."

Henrietta looked at me and raised an eyebrow. "I notice you used the first-person plural there."

I joined her by raising an eyebrow. "Harriet Sturgess, my contact who knew Dorothy, thinks she was married in the closing months of the war or in the years immediately after, but she can't remember exactly when. I'm working on the assumption it was between nineteen forty-five and nineteen forty-nine."

"So you want to look through the marriages columns of every paper for five years."

"That's my plan."

"Do you know how many papers there were over those five years?"

"Well, the paper publishes six days a week for fifty-two weeks a year. That makes three hundred and twelve. But we don't publish on bank holidays, so knock off six from that number which gives us three hundred and six papers a year. Multiply by five for five years. I make the grand total one thousand five hundred and thirty papers."

"Do you realise how long it will take to look through that number of newspapers?" Henrietta asked.

"If we do it quickly, I reckon that it'll take about thirty seconds for every paper. The marriages column is in the same part of the paper every day and there are rarely more than two or three entries. If we all do it, it shouldn't take more than about two and half hours. Less if we strike lucky early on."

"And longer if we don't find anything in the years you've mentioned and you want to extend the search," Henrietta said. "I really don't think we can spare that time. We're already behind with the clippings after helping yesterday. It would mean us giving up our lunch hour. But you can ask."

I looked at the Cousins. They were my last chance to crack the biggest story I'd had since joining the *Chronicle*. Since I'd started my career in journalism.

Elsie was licking the chocolate off her éclair. Mabel was sucking the real artificial cream out of it from one end. Freda was cutting her éclair into neat bite-sized pieces.

To gain their assistance, I needed to appeal to their finest qualities. To alert them to the big issues of justice and free speech which hung in the balance. To appeal to their sense of sacrifice for a noble cause. I needed to find the words that would motivate them to help me. I thought of Mark Antony and his friends, Romans and countrymen. I thought of Henry the Fifth and his band of brothers. I thought of Churchill and his blood, sweat, toil and tears.

I spoke: "Ladies, if you help me, I'll buy you cakes for a week."

As a call to action, I thought the speech, although short, went down rather well.

Elsie replaced her éclair on the plate. She said: "Down cakes, ladies, this is an emergency."

Mabel said: "I'm putting mine to one side."

Freda said: "As my éclair is in bite-sized pieces, I can eat it while we work."

Henrietta shrugged. "I'll show you where we keep the bound copies," she said.

There were four volumes of bound copies for each year, one for each quarter. Each volume was bound in thick covers with leather spines that smelt like old suitcases. I had to brush a thick layer of dust off each one before I took it off the shelf.

Elsie took the volumes for nineteen forty-six. Mabel took nineteen forty-seven. Freda took nineteen forty-eight. Henrietta took nineteen forty-nine. I took nineteen forty-five. I had a hunch it would turn out to be the year Dorothy married. When we all had our piles of volumes, I said: "We're looking at each copy's marriages column and we want to find a Dorothy Trumper and the name of the man she married."

Five bodies bent over old newspapers. Yellowed pages of newsprint rustled as they turned. Completed volumes thumped on to the floor. Nobody spoke.

Then Elsie said: "I'm in August nineteen forty-six and Mary Pyle is marrying Stephen Driver. If they chose a double-barrelled married name they'd be Pyle-Drivers."

Mabel said: "Back in May nineteen forty-seven, I had an Arabella Sweet marrying a Richard Hart. They'd be Sweet-Harts."

Freda said: "In January nineteen forty-eight, I had a Susan Fancy marrying a Leonard Pante. If they have children, they'll have lots of little Fancy-Pantes."

Henrietta said: "Ladies, concentrate please."

Silence descended again. Time passed. Pages rustled.

I reached the last volume of nineteen forty-five. Henrietta turned to the last volume of nineteen forty-nine. In turn Elsie, Mabel and Freda reached for their last volumes. More pages rustled.

I turned to the thirty-first of December nineteen forty-five. There were three weddings listed. None involved Dorothy Trumper.

Henrietta closed her volume. "Nothing," she said.

Elsie shut nineteen forty-six with a sigh. Nothing.

Mabel slammed the heavy board cover on nineteen forty-seven. Nothing.

Freda picked up her last bite-sized piece of chocolate éclair and popped in her mouth. She ate it noisily. It sounded like laundry rotating in a washing machine.

She turned a page. "I think I must have had more entries than you. But I'm up to December the eighteenth."

She turned a page. Nothing. She turned another page. We watched her. She stopped chewing. Silence.

"There's an ink blotch on this page," she said. "I can't read it very well."

She peered closer at the page. "I thought so." She read: "The marriage is announced between Dorothy Gertrude Trumper, daughter of..."

I shifted forward to the edge of my seat.

"No need to read it all," I said. "Just give me the name of her husband."

Freda looked up. "It's not one of the funny ones," she said.

"What is it?" I said.

"John Smith," she said.

Chapter 11

John Smith.

The most common name in England, and Dorothy Trumper had married one. She could have married a Clackworthy, a Featherstonehaugh or a Pine-Coffin. Any of them would have been easier to trace than John Smith. Thousands of them in Britain. Dozens in the Brighton area.

I thanked Henrietta and the Cousins and hurried back to my desk in the newsroom. The clock on the wall was showing twelve forty-three. Five hours seventeen minutes to the six o'clock deadline Figgis had set me.

I sat down at my desk and thought about what to do next. The newsroom was noisy with clacking typewriters, shouted conversations. Smoke spiralled up from cigarettes abandoned in ashtrays while their owners bent over typewriters and batted out deadline copy. From the bowels of the building I could feel the vibrations as the presses rolled off the last of the midday edition.

I pulled down the Brighton area telephone directory from the shelf beside my desk and turned to Smith. Ran my finger down the column looking for the start of the initial "J".

In the limited time I had, it was my best bet for tracing Dorothy Smith. If, that is, John and Dorothy Smith were still alive. If they were still living in the Brighton area. If they owned a telephone. If they hadn't gone away on holiday. Or out shopping. If they weren't ex-directory. And only if the telephone was registered under John rather than Dorothy's name. It was a worrying list of "ifs" but I had no alternative.

I found the Js and started counting. One, two, three... There were fifty-seven. I made a quick calculation. At two minutes a call, it would take me nearly two hours to ring the lot. That would take me until nearly three o'clock. But I wouldn't reach them all because at least a quarter would be out the first time around. So call-backs could take longer.

I picked up the phone and dialled the first number. I let it ring ten times. No answer.

I dialled the second number. A woman's voice answered: "Ruby Smith speaking."

I said: "Do you have a Dorothy Smith, whose maiden name was Trumper living there?"

She said: "Who are you?"

"My name's Colin. I'm trying to trace an old friend."

"No, I don't think I know a Dorothy Smith," she said. "You don't mean Doris, do you?"

"No, it's definitely Dorothy, unless she's using Doris as a shortened version of the name."

"She wouldn't do that. Dorothy and Doris are completely different names. Everyone knows that."

"Silly of me," I said. "Thanks for your help."

I put the phone down.

Picked it up again. Dialled the next number.

A man with a deep voice answered.

I said: "I'm trying to contact a Dorothy Smith. Have I got the right number?"

He said: "You're not that bald-headed bloke from the bus depot who's been bothering my missus."

"Is her name Dorothy?"

"No, it's Sadie."

"Sorry to have troubled you."

"Dirty little pervert," he said.

I put the phone down.

I picked it up again.

Made another call.

The minutes ticked by.

I made more calls.

Two o'clock came and went.

Some Smiths were out.

Some Smiths were in.

Some wanted to talk.

Some slammed the phone down.

Time passed.

My thirty-eighth call. A woman's voice. Well-modulated, almost musical and refined.

I said: "I'm sorry to trouble you. I'm trying to contact a Dorothy Smith, maiden name Trumper. Do I have the right number?"

"I'm afraid not. I'm Joan Smith. What name did you say?"

"Dorothy Smith."

"I mean her maiden name."

"Trumper. Dorothy Trumper," I said.

I sensed hesitation. "Did you ever know a Dorothy Trumper?"

"Would that be Arnold Trumper's sister?"

"Yes," I said. "The Arnold Trumper who owns the Krazy Kat miniature golf course on Brighton seafront."

She paused. "I did know her slightly. But perhaps I could ask what your interest is."

"I'm Colin Crampton, from the *Evening Chronicle*. Mr Trumper appears to have disappeared and we're trying to build up a picture of his background."

"Oh, he has more than enough background," Joan said.

I shifted uncomfortably on my chair. Joan had surprised me. It sounded as though she might know more about Trumper than I'd managed to discover.

"Do you know where Dorothy lives now?" I asked.

"I'm afraid not," she said. "We lost touch many years ago, after that horrid business with Mr Trumper's wife."

"You know about that?"

"I know all about that. At the time, I was the best friend of Abigail Farnsworth. That's how I got to know Dorothy. Abigail and Dorothy knew one another."

"And Abigail Farnsworth was?" I knew the answer but had to ask the question.

"The wife of Reginald Farnsworth, the man who was alleged to have killed Mildred Trumper."

I scribbled a shorthand note. Underlined "alleged". This was the first time I'd heard anyone suggest that Farnsworth may not have been Mildred's killer.

"You used the word 'alleged'."

"Not everyone thinks Reggie killed Mildred," she said.

"Who doesn't?"

"His daughter Mary."

"She lives in Brighton?"

"Hove, actually."

"Could you put me in touch with her?"

"I could but I'm reluctant to give you her address over the telephone."

"Could I come and see you?" I asked.

"If you wish."

I looked at the list of numbers still to call. Made a quick calculation.

"I've got some calls still to make but I could be with you at about four o'clock. Your address in the telephone book is listed as New Church Road, Hove. Is that correct?"

"Yes. At four o'clock then." She replaced her telephone.

I sat there for a minute thinking about what Joan had said. It would be natural for a daughter to believe her father was innocent of a murder. But if Joan believed that, too, perhaps there was more to it. Then I picked up the phone and made the thirty-ninth call.

I arrived at Joan Smith's house at quarter past four.

I had an hour and three-quarters to stand up my story and I seriously wondered whether this meeting was going to help. But I was running out of options.

Joan lived in a large mock-Tudor house in a part of Hove that regarded itself as several steps up the social scale from the mean terraces of central Brighton. The house itself looked as though it could do with a fresh paint job. But the front garden was neatly kept. The beds were planted up like an English country garden with foxgloves and nasturtiums and pansies. There was a covered porch which had been a later addition to the house. Honeysuckle had been carefully trained over the top of it. It was flowering and gave off a heady perfume. The front door opened as I approached.

Joan Smith was a tall and severe-looking woman who reminded me of an old-fashioned schoolmarm.

She said: "I saw your car draw up. You're late."

I said: "I'm sorry about that. I was held up at the office."

She said: "You better enter."

I entered.

The hall was a long gloomy passageway with a low ceiling and dark brown wood panelling. It was the sort of place you'd expect to lead to some dungeons.

Instead, Joan led me into a small sitting room at the back of the house, which was surprisingly bright. It had cream-coloured walls and French windows that opened out onto a small patio. There was a wooden table and chairs on the patio already laid with a jug of what looked like homemade lemonade. Joan poured us glasses.

I said: "Thank you for agreeing to see me at short notice."

"Not at all. You wanted to know Mary Farnsworth's address. May I know why?"

I drank some lemonade. It was not too sharp but cool and refreshing.

I said: "You mentioned that she believes her father to be innocent of Mildred Trumper's murder."

"She has never wavered in that belief."

"May I ask whether you share her view?"

Joan sipped at her lemonade while she thought about her answer. "The honest answer is that I don't know. I think there is reasonable doubt."

"Enough to have acquitted him of Mildred's killing if the case had come to trial?"

"Possibly."

"What makes you say that?"

"Reginald Farnsworth was no saint. He had an eye for the ladies. Rather too much of an eye in my opinion. But I don't believe he was a cold-blooded killer."

"Did his wife, Abigail, know about his wandering eye?" I asked.

"I think it's unlikely she wouldn't have known the kind of man he was. She'd have known that before she married him. So likely she was willing to take him with all his faults."

"But would she have known about his affair with Mildred?"

"I don't know. She certainly knew that he had casual flings with other women but I don't think she knew who the women were. Perhaps she preferred not to know."

I glanced at my watch. It had just gone half past four.

I said: "I have a very tight deadline. And I'd like to speak to Mary Farnsworth before it expires. Could you give me her address?"

Joan rose and walked back into her sitting room. I drained the last of my lemonade and followed. Joan went to a small bureau, unlocked the lid and took out a leather-bound address book. She sat down and copied out the address onto a small card.

"Here it is," she said. "But I don't know whether she will be willing to speak to you. Memories of her father still touch a raw nerve even after all these years."

I took the card. Mary lived in a flat in Palmeira Square, just off Hove seafront.

"Thank you for speaking so frankly," I said. "I feel I know Reginald Farnsworth a little better as a result."

We passed back through the gloomy hall and I left.

I climbed back in the MGB, made a U-turn in front of a builders' lorry and screeched off along New Church Road.

Mary Farnsworth lived in a second-floor flat on the west side of Palmeira Square.

The entrance to the flats was through a grand portico built in a time when ladies and gentleman would have swept up in carriages and had the front door opened by a liveried footman. Inside, the hallway and stairs were lit by low-wattage light bulbs. There was a pervading smell of furniture polish.

I climbed the stairs to the second floor. The door to Mary's flat was on a small landing. There was an electric bell. I pressed it and heard a shrill ringing inside the flat. I waited for half a minute and pressed again. Still no answer.

I was about to press a third time when the door on the other side of the landing opened. The head of a middle-aged woman wearing a hairnet peered round the side.

"Do you want something?" she said.

"I'm a friend of Mary's from London. Just in Hove for the day and thought I'd look her up."

"Well, I'm afraid you're out of luck," she said with evident relish.

"Why's that?"

"Because she's gone away for a few days. Left three days ago in a station taxi. She was carrying a holdall as well as a suitcase. And wearing those new shoes she bought at the Army & Navy Stores."

"Do you know where she's gone?"

"Of course not. Do you think I'm some kind of busybody?"

"Not at all. Do you know when she'll be back?"

"Not for some time. She's cancelled her milk and those yoghurts she has. And her *Daily Telegraph*."

"Thank you," I said.

She frowned at me and closed the door.

I reached in my inside pocket for one of my cards and wrote a brief note on the back. It asked Mary Farnsworth to telephone me at the *Chronicle* as soon as she returned. I pushed the card through her letterbox.

Then I went back down stairs and out into the street.

An *Evening Argus* delivery van drove past. The newsbill on the side read: Seafront development rumours.

In frustration, I kicked a nearby lamppost. I had a sinking feeling that Jim Houghton was going to scoop me again.

Chapter 12

As I stood in the street, a church clock chimed five.

I had one hour before I reported back to Figgis. It seemed impossible that I could locate Trumper in the time. The only long-shot was that he might have resurfaced at the Krazy Kat. I'd asked Barnet to contact me if Trumper got in touch, but I didn't trust him. Barnet said he'd stay on until the end of the week. So he should still be on duty.

I climbed into the MGB and roared towards the seafront.

I knew the Krazy Kat was closed as soon as I pulled into the kerb beside the ticket office. I could see the blind drawn down at the window.

I rummaged in my pocket and pulled out my notebook. Barnet had given me the address of the house in Kemp Town where he was staying. Perhaps he'd decided to bunk off work and stay at home. I couldn't blame him. After all, he'd not been paid. I pulled the MGB into the late-afternoon stream of traffic on Madeira Drive.

The clock on the top of the Aquarium showed seventeen minutes past five.

Barnet had rented a small flat in Sokeham Street, a row of mean-looking terraced houses in a run-down part of Kemp Town.

I pulled up outside the house and got out of the car. A young boy on roller skates shouted "Watch out, mister," whizzed past me and disappeared round a corner. Across the street, a fat woman beat a carpet she'd hung over some railings. An old bloke wearing a rat-catcher's cap and clips round his trouser turn-ups rode by on a butcher's bike. The smell of chips frying wafted out of a nearby house.

Barnet's flat was in the basement of a three-storey tenement that looked like the kind of dilapidated old ruin Darke usually bought. A rusting iron gate opened on to steep stone steps which led down to a covered portico below street level. I pushed open the gate and went down the stairs.

A faded sign next to the front door said "Garden Flat". The garden consisted of a tiny yard paved with chipped red bricks. There were a couple of large flowerpots which held dead geraniums. The area had filled up with litter that people had thrown over from the street. The place smelt of mildew and mangy cats.

I knocked on the door and waited. Nobody answered. I knocked again. Silence. And again. Nothing.

The flat had a small window which looked out over the yard. I moved across and peered through. It was a bedroom. The bed hadn't been made. The contents of the room were strewn about over the bed and the floor. Books from a shelf were scattered about, some lying opened. The bedside lamp was on its side. Drawers had been pulled open and the contents roughly thrown around. The room had been turned over.

I grabbed one of the flowerpots, upended it and stood on the top to get a better view into the room. I could now see the bed more clearly. The floor on the far side of the room was still obscured by the bed. But I could see a shoe protruding from behind the bed. The shoe was at a forty-five degree angle with the sole partly off the ground. It couldn't possibly rest in that position by itself without falling one way or the other to rest either on its sole or its uppers.

Unless it had a foot inside it.

I needed to get inside the flat. A fanlight window was ajar at the top. I checked to see whether I could open it wider. I could. But even if I could stick my whole arm through, I wouldn't be able to reach the handle that opened the main window.

I took the basement steps two at a time up to the street. I opened the MGB's boot and rummaged inside. I took out an adjustable spanner and pair of gloves – both part of my wheel-changing kit. I took a quick look up and down the street and slipped back down the stairs.

I put on the gloves and hoisted myself up on the flowerpot. I adjusted the claw of the spanner and eased it through the window. I didn't think it was going to be long enough. But by standing on tip-toe I could just reach the window handle. I worked the claw of the spanner round the handle and pulled gently upwards. The handle didn't move.

I pressed myself as close to the window as I could, gained an extra half inch and tried again. The handle shifted a little and then stuck. Carefully, I eased my hand a little down the spanner handle, gripped it more tightly and pulled again. The handle moved a little. Then it flew upwards in a sudden jolt. I slipped on the flowerpot and almost lost my footing. I grabbed the windowsill and held on. I manoeuvred the spanner out through the fanlight, stepped off the flowerpot and laid the spanner on the ground.

I pushed open the window and climbed inside, taking care not to disturb anything. A bluebottle rose from behind the bed and buzzed angrily around the room. I took a deep breath, steeled myself for what I might find, and looked behind the bed.

Barnet was lying there.

He was dead.

There was a patch of purple blood on the threadbare carpet beside his head. The blood had leaked from a deep cut on Barnet's forehead just above his right temple. His head was thrown back at an unnatural angle. There was a vivid welt round his neck, left by something that had been pulled so tight it had cut into the skin. It wasn't going to take Sherlock Holmes to work out how he died. He was knocked out by the blow to the head and then strangled.

I could feel my heart beating faster. I felt hot and flushed. My stomach churned and I belched. I didn't think I was going to be sick, but I turned away from the body and forced myself to breathe evenly.

I hadn't liked Barnet but he hadn't deserved to end up like this. Left for the bluebottles in a shabby little basement lodgings. It was a sickening end. For a moment, I wondered whether Trumper was also lying dead somewhere. But that was pure speculation. I needed to remember that I was a reporter – that my task was to collect facts.

I looked around the room. The place had been searched hurriedly. There was no doubt about that. I couldn't tell whether anything had been taken and I wasn't going to start moving things around and disturbing evidence.

Carefully, I stepped round Barnet's body and looked at his bedside table. There were a couple of books there – a law textbook on court procedure and a paperback western. There was a mug containing the dregs of some cocoa. And there was a bunch of keys. I recognised them from when Barnet had let me into the office at the Krazy Kat on Sunday morning. There was a Yale key, which I guessed might open the front door to the flat, a mortice which might be for Barnet's student digs and a third key which I'd seen him use to open the padlock which secured the door at the Krazy Kat.

I thought about that for a moment. There were boxes of old papers at the Krazy Kat. Perhaps there were papers that could throw light on Trumper's disappearance. I'd hoped to talk Barnet into letting me look through them. That wouldn't be possible now. But I felt I had to get back into the Krazy Kat office somehow. I thought about taking the padlock key but that would be too risky. It would be tampering with evidence. A serious criminal offence. No, the key would have to remain with the others.

I crossed the room and gently pushed open the bedroom door. The door led into a dark passageway with another door on the other side. I opened it and went in. It was Barnet's bathroom.

There was a small bathtub with a greasy ring round it, a lavatory with a broken seat and a small wash basin. A razor and shaving stick were on a small shelf beside the basin. There was a half-used bar of Lifebuoy soap on the basin. I picked up the soap and went back into the bedroom.

I crossed to the bedside cabinet and carefully picked up the key ring. I separated the padlock key from the rest and pressed it carefully into the bar of soap. I turned the bar of soap over and made a second impression with the other side of the key. I took out my handkerchief and carefully wiped the surplus soap off the key. Then I wrapped the bar of soap in my handkerchief and put it in my pocket.

I walked over to the window and closed it. I pushed back the fanlight so that it was in its original position. Then I went into the passageway and turned towards the front door. I glanced back to make sure I'd left the room exactly as I found it.

And noticed something I'd not seen before.

Lying on the floor beside the bed, partly covered by a blanket, was a small card.

I crossed the room, stooped to look at it. And almost slipped backwards in shock.

It was a business card. Printed in embossed ink. In gothic type. With a gold border. And announcing that its owner had been Septimus Darke, chairman, Darke Enterprises.

Carefully, I lifted the edge of the blanket to see whether there was anything else underneath. There was only the card.

My mind was buzzing like a chainsaw. What did it mean? Had Darke killed Barnet? Perhaps to make him reveal Trumper's whereabouts? Surely, he wouldn't leave his calling card? Not even a man as arrogant as Darke. But perhaps he thought he was untouchable. Maybe it was a warning to others who were thinking of crossing him. Or, perhaps, more mundanely, he had simply lost the card in the struggle with Barnet. Or maybe he had dropped it without realising.

I didn't think so. Darke was not the kind of man who did things without realising.

The bluebottle which had settled somewhere started circling the room again. It landed on Barnet's forehead. Crawled towards where the blood had clotted. I turned away in disgust and made for the door.

I opened the door and went out. I collected the adjustable spanner from outside the window and slipped up the basement steps. I went through the iron gate and closed it. I glanced up and down the street to see if anybody was taking special notice of me. No one gave me a suspicious look.

I went over to my car, opened the boot, took off my gloves and put them and the spanner back with the wheel-changing kit. I took the handkerchief-wrapped soap out of my pocket and hid it in the kit. I rummaged among the other stuff in the boot and found a printed card I needed. Then I closed the boot and walked briskly up the street.

I checked my watch. It was quarter past six.

There was a telephone booth on the corner at the far end of the street. I went in, dialled the operator. I asked for a reverse-charge call to be put through to the *Evening Chronicle*. When the *Chronicle* switchboard answered, I asked for Figgis.

I had to hold the phone for a couple of minutes before he came on the line.

When he did, he sounded angry. "Where in the name of effing misprints do you think you've been?"

I said: "That front-page story you've been pressing me for."

"What about it?"

"It'll be a murder headline."

"What the hell are you talking about?"

"I'm just about to telephone Ted Wilson at Brighton Police and tell him that I think Robert Barnet, Trumper's hired help, may be dead?"

"What do you mean you 'think' he might be dead?"

"I know he's dead because I've been inside his flat using means you may not want to hear about. I've left everything as it was and I don't think the police will reason they're not the first on the scene."

Figgis said: "You take some chances."

I said: "I'll delay my call to Wilson for ten minutes to give you time to get a photographer and back-up reporters down here before the cops arrive. I'm going to need someone to monitor the comings and goings at Barnet's flat and someone to go round the neighbours and ask them whether they saw anything. They won't have done, but we have to make sure."

"I'll get on that right away. And, as soon as you can reasonably do so, get back here. I want the copy for a front-page lead and an inside-page backgrounder on my desk by seven tomorrow morning."

I hung about in the phone box for a few minutes pretending to be looking up numbers in the telephone directory. Then I dialled Ted Wilson's personal number.

"Got a minute?" I said.

"It's you," he said. "Make anything of that disappeared golf man?"

"I think I might do. If you bring a team down to Sokeham Street in Kemp Town, I think you may find that Robert Barnet, the lad who reported him missing, is dead in his flat."

There was a brief silence while Wilson absorbed the information. Then he said: "I hope this is not one of your newspaper stunts."

"If it were a stunt, it would be in appallingly bad taste."

"Since when has that bothered newspapers?"

"Since it involved dead bodies," I said. "Are you going to get a team down here?"

"I'm on my way," he said. "Stay in the street."

He put the phone down.

I put down the receiver and took the printed card I'd retrieved from the boot of my car out of my pocket. I stuck it in the window of the phone booth. It read: "Post Office. We apologise that this telephone box is temporarily out of order." When the news got out, the locals would want to make calls to their friends to tell them about all the excitement and the box would get busy. But I'd need a ready line through to the *Chronicle* to phone in copy and I didn't want to hang around while the street gossip fed in four pence after four pence to spread the word.

The team from the *Chronicle* arrived a few minutes later in a taxi.

There was Freddie Barkworth, the paper's chief photographer, and two general reporters, Mark Hodges and Phil Bailey. We huddled in the street while I briefed them. Freddie would wait outside the house and get shots of the police going in and the body being brought out and driven away. Mark would stay with Freddie. He'd try to pick up odd snippets of information from cops coming and going about what they'd found inside. Phil was going on the knocker. He'd ask whether the neighbours had seen anything or whether any of them had got to know Barnet in the brief time he'd been lodging in the street.

The first of seven police cars arrived just as we were finishing our briefing. Wilson was in the third. He came over to me and looked at Freddie, Mark and Phil. "You seem remarkably well prepared," he said. "If I hadn't known better, I'd have thought you'd have set this up before you called us."

"We just happened to be in the area," I said.

"And I just happen to have floated in on the high tide perched on top of a digestive biscuit," Wilson said. "I'm going inside. Stay there, I shall want to talk to you."

By now the locals had realised that something was up. They poured out of their houses into the street. Women whispered fearfully to one another. Men pushed forward to get a better look. Mothers ushered children back indoors. Police stretched out tape and put a cordon round the house.

From the basement came the sound of splintering wood as Wilson and his team broke their way into the flat.

I spent a few minutes watching the movements up and down the basement steps. Then I walked back down to the phone box and called the *Chronicle*.

I asked for a copy-taker and dictated some notes to use in the story I'd write for the front page. I'd need to get Wilson's formal statement about the killing before I could write the peg, but it would save time to have the background ready to roll.

As I came out of the booth, I ran into Jim Houghton.

"I knew you were on to something," he said.

"Pure chance," I said.

"Sure. About the same as the chance of me editing *The Times*."

"Anyway, we're both on the same story now," I said.

"Are we?" he said. "I wonder. And you can take that notice out of the telephone box. I've got one of my own."

I walked back up the street and found that Wilson had just come up the basement steps.

He walked over to me and said: "I've been looking for you."

"Just had to phone through some copy."

"Barnet's dead," he said. "Knocked out, then strangled, I'd say. But we'll be waiting for the pathologist to pronounce on that."

"Anything else you can tell me?"

"We need to talk quietly," he said. "There's a boozer called the Red Lion round the corner. We'll go there."

We settled into a corner table at the Red Lion with our drinks.

It was small place with a neat L-shaped bar. The walls were hung with seafaring pictures. There was austere wooden furniture which explained why most patrons didn't seem to linger long over the drinks. We were served by a blowsy barmaid with blonde hair and a large bosom who seemed put out when she realised we didn't want sit at the bar and admire her cleavage.

Wilson said: "I need to know about the events leading up to you discovering Barnet."

I described my visits to the Krazy Kat over the past few days and why I'd gone to his flat. I left out the other visits I'd made including my encounters with Darke and Cross.

Wilson made a few jottings in his notebook. I took a generous swig of my G&T.

"And that's all," he said.

"That's all."

"And how did you know he was dead?"

"I looked through the window. I could see his foot poking out from behind the bed."

"We looked at that and we could only just see the shoe."

"I was standing on a flowerpot."

"Were you?"

He took a good pull at his whisky.

"And you did nothing else?" Wilson asked.

"I'd knocked on the door."

"Apart from knocking on the door."

"Not that I can recall," I said.

He wrote it slowly in this notebook. *Not…that…I…can…recall.*

He looked up: "I hope so," he said.

I lifted my glass and drained the drink.

I said: "Any clues about who the killer was?"

Wilson squinted at me over the top of his glass. He took a slug of his whisky and said: "Should there be?"

"I was just wondering."

"Let's just say that we'll be following up several lines of enquiry."

"Several?"

"Yes, several."

We fell silent for a moment. Wilson would have found Darke's card but he wasn't going to tell me what he made of it. At least, not yet. I'd need to work that out for myself.

So I said: "If there's nothing else, I've got to get back to the office."

"No," Wilson said. "There's nothing else. For the present."

I walked back into Sokeham Street.

Phil was just coming down the steps from one of the houses.

"Anything from the neighbours?" I asked.

"One or two bits of colour about life in the street. Nothing specific about Barnet," he said.

"We'll meet back at the office at ten o'clock to compare notes and plan coverage for the first edition tomorrow," I said. "Pass the word to Mark."

He nodded.

I walked on down the street, climbed back into the MGB and drove back to the *Chronicle*.

We had a front-page story that would surely reverse the circulation decline. But, somehow, I didn't feel as good about it as I thought I should.

Chapter 13

The following morning I was out of bed by half past six, even though I hadn't hit the sack until nearly one.

I had important business I wanted to get underway before serious work kicked off at the *Chronicle*. It would be a busy day at the paper.

Nobody stirred in the house as I crept down the stairs. Only the distant rumble of the Widow's antique boiler and ghostly knockings as airlocks shifted in the plumbing disturbed the silence. I left the house and walked round to the mews. It was going to be another hot day. The air was already warm. I took down the roof on the MGB, climbed in and drove off. I headed towards the seafront and turned towards Hove. A gentle breeze was coming in off the sea and the air smelt good. Fresh and salty. I still had the hot musty stench of Barnet's flat in my nostrils. A drive by the sea in the open-topped MGB would clear it.

When I reached Hove, I turned off the seafront and drove into First Avenue, a road of stately Edwardian villas. I parked the car halfway up the street and walked round the corner to St Johns Road. The road had once acted as a kind of mews for First Avenue. But that was long ago. Now the stable blocks had been turned into garages and workshops.

I glanced at my watch. It had just turned half past seven and the first places were opening. A mechanic's legs stuck out from under a Brown Humber. A young lad in green overalls had his head bent under the bonnet of a Morris. An older bloke was wrestling with the tyre from a baker's delivery van. The clang clang of metal on metal sounded from deep inside a dimly lit workshop. The sharp smell of oil cut through the sea breeze.

I strolled down the mews trying to give the impression I was deciding where to have my car serviced. I was looking for a man I'd heard about but never met. I'd been told that he worked out of a small garage in the mews but that he didn't make it easy for people to find him. I'd reached the far end of the mews and was retracing my steps before I spotted a black garage door with a wicket gate cut into it. The paint had worn off in places and the wood was rotting at the bottom. Unlike the other premises in the mews, this one had no sign outside advertising its occupant. There was a Judas hole in the wicket.

The man I was seeking valued his privacy. His name was Kenneth Jones. He'd been known among the Welsh criminal classes as Kenneth the Keys. But that was before the rozzers had made it clear that, as far as he was concerned, there was no longer a welcome in the hillsides.

I knocked on the wicket and waited. There was some movement behind the door and a slight darkening of the Judas hole. I was being observed. The wicket opened a crack and a man's head appeared. He was about sixty with a cadaverous face and a wart on his chin. He wore pebble glasses with thick black rims.

He said: "We're closed."

I said: "I was hoping you might be as I have private business to discuss."

He peered at me through the pebble glasses. His eyes were a brilliant blue. Magnified by the thick lenses they looked like jellyfish wobbling about in a fish tank.

He said: "How did you find me?"

I said: "I was recommended."

"By whom?"

"I'd rather not say. I understand discretion is everything in your line of work. Same in mine."

"You better come in," he said.

I ducked through the wicket. Inside, the place was in darkness except for a workbench illuminated by two bright Anglepoise lamps. The workbench contained a lathe and some other machinery I didn't recognise. There was a wooden stool in front of the bench. Kenneth sat on it.

He didn't offer me a seat so I stood.

He swivelled on his stool to face me and said: "What's your name?"

I said: "Percival."

Foolishly, I hadn't anticipated the question and it was the first name that came into my head.

I said: "I gather you make keys."

"So?"

"To special order."

"What's your problem?"

"Unfortunately, I have lost the key which unlocks the padlock on my bicycle shed. I was wondering whether you could make me a replacement."

"Might do. But be cheaper to get a locksmith to cut off the old padlock and fit a new one," he said.

"I had considered that, but I want to keep the existing padlock which fits very well."

"Of course you do, Percival." He laid extra stress on my name.

"Can't normally copy a padlock key without an original to work from," he said.

"I appreciate that difficulty," I said. "I may be able to resolve it."

I pulled out the handkerchief with the bar of Lifebuoy soap wrapped inside.

"Fortunately, I'd made an impression of the key just for this unhappy eventuality," I said. I handed him the soap.

"Very forward thinking of you," he said.

"Prudence is my middle name."

"Percival Prudence," he said. "Has a certain ring to it."

His voice had a musical Welsh lilt which didn't go with his appearance. I wondered whether he'd ever sung in a male voice choir. Kenneth rummaged on his workbench and found a magnifying glass. He studied the soap for at least a minute, making a minute inspection of both sides.

"I think I can do that," he said.

"That's good news."

"It'll cost twenty-five pounds."

"That seems rather steep for a single key."

"Could always call the locksmith with the bolt cutters."

"No. On reflection, considering a man of your experience, and the skill you bring to the work, I'm sure the price is reasonable," I said.

"Only price you'll get."

"I'll take it," I said. "Fifteen pounds now and ten on delivery."

"Seems fair," Kenneth said.

I took out my wallet and handed over three fivers.

"Be ready by noon tomorrow," he said.

"I'll collect from here."

"No. I don't keep finished goods on the premises."

"Very sensible," I said. "There's a pub up in the North Laine area of Brighton called Prinny's Pleasure. I'll meet you there at twelve-thirty."

He scribbled a note on the back of an old cigarette packet.

I said: "Don't be late."

"Punctuality is the politeness of princes," he said.

"Let's hope it also applies to locksmiths," I said. "I'll show myself out."

I ducked back though the wicket door and closed it behind me. I spent the time walking back to the car thinking of ways I could disguise a claim of twenty-five pounds for illegal key-cutting on my expenses.

I arrived at the morning police press briefing twenty minutes later just as Ted Wilson was walking in.

The room was more crowded than usual. Apart from the regulars – Jim and me – there was a young woman from the *Brighton & Hove Herald* whose name I'd forgotten, a genial bloke with a beard and big smile called Harry from a local news agency, and three stringers that were representing nationals.

As there was a murder to announce, Wilson had been drafted in to front the briefing. Fairbrother was there to carry his notes and hand round the tea.

Ted started by reading a statement written in the kind of official language which the police use to make it look as if they're in complete control. "Police officers attended a call at an address in east Brighton… They had occasion to use force to enter the premises… A body was discovered on the premises which showed signs of violence… The police are treating the incident as suspicious…"

When he finished, Ted called for questions.

I decided to keep my mouth shut. You can give away what you already know in a carelessly worded question. And I didn't want Jim and the others getting a hint that I knew more than they did.

So as Ted scanned the room looking for questions, I kept my hand down.

Jim asked: "Are you looking for any particular suspect?"

Ted shuffled his papers a bit and said: "At this stage, we're pursuing a number of lines of enquiry."

I whispered to Jim: "He means, 'we don't have any names at all in the frame'." Jim grinned.

So did I. When you've got an exclusive lead into a story, there's no harm in misleading the opposition.

One of the stringers asked: "Do you have any theories about the motive for killing Barnet?"

Ted said: "We're keeping an open mind on that."

I whispered to Jim: "We don't know what to think about it."

Harry, the news agency guy, asked: "How did the killer get into the victim's flat?"

Ted said: "We're examining a range of possibilities."

I whispered: "It's as much a mystery to us as it is to you."

And on that inconclusive note, the press briefing broke up.

I was first out of the door before Jim could collar me. I had the edge on him with this story so far. And I hoped that my whispered asides would persuade him that I knew nothing more than he did. But the next big break would be nailing the killer. And I wanted to be the first to break that story, too.

In a strange way, I felt I owed it to Barnet.

When I walked into the *Chronicle* newsroom ten minutes later, there was a big-story buzz about the place.

The day before, the newsroom seemed to be running in slow motion. Now there was real tension in the air. Phil Bailey barked questions down his phone. Mark Hodges hit the keys on his battered typewriter with deadline vigour. The copy boy bustled about with a snap rather than a shuffle.

I walked over to my desk and batted out a couple of pars about the press briefing to add to the copy I'd already written. I called for the copy boy and sent the folios up to the subs.

Then I sat back and thought about my next move. Figgis would be expecting a running story which meant something strong enough for the front page tomorrow. Another splash. But there were puzzles about this story I couldn't unravel. For a start, I couldn't work out why Wilson hadn't arrested Darke. The business card at the flat at least had to point the finger in his direction, even if Darke had an explanation for it – which he certainly would. Perhaps Wilson didn't think that Darke had been behind the killing. I'd only had a few minutes to look round Barnet's flat. Wilson and his team had had hours to conduct a thorough search. Perhaps they'd discovered something which turned their suspicions in another direction. If so, Wilson wasn't saying at the moment.

Then there was the question of Trumper's disappearance. Was Darke behind that? It had originally seemed likely to me, but Wilson's failure to arrest Darke made me wonder. Perhaps

Trumper had merely disappeared to get himself out of Darke's way. If so, finding him could be the key that unlocked the mystery of this story. But I simply couldn't begin to think of where to look. Trumper could have gone to ground anywhere. Trumper's sister should surely be able to shed some light on the mystery, but as I didn't know where she lived, I couldn't ask her. I couldn't think of a way to trace her, although I had a nagging feeling at the back of my mind that Harriet Sturgess, Trumper's neighbour, had said something which could have helped. But I couldn't remember what it was.

I was thinking about all this, when my phone rang.

I lifted the receiver and said: "Colin Crampton."

A woman's voice said: "Mr Crampton, I've got your note."

I said: "Who's speaking, please?"

She said: "It's Mary Farnsworth. You left a note at my flat yesterday. I've been away and returned this morning."

"Of course, I did. Sorry."

"The note said you wanted to see me about my father."

"Yes, if I could. I spoke to your friend Joan Smith."

"She was my late mother's friend. But we've kept in touch."

"Anyway, I was wondering whether I could talk to you about your father."

"Why do we have to rake up that business again?" she asked. There was pain in her voice.

"It appears that Arnold Trumper, whose wife was killed, has disappeared. His employee has also been killed," I said.

"I can't see how this is relevant to my father after all these years."

"I've written a background piece for today's paper and I've mentioned the story about Mildred's murder. But Joan told me yesterday that both you and she don't believe your father was guilty of the killing. I've suggested in the piece that the idea that the case was open and shut was wrong."

"Have you?" She sounded surprised in a good way. "I haven't

seen today's *Chronicle* yet."

I glanced at the clock. It was twelve minutes past ten.

I said: "The presses will start printing the midday edition in three minutes. If you like, I could bring one round to you. I'd like to speak to you anyway."

There was silence on the line for a moment while she thought about that. Then she said: "I could see you in about an hour if that's convenient."

"I'll be there," I said.

I replaced the receiver. I sent the copy boy to collect some copies of the midday edition.

Mary Farnsworth was a young woman turning into an old woman before her time.

She had black hair which already showed the odd fleck of silver. She had an attractive open face but there were more frown than smile lines around her brown eyes and her small mouth. She was wearing a cream blouse and tan slacks. She had a crucifix on a silver chain round her neck.

The sitting room was at the front of the flat and looked out over Palmeira Square. Sun was streaming in the windows so the room was brightly lit. It was not flattering to the three-piece suite covered in some worn red velvet material. The musty smell of old cooking clung to the fabric. A Siamese cat slunk around in the background.

I handed Mary a copy of the *Chronicle* and said: "The background piece is on page three."

She sat down in an armchair, took up her glasses from a side table and turned to the page. I sat down opposite and waited while she read the article.

She took off her glasses and looked at me.

"It's painful to have all this brought up again," she said. "But at least you've been fair to father."

She got up and crossed to a bookcase. She took down a

picture of a tall man in a private soldier's uniform.

"This is father… Reggie," she said. "Taken the day before he left for France. He was a corporal in the Sussex Rifles."

I took the picture from her and looked at it. The family snap had been taken on the seafront. I could see the Palace Pier in the background. He was a handsome man with even features and a dimple in his chin. He had fair wavy hair. He wore his uniform well. He was smiling but I thought I could detect worry lurking at the back of his eyes. Perhaps he was thinking about what might await him in France. Or what Mildred had in store. I handed the picture back to Mary.

"A good-looking man," I said.

"Yes," she said.

I said: "It's difficult for me to ask this question, so let me just do it a simple way. The evidence implicating Reggie in Mildred's murder was circumstantial but strong. What makes you believe he was innocent?"

"A daughter's intuition," she said.

"Intuition is not evidence."

"No, it can be better. Because it's knowledge that comes from the heart."

"Lawyers wouldn't say so."

"Lawyers never got a chance to test the evidence. That's the damnable thing. Because father died before he could answer the charges, he never had the opportunity to refute them."

I thought about that for a moment. Then I said: "We have Magna Carta. Everyone is innocent until proven guilty. Reggie was never charged, tried and convicted. Therefore, he is innocent in the eyes of the law."

"But not in the eyes of the public."

"Does that really matter?" I asked.

"It does to me. The police at the time said they weren't looking for any other suspects."

"It was wartime. The country was facing invasion. The police had other things to do."

"That's not good enough. It's not enough to stain a good man's character when he's dead."

"If he's dead, can it hurt him?"

"It hurts me." There was a catch in her voice. Her eyes shone with unshed tears.

I said: "Can I get you a glass of water?"

She said: "No, thank you. I'm all right."

I tried another approach. "When Arnold Trumper discovered Reggie's affair with Mildred that must have caused difficulties for his business. Wasn't he doing some work at the Krazy Kat at the time?"

She sighed. "There were always difficulties. But, yes, I believe Mr Trumper refused to pay father and told him he wouldn't be allowed to finish the work. It was particularly difficult because father had almost completed the work there and was owed quite a lot of money."

"What did Reggie do about that?"

"There wasn't much he could do. Besides, within days he left for France."

"Do you know how Trumper completed the work?"

"I recall somebody telling me that after Mr Trumper had fired my father, he finished the work himself. But, you must remember, I was very young at the time, and most of what I know I learnt later."

I said: "If Arnold Trumper is found, I may have to write about it and that may mean mentioning Reggie again."

She frowned. "Journalists – like vultures. Picking over the bones of an old hero."

I ignored the bird reference. It was far from the worst I'd ever been called. Instead, I said: "Yes, I'd heard that Reggie had been heroic in battle. Tell me about that."

She said: "It was in June 1940. Dunkirk. The army was being evacuated from the beaches, but not all of them. Some of them were ordered to stay behind and fight off the Germans."

"To give the others time to get away."

"Yes. Father was in a detachment that was defending a farmhouse. It was on an important road leading towards the beaches, so it was vital to hold it and prevent Germans advancing up the road."

"A rearguard action."

"Exactly. After a couple of days, the Germans decided they'd try to take the farmhouse by sending tanks up the road to shell it. Three tanks opened fire on the farmhouse and started to demolish it. The only way to save the farmhouse and protect the road to the beaches was to destroy the tanks."

"A desperate situation," I said.

She nodded. "Reggie crawled along a drainage ditch beside the road. He was under fire from the leading tank's machine gun and wounded twice, once in the side and once in his right leg. But he crawled near enough to the tanks to throw anti-tank grenades at them. He put two of them out of action and the third retreated. It meant the others in the farmhouse could hold out for another day and prevent the Germans reaching the beach. Thousands of men were saved because of his action."

"But he died?"

"Yes, there was sniper on the turret of the third tank. He shot father in the head before the tank retreated."

"And your father was decorated?"

"That's the injustice of it all. There was talk of awarding him the VC posthumously. But when the police announced they weren't looking for any other suspects, the talk soon stopped."

"I'm sorry," I said.

"It's not fair." She was crying now. Her shoulders heaved as some deep emotion inside her broke loose.

I reached inside my pocket and handed her my handkerchief. She used it to dab her eyes. She was breathing deeply trying to get her grief under control. She blew her nose. Wiped her eyes again.

"Thank you," she said. "I'm sorry."

"You've no need to be. It is unjust. It should be put right."

She managed a thin smile.

"I can tell you one thing," I said.

"What's that?"

"I shan't refer to Reggie as Mildred's killer in any copy I write. Not unless there is unanswerable evidence that he is."

"Thank you," she said.

"Can I come and see you again if I get any more news about Reggie?"

"Yes," she said. "I'd like that."

I got up and moved towards the door. She followed me. I stepped onto the landing, turned to say goodbye.

She said: "You know that bit about the sins of the fathers being visited on the sons?"

I nodded.

"It's also true of the daughters."

She shut the door.

Chapter 14

After I'd left Mary Farnsworth's flat, I climbed into the MGB and sat there for five minutes.

I was thinking about my next move. Before I'd visited Mary I'd been considering my options. One of them was so risky I wasn't sure I should chance it. But my meeting with Mary had helped me to make up my mind. There'd been two murders in this town and nobody had yet uncovered the truth about either of them. Mildred's had been allowed to fester, possibly as a simmering injustice. Barnet's, I was convinced, was linked to the corrupt casino development Darke was planning for the Krazy Kat site. I admired Ted Wilson, but I wasn't optimistic he'd get to the bottom of Barnet's murder if Darke was involved. Darke just had too much influence in the town. He owned too many people. And those he didn't own, he intimidated.

But he didn't own or intimidate the *Chronicle*. I'd made my mind up. I would take the risk and, if it came to it, the consequences. But to do so, I would need Shirley's help.

I glanced at my watch. Twelve-fifteen. She'd be working at the restaurant. With luck, I'd be able to get her alone for five minutes to explain what I had in mind. I turned the ignition key. Revved the engine a couple of times. Then I took off towards the seafront.

"Are you crazy? That's the loopiest scheme I've ever heard."

Shirley and I were standing in the back yard of the Happy Tripper restaurant, a seafront eating house for holidaymakers, where she worked as a waitress. The menu promised "home cooking". It didn't mention whose home.

I'd walked in as Shirley was serving up two plates of meat and three veg to a couple of likely lads dressed in sporty shirts and kiss-me-quick hats. They seemed more interested in Shirley than the stuff on their plates. I could hardly blame them.

Shirley did a double take as I walked through the restaurant. "What are you doing here?"

"I need to speak to you. Urgently."

"I'm working."

"I know."

"Then nick off."

"This is important."

"So is my job."

"This can't wait."

Shirley frowned. "Go out the back. I'll see if Marco will give me a five-minute break."

I'd only had to hang around among the dustbins and crates of empty beer bottles for a minute before Shirley came through the back door like a one-woman whirlwind.

And that's when I'd explained my plan. And taken the full force of her explosion.

"It's not crazy and it's not loopy," I said. "It's the only chance I have to get the information to link Cross to Darke and then find what they've done with Trumper."

"But you intend to search Cross's dustbins?"

"Yes."

"At his own house?"

"That's where he keeps them."

"The guy will kick your arse right out into the street," she said.

"He won't know I'm there."

"You going to disguise yourself as a fruit fly?"

"Don't be ridiculous. I shall do the search at night."

"Under cover of darkness."

"That's the plan. And that's where you come in," I said.

"Count me out, bozo. No way I'm rootling about in someone else's garbo."

"You won't have to rootle in any garbo. I need you as a look-out in the street."

"And what exactly would I be looking out for? Apart from a nutcase with his head in a dustbin."

"I'll be at the back of Cross's house. I won't be able to see what's happening in the street."

"And you want me to do this, just so you can take down some little chiseller."

"There's more to it than that."

I told her about my visit to Mary Farnsworth. I talked about the deep sense of injustice Mary felt. I spoke about the need to find the truth. I described the corrosive way the likes of Darke and Cross were ruining people's lives in Brighton. I said I was going to do it anyway whether she helped or not. Shirley's face moved from outrage to concern as she listened.

"That's why I'm risking my career to do it," I said.

She put her hands on her hips and sighed. "Well, if you're determined, I guess someone's got to be there to bail you out when the blue meanies grab you."

"You'll help?"

"I've got a nasty feeling I'm going to stick out like a koala without a gum tree."

Marco's head appeared round the kitchen door.

"Hey, Shirley, we've got nine plates ready for service," he said. "And those two guys with the funny hats want to know when you get off work."

Shirley made her way towards the kitchen.

"Tell them November," she said.

I met Shirley at nine o'clock after she'd finished her evening stint at the restaurant.

We went for dinner at Antoine's Sussex Grill, where the food was always delicious. A treat before the dangerous work to come.

"The condemned man ate a hearty dinner," Shirley said as I cut into my chateaubriand.

"He ate a hearty breakfast," I said.

"Who cares if it's the last supper?" she said.

"It may well be for me if tonight's plan doesn't work out."

Shirley popped a last slice of rare fillet into her mouth, chewed and swallowed. "That was great tucker." She put down her knife and fork. "So what's the dastardly plan, Moriarty?" she said.

I said: "Cross lives in Dyke Road Avenue. It's a posh area, as you'd expect with an estate agent and councillor on the make. Think Nob Hill with lawnmowers."

"I get the picture."

"I conducted a quick reccie this afternoon. His house is a big detached place. There's a passageway up the side and a gate that leads round to the back. I don't think the gate will be locked, but I should be able to climb it, if it is."

"This I've got to see."

I ignored that and said: "The problem is that Dyke Road Avenue is quite a busy road. There'll be traffic on it all night. So I need you to keep watch and give the all clear when I come out."

"How do I do that?"

"I don't know. Some kind of pre-arranged signal. Perhaps you could make a call like a duck-billed platypus."

"They don't make calls."

"Then whistle a couple of bars of 'Waltzing Matilda' as the all clear."

"So the jolly swagman can appear."

"Yes."

"And I suppose while you're playing swagman I'm going to stand out like a polar bear on Bondi beach," Shirley said.

"That's where we've had a bit of luck. There's an old tram shelter about twenty yards from the house. You can hide in there and nobody will see you. Not unless they walk right by and look in. Which is unlikely."

"For your sake, I hope so," she said.

"One last point," I said. "We'll obviously have to leave our visit until Cross and his household are in bed and they've fallen into the land of nod. So I suggest we don't start until around two."

"What are we going to do until then?" Shirley asked.

"I thought we could sit it out at your place."

"*Sit* it out?" Shirley said.

"Well," I said. "Not exactly *sit*."

We left Shirley's flat at five to two.

We climbed into the MGB and drove out of central Brighton. The town centre was busy but after we passed Seven Dials, the traffic thinned. We saw only three other cars while driving up Dyke Road. I parked in a side street close to Cross's house to get the car off the main drag. We got out and walked towards the house.

We turned into Dyke Road Avenue. There was no traffic. In the distance, a late-night dog walker was silhouetted by a street lamp. He turned into a side street and disappeared. We were alone.

I pointed to the tram shelter. "Wait in there and keep a sharp eye open," I said.

After much discussion, we'd agreed that Shirley would give one long low whistle if she saw anything that was likely to cause trouble.

"I must be as hare-brained as you to get mixed up in this cockamamie scheme," she said.

"It'll be fine," I said.

Shirley took up her post in the tram shelter and I made my way towards Cross's house. In my pocket, I had a pair of rubber gloves and a small torch. I was carrying three old newspapers under my arm – copies of the *Evening Argus* in case I had to drop them and make a run for it.

I reached Cross's house, stood behind a tree and studied the building. There was a faint light on in the hall but the remaining rooms were in darkness. I thought the hall light was probably left on for security. The bedrooms at the front of the house were dark.

I moved forward, opened the front gate and crept up the driveway. I walked round to the side of the house and found the gate. I tried the handle. It didn't move. It felt locked. I tried it again. This time harder. It clicked open with a sound that echoed off the walls of the neighbouring houses. I stood rigid and cursed my carelessness.

I waited for two minutes and listened intently. There was no movement in the house. I heard a car drive by in Dyke Road Avenue heading towards the town. No low whistle.

I moved round to the back of the house. Cross had a large garden. I could see a lawn which stretched away into the darkness. I looked along the back of the house for the dustbins. There weren't any. There was a pathway along the back of the house. I followed it to the far end of the building and looked out into the garden. No sign of dustbins. I stood still, wondering what to do.

A light came on in the house immediately above me. It was on the first floor. I looked up. A fanlight was open in the illuminated window. I crept into the shadow of the wall and waited. There was silence for half a minute. Then the sound of a lavatory flushing. Cross, or one of his household, was paying a nocturnal call of nature.

The light went out and I waited quietly for another five minutes. Then I turned round the corner and examined the passageway which ran down the far side of the house. Halfway down was a door. I peered in. The room was partly lit by the light from the hall. It was the kitchen.

I crept on and found the dustbins just beyond the kitchen door. There were two of them, round metal bins with lift-off lids. I took out my torch, switched it on and had a closer look at them. They were old and stained. The lid handle had come loose on one of them. I moved closer.

Something rushed out from between the bins. It flew between my legs. I jumped, knocked against one of the bins. It rattled. A fat rat scurried down the passage and disappeared into the garden. I took a deep breath and listened carefully again. Nobody stirred in the house. In the street, I heard another car. This time it sounded as though it was heading out of town. No low whistle.

I lifted the lid on the first bin. A dragon's breath of rotting vegetables and curry sauce rose up to greet me. I stepped back and gagged. I took a deep breath and moved forward, shone the torch into the bin. It was about a quarter full. Mostly food leftovers and old packaging as far as I could see. I replaced the lid.

In the street, another car drove up the road out of town. Immediately, another came the other way. I heard it decelerate and stop. A moment later two car doors slammed. I strained to hear. No low whistle. Probably neighbours returning from a night out.

I moved to the bin with the broken handle lid. I carefully took off the lid and put it on the ground. I shone the torch in. This bin was full. The smell wasn't so bad, and I guessed that perhaps they kept the other bin for kitchen refuse and this bin for general household waste.

I laid out a couple of the old newspapers on the ground and started to empty the bin item by item on to them. Two copies of *The Daily Telegraph*. A shoe box. An invitation to a dog show. Some advertising circulars. A squeezed toothpaste tube.

As I took out the items, I laid them on the newspaper in lines so that I could put them back in the reverse order to which I'd taken them out. That way, if anybody looked, they wouldn't know that a bin bandit had been at work.

I continued my search. A couple of spent batteries. A light bulb. Three ladies' stockings. A few birthday cards. (Mrs Cross's.) An empty aspirin box. A pair of underpants with a large hole. A back issue of *Golf Monthly*. A paid electricity bill. Some old envelopes.

I shone the torch on them. A couple were blue Basildon Bond hand addressed. They looked like personal letters. There was an envelope from the gas board. Another from Sussex County Cricket Club. A third buff envelope which could have come from anywhere. The final envelope was larger than the others. It was white and made out of better-quality paper. It was addressed to Mr Derek Cross. The back of the envelope was printed with the name of the sender: Mulholland & Steer, Private Bankers, Leadenhall Street, London EC3.

I'd never heard of Mulholland & Steer, Private Bankers. I wondered what Cross was doing with a private bank account. There was a bulge in the bottom on the envelope. I peered in. It was hard to see by torchlight, but it looked like torn-up pieces of paper. Possibly, I thought, the letter the envelope had contained. I pocketed the envelope and continued my search. I found nothing else of interest in the dustbin.

I replaced the contents of the dustbin item by item. Then I retraced my steps round the back of the house, down the passage and out through the gate. I listened for any passing traffic before walking quickly down the drive and out into the street. I hurried to the tram shelter to meet Shirley.

The shelter was empty. I looked up and down the street. Nobody was about. I called Shirley's name softly. Then more loudly. I walked back to the car in the side street. She wasn't there. My mind was racing. What had happened to her?

She'd not made the signal. In real danger, she could have shouted for help. I didn't know what to think. I walked back to the main road. Walked two hundred yards up and down the road. She had vanished. I could only think of one explanation. She must have been spooked by the whole experience. She'd chickened out. Walked back into town. She'd be back at her flat. Tucked up in bed. Sound asleep. That had to be the answer.

She'd tired of hanging about and bunked off home. But there was no point being angry about it. I'd accomplished what I set out to do. Mission completed. And successful. I had a lead into Cross's financial affairs which I could follow in the morning. I glanced at my watch. Of course, it was already the morning.

I walked back to the side street, climbed into the MGB and drove back to my flat. I was eager to take a closer look at the envelope and the paper it contained. I'd call Shirley in the morning. She'd feel happier after a good night's sleep in her own bed.

I walked into my flat just after three o'clock.

It was so late even the Widow had gone to bed.

I felt tired but I had to examine the paper in the envelope before I could sleep. I tipped the pieces of paper out onto the table. It looked as though they had originally consisted of one sheet of paper which had been torn four or five times. I started by putting them all the same way up. Then it was just like doing a jigsaw puzzle except there was no picture on the lid of the box for guidance.

Within five minutes I'd assembled the pieces into the original sheet of paper. It was a sheet of quarto-sized notepaper from Mulholland & Steer. It contained a letter to Mr Derek Cross and it read:

Dear Mr Cross,
This is to inform you that the sum of £1,000 received from Beaupassin & Cie has been transferred to Traverser Nominees c/o Séjourné & Associates, notaries, Luxembourg.

It was signed by a squiggle which could have been anything.

I'd never heard of Beaupassin & Cie or Traverser Nominees or Séjourné & Associates. But as soon as I'd had a few hours' sleep, I was going to find out.

Chapter 15

I was awake, showered and dressed by half past six the following morning.

The envelope with the torn letter I'd liberated from Cross's dustbin was on my bedside table. I picked it up and put it in my jacket pocket. While I was shaving, I'd been puzzling some more about how I could pick apart Cross's tangled financial dealings. I would have to make it my top task when I reached the office.

But first, I decided to thank Shirley for her help last night by going round to her flat and taking her out to breakfast at Marcello's. Last night, I'd been annoyed that she'd cleared off and left me without back-up. But driving home after my raid on Cross's dustbin, I'd realised that I'd asked too much of her. It hadn't been fair to ask her to lurk around in the street like a nark.

It was another sunny day. I drove along the seafront in the open-topped MGB and turned into West Street. A cleaner was washing the steps outside the ice rink. An early-morning dog walker dragged a reluctant Labrador towards the beach. As I passed the clock tower, the copper who patrolled the junction was adjusting his white summer helmet.

A few minutes later, I pulled into the kerb outside Shirley's flat. I looked up at the second floor where Shirley occupied flat five. The curtains in her bedroom window were already drawn back. She must be up.

I climbed out of the MGB and made my way into the building and up the stairs. My shoes clunked on the bare boards. Somewhere, one of the tenants was frying bacon.

I knocked on the door to number five. There was no sound from inside the flat. I put my ear to the door. In the morning, Shirley listened to the radio. It wasn't turned on. I knocked again and shouted through the door. "Shirley, it's me." No response.

I stood on the landing thinking about my next move. It

seemed unlikely that she'd gone out so early. But it was just possible. I was wondering whether to wait or come back later when the other door on the landing opened. A dark-haired girl with sleepy eyes stood in the doorway. She was wearing a mauve dressing gown over a yellow nightdress patterned with tiny teddy bears, and fluffy pink slippers.

She said: "Were you looking for Shirley?"

"Yes."

"You're the second person asking about her this morning."

"I am?"

"I was woken up at half past five."

"By whom?"

"It was the police."

"Looking for Shirley?"

"Not looking for her," she said.

"What then?"

"They wanted to confirm that she lived here."

"Why?"

"Because she's at Brighton Police Station."

"Did the police officer say why?"

"I understood she's been arrested."

She closed the door. I stood on the landing staring at the door with my mouth hanging open.

Confused thoughts tumbled through my mind. How had Shirley been arrested? And when? Why were the police holding her?

I ran down the stairs. Sprinted for the MGB. Jumped in, started the car and screamed off towards the police station.

I parked about a hundred yards from the cop shop and ran towards it.

By the time I reached the front office counter, I was breathing heavily. I recognised the sergeant on duty but couldn't remember his name. He was a chubby man with flabby cheeks and thick lips that twisted upwards in a kind of smirk.

I leaned on the counter to get my breath back and panted: "I believe you're holding a Shirley Goldsmith in the station."

He slid off his stool and pushed through a frosted glass door marked "Private". He looked back over his shoulder and said: "Wait there a minute."

I paced back and forth in the office while I was waiting for him to come back. He returned with the smirk glowing more brightly than before.

"We do have Shirley Goldsmith here," he said. "She's in the cells. Apparently, she was arrested last night for loitering with intent."

I said: "Is Detective Inspector Ted Wilson in the station? If so, I want to see him. Now."

His smirk twitched and his eyes bulged unpleasantly.

"I'll see," he said.

He disappeared through the glass door again.

I thought about Shirley languishing in the cells with the usual collection of tramps, drunks and street-corner tarts. I was thinking about what I was going to say to her when Ted Wilson came through the door with the sergeant. Ted wasn't smiling. And the sergeant wasn't smirking.

Ted walked round from behind the counter and said: "Here's a nice mess you've got Miss Goldsmith into."

I said: "You can leave the Laurel and Hardy impression for later. Have you seen Shirley?"

"I've just been to see the custody sergeant. He's releasing her now."

"Without charges?"

"Without charges," he said.

"Why was she arrested in the first place?"

"She was found by a couple of patrolling officers in a tram shelter in Dyke Road Avenue around half past two in the morning."

"That's not a crime."

"No."

"So why the arrest?"

"Apparently, when they asked her what she was doing, she got a bit mouthy. So they decided to teach her a lesson."

"That's outrageous."

"Possibly. In any event, the officers will be spoken to and told they're not to pursue private vendettas."

I wondered how much Shirley had told the police.

Anxiously, I asked: "What did Shirley say she was doing?"

Ted said: "According to her, you'd both been going for a late-night drive when you suddenly remembered you had to have a private meeting with one of the paper's contacts. You left her at the tram shelter while you went for the meeting and were going to pick her up later."

He raised an eyebrow to indicate he didn't believe a word of it. The tension I'd felt eased a little. Shirley hadn't given me away.

Ted pulled me over to the far side of the office. Looked back to make sure the sergeant couldn't overhear. An elderly woman had come in and was bending his ear about something. She was wagging her finger in his face and berating him about cyclists who rode on the pavement. He wasn't smirking.

Ted lowered his voice: "What I'd like to know is what the pair of you were really up to."

I winked at Ted. "You know I can't betray my sources."

Ted frowned. "To be frank, I'd like to give you a piece of my mind. But as Shirley will be up from the cells in a minute, I think I'll leave it to her. Somehow, I don't think I could match her passion. Or vocabulary."

Shirley was blazing like a bushfire when she came up from cells.

She ransacked the dictionary from A to Z to describe me, my plan, my profession, my personal life, and my performance in bed. Then she went back to the beginning of the alphabet and started again. The sergeant with the smirk loved every minute of it. Ted had the decency to go back to his office.

Eventually, the bushfire burnt itself out. Shirley collapsed onto my shoulder and started to sob. I put my arms round her, held her close and whispered comfortingly in her ear.

"Everything's all right now," I said. "And I'll make it even better."

Through tears, Shirley said: "You bastard." But she held me tighter.

We left the police station and drove to Marcello's. By the time we were sitting inside and drinking steaming cappuccinos, Shirley seemed more cheerful.

Over scrambled eggs and bacon, we talked about how she'd been arrested and what it had been like in the cells. I tried to persuade her that her sacrifice had been in a noble cause. But Shirley had had more than enough of noble causes. So I pointed out that the expedition had given me a lead which might finally help me to expose Cross and stop Darke in his destructive tracks.

I said: "If I can crack the story this morning, I think it will make me the front-runner at the *Daily Mirror* interview this evening. I'd be a shoo-in for the job."

"If that's what you want," she said.

"It is."

I ate some scrambled egg. It was creamy and savoury, just how I like it.

I said: "I've had an idea. Why don't we plan a celebration? I owe it to you."

Shirley sipped her cappuccino. "What have you got in mind? A night in the torture chamber at the Tower of London?"

I grinned. "Better than that. We'll have a night to remember in London after my interview. We'll go to a show, have supper at the Savoy Grill afterwards and then stay in a swanky hotel. We'll meet at Piccadilly Circus at half past seven this evening."

"You're tempting fate. You might not get the job."

"If I can land this story, it's in the bag," I said. "And if I do, we'll take a trip to Paris as soon as I can get some time off. Then you can go up the Eiffel Tower."

Shirley grinned. "You certainly know how to bribe a girl," she said. "I don't know why but I'm willing to risk a foreign trip with you."

"Why risk?"

"Knowing you, you're probably one of those people who'll lose the airline tickets and forget your passport."

I put down my knife and fork. "You can keep the tickets and, as for the passport, I always have it with me."

I reached inside my jacket and fished out the blue-bound document.

"Weird," Shirley said. "Do you need it before they let you into Hove or something?"

"Old journalist ploy," I said. "If your press card doesn't get you in somewhere you need to be, your passport will. Nobody likes arguing with Her Britannic Majesty's principal secretary of state," I said.

"Well, when you've got that job, Paris here we come," Shirley said. She drained her cappuccino.

"I could do with another," she said. "For some reason, they don't have a coffee bar in the cells."

When I reached the *Chronicle* offices, I went in search of Susan Wheatcroft, the paper's business correspondent.

I found her carrying a mug of coffee and sticky bun back from the tea room.

"Can you spare a minute?" I said.

"As many as you like, honeybunch," she said.

Susan was a chubby five foot nothing with curly red hair which she tied back with a ribbon. She had a big smile and a couple of wobbly chins. Her fawn slacks strained in creases around her waist.

We threaded our way through the newsroom to her desk. It was at the far end of the room from mine. She sat down in her chair and I perched on the edge of her desk.

She took a big bite out of her bun. It was a large pastry with plenty of currants and a lot of sugar on top. The Clipping Cousins would have loved it.

I said: "Have you ever heard of a bank called Beaupassin & Cie."

She said: "No, but it sounds like a Swiss bank. The '& Cie' bit is the giveaway. It means 'and company' in French."

"And Swiss banks are renowned for their secrecy?"

"Switzerland: not so much a country, more a private club," Susan said.

"Which only the rich can join."

"That's about the size of it. And it helps if you're a renegade Nazi, an African dictator or a South American drug baron. The Swiss have no qualms about minding dirty money and charging you a princely sum for doing so."

Susan took another large bite of the bun. Bits of sugar cascaded on to her desk. She brushed them on to the floor.

"Is there any way I could find out who owns a particular account in a Swiss bank?" I asked.

"No way," Susan said. "When the Swiss say something's secret they mean it. The names of the account holders are locked up tighter than Frank Figgis's wallet."

I laughed while Susan had a slurp at her coffee. "Another question. What would you make of a company called Traverser Nominees registered at a lawyer's office in Luxembourg?"

Susan took a huge bite of her bun. She had so much in her mouth her cheeks wobbled in and out.

She swallowed, took another noisy slurp of coffee and said: "Name sounds foreign. Nominee companies in Luxembourg are often the front for some big wheel who wants to hide his money away from the tax man."

"A sort of front company?"

"Exactly. The company won't actually do anything except provide a smokescreen for the big wheel's private wealth."

"A kind of personal piggy-bank," I said.

"Beauty of the arrangement is that only the lawyer knows who owns the pot of cash in the nominee company. And Luxembourg law says that he doesn't have to tell."

I slid off Susan's desk. "That's very helpful," I said.

"Don't mention it, honeybunch," she said. "Hey, where are my manners?"

She held up the remains of the bun.

"Like a bite?" she said.

"I'm trying to give them up," I said.

"Oh, well. If you ever feel like a nibble, you know where to come."

And she sent me on my way with a big fat wink.

I sat down at my desk and took out the pieces of the Cross letter.

I arranged them in order. I read the brief text again. I tried to get clear in my mind what I knew as fact and what remained as speculation.

The letter described a clear set of actions. A sum of one thousand pounds had been sent from a Swiss bank account to Cross's account at Mulholland & Steer in Leadenhall Street in the City of London. The City boys had then transferred the same sum into the account of Traverser Nominees, a company fronted by a Luxembourg lawyer.

I was as sure as I could be without him admitting it that the Swiss account must belong to Septimus Darke or one of his front companies. But I couldn't think of a way to prove it. If Susan was right, there was no way I'd be able to penetrate the secrecy of a Zurich bank from a newspaper office in Brighton. I considered trying to blag information out of the bank over the telephone. But there would be a high risk that I'd fail. Then the bank would warn the account's owner – presumably Darke – that someone was making enquiries. It wouldn't take him long to work out that it was me. Fat Arthur would be on my case. Which was the last thing I needed at this stage.

So I had to try and crack the mystery from the other end. Why was Cross transferring the money from his Mulholland & Steer account to Traverser Nominees? I thought I knew the answer to that question. To get it out of the clutches of the tax man. But why not just transfer the money from Switzerland to Luxembourg and leave London out of it completely? Perhaps Cross didn't want the lawyer handling Traverser Nominees to know where the money originally came from. A lawyer who made a career out of being a front man for nominee companies wouldn't necessarily be a shining example of honesty and probity. In fact, he might well be as bent as the people he was representing. Probably was. Perhaps he was not averse to picking up a little extra in blackmail pay-offs on the side. Maybe Cross feared that danger and used Mulholland & Steer as a cut-off between him and the original source of his funds. That was a clever move.

But it would strengthen the evidence that the original source of the funds was corrupt.

Susan had said that nominee companies were fronts for wealthy men. She'd also said that Luxembourg lawyers didn't have to say who owned the funds they fronted. So that would be another cut-off for Cross. If anyone ever discovered his Mulholland & Steer account, he could always claim that the funds were passing through it to Luxembourg on behalf of a business associate. It would be a thin excuse but nobody would be able to disprove it, because the Luxembourg lawyer wouldn't be talking.

But who were Traverser Nominees? I'd assumed they must be a front for Cross's funds. But perhaps they weren't. Could they belong to somebody else? Perhaps somebody that Cross was paying for unknown services rendered?

I drummed my fingers on the desk in frustration.

I had thought the letter would unlock the secret of the whole story. But it just seemed to have added more mysteries. There seemed to be no way in which I could penetrate the chain of secrecy that stretched from Switzerland to London to Luxembourg. But a chain is only as strong as its weakest link.

I stared at the letter harder as if there were some hidden message in its words. There wasn't. The words were the hidden message. I shifted the pieces of the letter around on my desk like a jigsaw puzzle as though they might reveal another picture. Of course, they didn't. They just looked like torn-up pieces of letter in the wrong order.

And then I saw it. I thumped the edge of my desk in triumph.

There was a hidden meaning. It was in one of the names. I summoned up my schoolboy French. The word was Traverser. It was a French verb. It meant "to go through". But it also had a second meaning.

"To cross".

Cross had used a French translation of his name as the title of his nominee company. No doubt, he thought he'd been extra clever. The obvious translation for Cross would be *croix*, the noun meaning "a cross" rather than the verb meaning "to cross". The usage he'd chosen was more obscure. But not obscure enough. The man had created a complex chain of cut-offs but given himself away in the choice of name for his nominee company.

At first, I thought it was stupidity. But Cross wasn't a stupid man. It was arrogance. Sheer bloody-minded arrogance. He thought he was so clever that he could get away with it. That nobody could touch him. But now I knew I could. I collected the pieces of the letter and put them with the envelope in my pocket. I stood up and wove my way across the newsroom towards the door. On the way, I passed Susan making her way back to the tea room, no doubt in search of another bun.

I seized her shoulders and planted a big kiss on her cheek. "You're a genius," I said.

She grinned and her chins wobbled with delight. "Does this mean we're engaged, honeybunch?"

I could hear the rest of the newsroom laughing as I went through the door.

Chapter 16

As I drove up Dyke Road Avenue towards Cross's house, I tried to clear my mind.

I felt like a poker player staking all his chips on a weak hand in the hope that his opponent held even lower cards.

I didn't know everything. But I thought I could shock Cross into believing I knew more than I did.

My main worry was that I wouldn't find Cross at home. I hadn't wanted to call ahead because I didn't want to alert him that I'd have some awkward questions for him to answer.

When I pulled the MGB onto his driveway, Cross was getting into his car, dressed for the office. He was wearing a grey pin-striped suit and a brown trilby hat that made him look like a bookie's runner. I parked the MGB in front of his Humber so that he couldn't leave. He leapt out of his car with a furious look on his face. His eyes were wide with anger. He strode towards me waving his arms about.

"What the hell do you think you're doing?"

I took my time getting out of the MGB. Closed the door carefully. I made a big performance with my keys of locking it. He stomped up until his nose was two inches from mine. I could smell the last cigarette on his breath.

"Get that car off my drive," he screamed.

"Can't be too careful with all these crooks about, Derek," I said.

"Don't you Derek me. It's Councillor Cross to you."

"Councillor Cross," I said. "Not for much longer, I suspect."

"I don't care what you suspect, now get that car out of the way before I call the police."

"I don't think you'll want to do that."

"Don't you. And why not?"

"Because I want to talk to you about Beaupassin & Cie."

"Never heard of it."

He was good. I had to admit it. He responded with barely a flicker of the eyes or a change in his voice. But I'd seen the muscles tense slightly around his neck.

I said: "I expect you've heard of Mulholland & Steer, the private bankers in Leadenhall Street. You have an account there."

His eyes narrowed. "What's that got to do with you? I can bank where I like."

"True," I said. "And you also seem to have money at a nominee company in Luxembourg. Traverser Nominees. A clever translation of 'cross' into French. But not quite clever enough. It points the company straight at you."

Now the colour had drained from Cross's face. He had the complexion of the uncooked tripe – pale and pock-marked – my mum used to boil up for supper on Friday nights. His eyes darted from side to side. He was worried. But he was also calculating. He was wondering how much I knew. Whether it would be enough to sink him. Whether he could talk his way out.

It was time for me to stake the pot on my final cards.

"I know everything, Cross," I said. "I know how Septimus Darke sent money from his Swiss bank to your account at Mulholland & Steer and how you passed it to your nominee company in Luxembourg. I've got evidence for the full trail. And I'm going to write a story about it. But what that story says largely depends on what you tell me."

Cross slumped against his car. He put his hand on the door to steady himself. His mouth worked up and down but no sounds came out. His breathing was shallow and fast. Red blotches had appeared on his neck. He looked as though he might be about to throw up. He fumbled in his pocket. Pulled out a paisley pattern handkerchief, mopped his brow, wiped his mouth. He looked like a man about to collapse. But that wouldn't suit me. I needed more information from him. I knew enough to frighten him. Not enough to sink him. And, most important of all, not enough to write the story I had in mind.

As these thoughts ran through my mind, the front door of the house opened and a woman stepped briskly out. Geraldine Cross was tall with a slim but shapely figure. She had blonde hair cut so that it just brushed her shoulders. She had high cheek bones and a wide mouth. In most cases, such a woman would be regarded as warm and sensual. But she had the eyes of an ice maiden. She was wearing a calf-length dress with a sort of floral pattern than involved roses and leaves. The chiffon scarf round her neck trailed behind her as she stormed across the drive.

She marched up to Cross and said: "Why are you still here?"

Before he had time to answer, she turned to me and said: "Who are you?"

I said: "I'm Colin Crampton, Mrs Cross. I'm the crime correspondent of the *Evening Chronicle*. We've spoken on the telephone a couple of times."

She said: "Crime correspondent? Is my husband in some kind of trouble?"

I said: "I have a few facts that I need to check with him."

"And what facts might they be?" she said.

"Facts about money he's received from Switzerland and sent to a company he owns in Luxembourg."

She laughed and it sounded like ice cubes tumbling into a glass. "That's nonsense. The only thing Derek knows about that country is Radio Luxembourg. And he's so inept with machines he can't even tune into the station on the wireless."

Cross moved towards us and laid a hand on his wife's arm. Her eyes flashed at him as though he'd just goosed her in the middle of Brighton promenade.

"It's all a misunderstanding, Gerry. I can clear it up."

"I think you better, Derek," she said. She brushed his hand off her arm as though it were a fly. "I hope this isn't going to involve a woman, again. You know what the consequences will be."

It was time for me to take firm control. If I didn't get a grip, the situation was going to degenerate into a domestic spat.

I said: "Would it be possible to talk about this indoors?"

The Crosses looked at me as though I'd just suggested setting fire to the house and roasting a few chestnuts in the flames.

I noticed a furtive movement in the next-door garden. So I added in a loud voice: "I'm sure the neighbours aren't interested in listening to what we have to say about these very personal matters."

As if on cue, the woman's head I'd just glimpsed popped up over a hedge and said: "Morning, Gerry. Morning, Derek. Everything all right?"

Gerry said: "Perfectly, Mrs Turnbull."

Under her breath, she muttered: "Nosy old cow."

Like a troop commander, Geraldine commanded: "Derek, lock the car and bring your briefcase inside."

Derek did as he was told. We trooped into the house.

The hall was an impressive room with a polished wooden floor. There were oak doors off to other rooms and a curving staircase with a carved wooden pineapple on top of the newel post. An old-fashioned barometer hung on the wall. I gave it a tap as I passed. The pressure fell. There was an elephant's-foot umbrella stand in the corner. I thought: *Somewhere in Africa a three-legged elephant is hobbling around just so the Crosses have a handy place for their brollies*. Of course, it was a ridiculous idea but this story was taking some bizarre turns.

Gerry led our little procession – Derek second, me bringing up the rear – though the hall and into a long sitting room. This room was a clash of his and her tastes. I reckoned she'd contributed the chintzy sofas and chairs and the Louis Quinze-style occasional tables and cabinets. He'd contributed the tubular steel and glass bar at the end of the room. I had a good look as I walked past. It was well stocked with single malt whiskies and the kind of exotic liqueurs in primary colours that nobody ever seems to drink.

We sat down. I chose an armchair. Cross sat on the sofa. Gerry made a point of choosing a winged chair so she didn't have to sit next to him.

A high-pitched voice said: "Silly bugger."

I looked round. A cage with a blue budgerigar hung in the corner of the room.

"Bertie," Derek said. "Our pride and joy."

"Your pride a joy," Gerry said.

"I've taught him to speak," Derek said.

"Inane profanities," Gerry said.

"*Silly bugger.*"

Bertie set to work sharpening his beak on a cuttlefish bone. I turned back from the budgie and got their attention by pulling out my notebook and licking the tip of my pencil. A little of the colour had returned to Cross's face. I was pleased. I didn't want him falling to pieces before I'd drained him of useful information.

He said: "Gerry dear, I'm sure Mr Crampton won't want to bother you with this, so please don't let us hold you up if you were planning to go shopping."

She said: "I think I'll wait and hear what this money from Switzerland that now appears to be in Luxembourg is all about before I go shopping. It might change my view about how much I can afford to spend."

Cross said: "I need a drink." He got up and walked over to the bar, poured himself three fingers of scotch. He didn't offer me one. He took a large slug of the drink and came back to his seat.

He said: "I think I can provide a perfectly satisfactory explanation about these financial movements."

Gerry said: "This I've got to hear."

I said: "I'm listening."

"*Silly bugger.*"

Cross said: "If you'd give me a week or two, I'll get my accountant to prepare some information for you."

"I've got a deadline to meet. That won't satisfy me," I said.

"Nor me," Gerry added.

I said: "I'm going to write this story anyway. Best you give me your spin on events before I do."

Cross slumped back on his seat. He spoke in a whisper: "You're right that the payment was from Septimus Darke. It was a consultancy fee for property advice I've provided on his proposed casino development."

"Speak up," Gerry commanded.

"*Silly bugger.*"

"What sort of advice?" I said.

"Advice about possible sites, planning regulations. That sort of thing."

"And you didn't think that created a conflict of interest with your post as chairman of the Planning Committee?"

He said: "I adopt the highest standards of professional probity in everything I do."

I said: "But that doesn't include declaring a financial interest in the project at the Planning Committee. That's a criminal offence."

"Surely not that harsh. A mere administrative oversight."

"*Silly bugger.*"

Cross drank another slug of his scotch.

"Tell me why you sent the money to Luxembourg," I said.

"I'd like to know that as well," Gerry said.

"I thought it would be useful to build a fund of money which I could use to develop my business interests on the continent."

"And which you've kept hidden from me," Gerry said.

"And which you haven't declared to the Inland Revenue," I said. "Was that another administrative oversight?"

"I'll speak to my accountant about it today," Cross said.

"How long have you had this Luxembourg account?" Gerry said.

"I'll tell you later."

"No, tell me now."

Cross looked at his glass. Realised he'd drunk the whisky. Thought about getting another, glanced at Gerry, decided against.

"Four years," he said.

"And how much money is in it?" I asked.

"That's my business."

"It won't be when the Inland Revenue prosecute you for tax evasion."

"I want to know as well," Gerry said.

Cross pulled out the paisley handkerchief and mopped his forehead.

"*Silly bugger.*"

"Just over twenty-three thousand pounds," Cross said.

I said: "Has all of that money come from Darke?"

"Most of it."

"Most?"

"All of it."

Cross decided he needed another drink. He started to get up.

"Sit down," Gerry said. Her voice had a crack like a riding crop. "You don't need more whisky."

"So what has Darke been paying you for?" I asked.

"I've been advising him on his property interests for nearly four years."

"Without once declaring your conflict of interest to the council."

"No."

I said: "Did you advise Darke that the Krazy Kat site could be suitable for a casino?"

"I might have done."

"Did you or didn't you?"

"Yes."

"And were you aware that Arnold Trumper had turned down Darke's offer to buy the property?"

"Yes."

"Arnold Trumper has disappeared. Do you know where he is?"

"No."

"I think you do."

"I don't. I swear it."

"Silly bugger."

"You know that Trumper's assistant has been murdered?"

Cross's hand flew to his mouth. For a minute I thought he was going to throw up.

"Don't dare be sick on the shag pile," Gerry commanded.

Cross swallowed hard.

"Darke will inevitably be a suspect," I said. "You understand now why your dealings with Darke won't look good in the eyes of the police."

I hardly heard his whispered reply. "Police?"

I closed my notebook. "Well, no doubt the police will ask you how much you knew about Darke's business affairs."

"Affairs?"

"I can imagine they'll be round here to interview you like whippets after a hare when they've read my article. They'll want to talk to you about corruption. If Darke has intimidated Trumper – or worse – you'll be implicated in that as well. And the boys from the Inland Revenue won't be far behind to go through your books and bank accounts."

"I don't want the police here." Gerry had decided it was time she joined the conversation.

"Perhaps there's a way they don't have to come," I said.

"A way?" The first hint of hope crept into Cross's voice.

"It would mean your complete co-operation," I said.

"Of course," he said.

"My target is Darke. If I can't get him I'll have you instead. But if you can hand me the evidence that will put Darke in jail for a good long period, I'm prepared to delay writing my front-page story until you've been able to make – how shall I put it? –

travel arrangements."

Cross looked like a drowning man who's been handed a lifebelt but told he's got to blow it up himself. I watched as a lifetime's worth of emotions chased across his face. Hope. Disappointment. Fear. Anger.

And, finally, resignation.

He looked at Gerry: "We could go to Spain," he said. "Start again. Perhaps rent villas to tourists. A new life."

Her eyes looked like frozen pools. "You can go to hell as far as I'm concerned. You can rent furnaces to the Devil for all I care. I'm staying here. I'm not ruining my life because you've been greedy and stupid."

Cross's face hardened. "Damn you," he said.

I said: "My offer depends on you providing me with evidence that will nail Darke. Can you do that?"

Cross turned back to me: "I've never trusted Darke. I've kept everything. Every letter, every note, every bank transaction. It's all in a folder. I keep it in the safe in my study. It was my insurance. Darke is a violent man. I curse the day he walked into my office."

I said: "I don't have much time. Do you want to give me what you've got?"

Cross said: "It looks as though I've got no choice."

"I can give you twenty-four hours before I go to print."

"I need more time. A week at least."

"The time limit is not negotiable. Today is Thursday." I glanced at my watch. "It's just before noon. The *Chronicle* will run this story in the mid-afternoon edition which hits the streets at two o'clock on Friday."

Cross shook his head in despair. A single tear welled in his right eye and ran down his cheek. The future mayor was thinking about what might have been. He brushed the tear away. Then he stood up and shuffled towards the door. His shoulders slumped and his head drooped forward.

"I'll fetch the folder," he said.

As he left, a voice said: "Silly bugger."

This time, it was Gerry speaking.

I left Cross's house with a thick black folder, but without a song in my heart.

The folder contained letters, bank statements, copies of cheques that had passed between Darke and Cross. There were more than one hundred pages of it. I needed time to study the folder carefully. And I didn't relish the paper's lawyer getting involved when I came to write the story. Still, it would make another splash. And that would keep Figgis happy. For the time being.

Cross's confession was a step towards cracking the story. But I still hadn't answered the most important question: where was Trumper? If only I could find where his sister lived, I felt sure she'd be able to throw fresh light on what was happening. I had a niggling feeling that Harriet Sturgess had said something that would help me trace Dorothy. But, try as I might, I couldn't think what it was.

But there was still one way I could move the story forward. I hoped a clandestine visit to the Krazy Kat would provide some new clues. But to enter the Krazy Kat, I needed the key to the door. I glanced at my watch. Kenneth the Keys was due for our meeting in Prinny's Pleasure in ten minutes. I climbed into the MGB, scuffed the gravel on Cross's driveway and headed down Dyke Road Avenue towards the town centre.

The dead fly was still in the glass case on the counter when I walked into Prinny's Pleasure.

The cheese sandwiches had gone, but the fly now had a sausage roll and a Scotch egg for company. A spider was busy clambering into the sausage roll.

"Having your lunch here today?" Jeff said. "You could do

worse, you know."

I said: "I know. I could be eating with Lucrezia Borgia."

He gestured towards the glass case. "How about a Scotch egg?"

The thing looked like a squashed sporran. But not as appetising.

"You'll never sell that," I said. "I'd rather have the fly."

"Bet you a quid I sell it by the end of the week."

"Even Banquo's ghost wouldn't eat that."

"So you'll take my bet?"

"Just to teach you a lesson."

Jeff mumbled something to himself while he poured my G&T and put it down on the counter. I took a swig and glanced round the bar. There was no sign of Kenneth the Keys. I hoped he hadn't taken my money and disappeared. But I didn't think so. He had a reputation to live down to.

I left Jeff trying to scrape out some of the dirt from under his fingernails with the wrong end of a teaspoon and took my drink to a table. I chose a seat where I could keep an eye on anyone who came in. Not that many ever did.

Kenneth the Keys showed up five minutes later. He came straight over and sat down opposite me.

"Get you a drink, Kenneth?" I said.

"Never touch it when I'm working, Percy," he said.

"Do you have my special order?" I said.

"It proved more difficult than I'd expected," he said.

"Problems?"

"Some. With the soap. It was wet when you made the impression, so some of it dissolved slightly afterwards. The impression might not have been completely accurate when I used it. I've made the key but it may not work."

"What use is that?" I said.

"I think it will work. But you can never be certain with a job like this."

"That's most unfortunate. I was hoping to get my bike out of the shed later and go for a cycle along to Hove Lagoon."

"Tell you what I'll do. If you don't want the key, I'll keep the fifteen quid you've given me but won't charge you the other ten. Can't say fairer than that."

I said: "I need my bike badly. I'll take a chance."

I reached for my wallet, opened it and gave him two fivers. He took the money, shoved it in his trouser pocket and handed me the key. He stood up.

"About the guarantee," he said.

"You give a guarantee?" I said.

"No. You give me the guarantee."

"For what?"

"I don't want any comebacks from the use of the, er, merchandise." He balled a fist and studied his fingernails. Decided he'd seen enough. Switched his attention back to me.

"There could be unpleasant consequences if there are," he said.

"No need to worry on that score," I said. "If I have to reveal where I got the key, I'll say I bought it from a man in a pub."

I left Prinny's Pleasure in a quandary.

Should I go back to the office and study Cross's folder or head straight to the Krazy Kat and try out the key? If I went back to the office, there was no telling what I might get involved in. No doubt Frank Figgis would have something that he wanted me to look into. He'd be angry that I hadn't been around all morning, but he'd calm down when he realised what I'd got. Besides, mining what I hoped would be a rich seam of information from the Cross folder could take hours. So I climbed back into the MGB and headed for the seafront.

I parked about two hundred yards along Madeira Drive from the Krazy Kat. I didn't want the car seen too near the place in case it was spotted by someone I knew.

I climbed out of the car and walked slowly back along the Esplanade. The breeze was freshening. A storm was coming in from the west. A seagull rode the wind. It looked as though it was suspended above the beach. A couple of tourists picked over the postcards in a stand outside a shop. An old newspaper blew across the road and wrapped itself round a lamppost, flapping like a pennant.

There was no sign of activity at the Krazy Kat. I'd been concerned that there might be a permanent police presence at the place. But I guessed that Wilson regarded it as peripheral to his enquiry. I walked round to the door. I reached into my pocket for the key. I took it out and inserted it in the padlock. It slipped in easily enough. I turned the key but it wouldn't budge. It looked as though Kenneth might have been right. Perhaps the soap had distorted the impression.

I took the key out, gave it a quick rub to remove some grit and slipped it back in again. This time I didn't push it right in. I gently turned the key to the right. It moved, snagged, and then turned completely. The padlock sprang open. Colin Crampton, master cracksman.

I removed the padlock, opened the door, went in and pulled it shut behind me. The ticket office smelt damp and musty. A thin film of dust had settled over the ticket machine and the other equipment. But there was no dust on some of the other surfaces. They'd had things on them which had recently been moved. It looked as though the police had been here and conducted a perfunctory search.

I went into the back room. The boxes were all over the place, some partly unpacked, others stacked from floor to ceiling. There was a large pile of old *Evening Chronicles* on the floor. I picked up the top copy. It was from June nineteen forty. The third lead on the page was a story about Mildred's disappearance. It said the police were investigating and that there were some "disquieting circumstances". The piece mentioned that Mildred was the wife of Arnold Trumper, the owner of the Krazy Kat. In the absence of photographs of Mildred or Trumper, the paper had used a picture of the Krazy Kat, which didn't reveal much. The photo showed the place surrounded by hessian screens, presumably erected during the building work which Farnsworth was supposed to be working on when he wasn't canoodling with Mildred.

I picked up another back issue of the *Chronicle* from the pile. This time the story was second lead. The police were still hunting for Mildred. But now they were concerned there might have been "foul play". The report said police had searched the room at the guest house where Mildred had been staying and taken away "some letters". It didn't say what they were but they were bound to be letters between Mildred and Farnsworth. I thought it was likely they revealed that Mildred was threatening to blow her affair to Farnsworth's wife. That would certainly put Farnsworth in the police's frame as a possible suspect.

A third copy of the *Chronicle* had a story that the police wanted to question an unnamed man – that would have been Farnsworth – in connection with Mildred's disappearance. So they'd read the letters and drawn the appropriate conclusion. There were other copies of the *Chronicle*, each containing items about Mildred. The story had run on for more than a month until a final article said that the man whom police had been hunting had been killed in action in France. From the way the pages in the newspapers had been folded back, I guessed Barnet had been going through the copies and following the story as it developed. I didn't bother to study the papers too closely as there would be copies back in the *Chronicle*'s morgue.

Besides, I was looking for the box labelled Ministry of Food: National Dried Milk. It was the one that Barnet had had his head in when I'd surprised him on my second visit. The one he'd hurriedly closed to prevent me seeing inside. It had vanished.

I started to search through the pile of boxes on the floor when

I heard a scratching outside, underneath the window. I froze. Moved to the side of the window where I couldn't be seen. I held my breath.

The scratching started again. Then a bark.

Ruff, ruff.

A dog. Nearby there would be an owner. The last thing I wanted was a dog walker nosing round the place and noticing the door wasn't locked. I willed the mutt to clear off, but the scratching got louder.

A voice called out from the other side of the building: "Lassie."

That was all I needed. Somebody poking around outside and an eponymous Hollywood hound bent on a starring role. It'd be just my luck if the creature emulated its namesake, burst through the door and pinned me to the floor while its owner called the cops.

I pressed myself harder into the wall.

"Lassie, here boy."

Lassie scuffled outside. A figure paused by the window. A shadow fell across the room.

"Ah, there you are."

Ruff, ruff.

"Naughty boy for running off like that."

Ruff, ruff.

"Now, what's in here?"

I turned my head slowly. A woman had pressed her face against the window. The glass distorted her features. The nose was bulbous. The lips were thick. The eyes were bloodshot. They were magnified by the glass. She was peering round the room. She was bound to see me.

I edged along the wall away from the window, towards the corner of the room. My hip connected with the table. I couldn't move any further. She couldn't fail to see me if she looked this way.

Ruff, ruff.

"Now what's that you've got?"

Ruff, ruff.

The face disappeared from the window.

"Nasty. Dirty. Put it down, boy."

Ruff, ruff.

"I expect you'd like a run on the beach."

Ruff, ruff, ruff.

Slowly, I let out a deep breath.

Feet and paws crunched on shingle as they moved off.

Carefully, I moved to the window and peered out. Mistress and mutt were bounding across the pebbles.

But if I'd needed any persuading, I now realised I needed to work quickly. There was no telling who else might turn up. Even Wilson and his finest having a second look.

I moved over to the tallest pile of boxes and started to lift them on to the floor. It was heavy work. Within a few minutes, I was sweating, scrabbling around over boxes and covered with dust.

I found the National Dried Milk box five minutes later. It was right at the back in a corner. It was behind three piles of other boxes. A casual searcher would never have noticed it. I didn't think that Wilson would have ordered all the boxes searched. I heaved the box out. It was heavier than I'd expected. I humped it over to the table and thumped it down. I pulled back the flaps of the lid and peered in. It was full of bundles of old scorecards from the course. I lifted the bundles out one by one. They felt damp and smelt of mildew. It looked as though the box was full of them. I wondered whether Barnet had taken whatever he'd secreted in the box and refilled it with the scorecards.

But I didn't think so. Because, then, there would have been no point in hiding the box under all the others in the corner.

I found what I was looking for at the bottom of the box, underneath a faded poster advertising the Krazy Kat. There was a small pile of letters and an old copy of the *Chronicle*. I took them out and looked at them. It would take me time to read them and I didn't want to hang about in the ticket office longer than necessary.

I put them to one side and refilled the box with the old score-cards. I hefted the box back into the corner and heaved the other boxes back into position as best I could. By the time I'd finished, I was breathing heavily and the collar of my shirt felt damp.

I left the storeroom as close to how I found it as I could remember, slipped through the ticket office, and went out. I refixed the padlock and locked it. I glanced up and down the Esplanade. Nobody looked askance or pointed and whispered behind their hands.

I crossed the road and went into Marcello's. Suddenly, I was feeling very hungry.

Chapter 17

I sat in Marcello's eating cheese on toast and studying the papers from the Krazy Kat.

At the other end of the café a young couple sucked at strawberry milkshakes and stared into each other's eyes. An elderly woman in a thick coat and a felt hat dunked digestive biscuits into a mug of tea. A business sort with a whispy moustache munched a ham sandwich and puzzled over the *Chronicle*'s crossword.

I doused my cheese on toast with Worcestershire sauce, took a bite and picked up the papers I'd taken from the National Dried Milk box. There were four Xeroxed sheets held together with a paperclip and a note written on a single sheet of blue Basildon Bond notepaper. There was also an old copy of the *Evening Chronicle*.

I looked at the Xeroxes first. They were all copies of letters from Mildred to Arnold Trumper. They were all written on the notepaper of the Sillwood Guest House ("no animals or children, running water in all rooms"). The first was dated Tuesday the fifteenth of April, nineteen forty. It read:

Dear Grump Face,
I've got your latest letter. It's no use you complaining about me and my little bit of fun. You can't talk. I know what you've been getting up to with that Enid Knightly from the Wellington Boot. Twice knightly, if you ask me. Her knickers go up and down so fast it amazes me they don't catch fire. The little trollop. Just your type. So don't you start on me. And don't you think I'm not going to stand by my rights. I've as much right to my half of the Krazy Kat as you, you mean stinker. So you sort it out and give me my share of the money. Or else you'll know what for.
Yours truly,
M Trumper

Mildred had a colourful turn of phrase and a forthright feminist attitude. With a little training, I could have seen her making a career on the *Chronicle*'s woman's page.

I ate some more cheese on toast and turned to the second letter. It was dated Friday the eighteenth of April, nineteen forty and must have been written in reply to one from Trumper. It read:

> *Dear Smelly Pants,*
> *Have received yours of the seventeenth inst. Now listen to me. You and your wandering willy are not going to diddle me out of my share of the Krazy Kat. It's my name on the title deeds of the property as well as yours. I own half of it and I'm going to have it. So just you try to stop me. Get the money and let me have it. If you can drag yourself away from that public bar whore.*
> *Yours truly,*
> *M Trumper*

I was beginning to build up a picture. This was a lady who knew her rights and was determined to have them. I crunched on through the cheese on toast and picked up the third letter. It was dated Monday the twenty-second of April, nineteen forty. It read:

> *Dear Seagull Poo,*
> *In fact, seagull poo has got more class than you have. Especially in your choice of bar-room tarts. This is to let you know that I've been to see a lawyer and he says that I can sue you if you don't pay up. I may even get the whole thing, because you'll be stuck with the legal bills when I win my case. (Ha! Ha!) So I'm giving you until the end of the week to give me my rights and hand over the money. Or else it's the courts for you, you warty old toad.*
> *Yours truly,*
> *M Trumper*

The final letter was dated Friday the twenty-sixth of April, nineteen forty. It read:

> *Dear Whelk Slime,*
>
> *Well, I was pleased to see from your latest letter that at least you're seeing sense. I don't know where you've got five hundred pounds to pay me, what with the money you spend on that primped-up prossie, but I don't care. You always were a sly one, Arnold Trumper, and I should have listened to my mother before I married you. I will come round to the Krazy Kat at half-past seven tomorrow. There better be no tricks and you better have the money. Or else.*
>
> *Yours truly,*
>
> *M Trumper*

I pushed the remainders of my cheese on toast round the plate and called over to Marcello for a coffee. He nodded and set the espresso machine hissing and bubbling.

So Trumper had been having an affair before Mildred indulged in her storeroom dalliance with Reggie. And she owned half of the Krazy Kat. I wondered whether the police officers investigating the case in nineteen forty had realised that. Perhaps it was a secret known only to Trumper and Mildred. And Trumper would have a strong motive for keeping the information to himself. If he let it out, the police could well decide he had a motive for killing Mildred. But Wilson had been adamant that the investigating officers were certain Farnsworth had committed the murder.

Marcello brought over my coffee, then wandered back to his espresso machine.

I picked up the newspaper. It was dated Thursday the twenty-fifth of April, nineteen forty. A triple deck headline read:

HEAVY FIGHTING IN NORWAY

Three armed trawlers sunk

TWO BRIGHTON MEN MISSING

I glanced down the story. It was a rewrite of agency copy about the Royal Navy's campaign in Norway. A *Chronicle* reporter had added local comment from friends and relatives of the missing men. At the bottom of the story, there was a trailer: Sussex Rifles go to war, page five.

Sussex Rifles. Mary Farnsworth had told me her father Reggie had served in the Sussex Rifles.

I turned to page five. The report described how the regiment had marched up Queen's Road to Brighton station, with cheering crowds lining the pavements. There was a picture of the regiment marching along the road. Another of a soldier leaning out of a train window. He was kissing his wife goodbye.

I recognised the face immediately. I'd seen it framed at Mary Farnsworth's house. Besides, the caption writer had spelt it out for me: "We'll meet again: Corporal Reginald Farnsworth says goodbye to his wife, Abigail."

I looked again at the date on the newspaper: Thursday the twenty-fifth of April. I picked up the last of Mildred's letters: Friday the twenty-sixth of April.

I checked the dates again.

That couldn't be right.

If Reginald had killed Mildred before he left for France on the twenty-fifth, she couldn't have written a letter on the twenty-sixth.

I had to allow for the fact that Mildred might have dated her letter wrongly. But I didn't think so. She was making arrangements to pick up the cool sum of five hundred pounds. That was important to her future. She wouldn't get the dates wrong.

Which had to mean that Farnsworth was innocent.

Somebody else had killed Mildred.

And there could only be one culprit. Trumper had killed Mildred because he didn't want to pay over her share of the money from the Krazy Kat. More likely, he couldn't afford to pay it without selling the property. Which would be worth a fraction of its value in wartime.

I sat there feeling sick. And not from the cheese on toast. The full horror of Trumper's crime had just struck me.

If he had killed Mildred, could he also have murdered Barnet?

I picked up the blue Basildon Bond note. It read:

Robert,
Don't come to my sister's house. I will bring the money to your place in Sokeham Street at nine o'clock. Make sure you have all the letters.
A Trumper

I read the note a second time. Then a third.

It was hot in Marcello's, but I shivered.

I let the remains of my cheese on toast congeal on the plate while I thought about what it all meant. Barnet had read about Mildred's murder and the police investigation in the old copies of the *Chronicle* I'd seen on the floor of the storeroom at the Krazy Kat. No doubt he'd taken a law student's forensic interest in the details of the case. Then he'd come across Mildred's fruity letters while sorting through the other boxes. He'd noticed the disparity in dates between the copy of the *Chronicle* with the picture of Farnsworth going off to war and Mildred's last letter. He'd realised that Farnsworth had to be innocent. Like me, he'd guessed that Trumper was guilty of Mildred's murder. And he'd decided to blackmail Trumper. I remembered that he'd complained several times that he was short of money for his law course. Somehow, he'd found out where Trumper was staying. It was likely that somewhere in the boxes he'd found information about Dorothy Trumper's address. Perhaps he'd guessed that Trumper would be holed up there. Or perhaps Trumper had inadvertently given himself away. Either way, Trumper would not have been pleased to know that somebody had discovered his hidey hole. The only way to keep his secret was to kill Barnet.

But Trumper had had a card up his sleeve to throw police off the scent. Darke's business card. No doubt he'd been given it at the meeting Barnet overheard in the storeroom. Trumper had used the card to point the police towards Darke.

So Trumper, the disappeared golf man, was a double murderer.

I was as sure as I could be that my reasoning was correct. The problem was that although Mildred's letter proved that Farnsworth had not been her killer, it didn't prove that Trumper had murdered her. The only way I could prove that would be to find Trumper, confront him with what I knew and force him to confess.

And there was another question which nagged at my mind. Trumper had tried to throw suspicion for Barnet's murder on to Darke. Darke already had a strong reason – his casino project – for removing Trumper from the scene. But now that Trumper had tried to frame him for Barnet's murder, he had an even stronger motive. Darke had carved out his property empire by paying for information. I had little doubt that he had a nark inside Brighton Police – one of Wilson's less trustworthy colleagues – who would have told him about the business card found in Barnet's flat. That would have driven a man like Darke to irrational fury. He would use every contact he had – and in Brighton he had plenty – to find Trumper and silence him.

I thought about how Mary Farnsworth had lived a life of grief because she believed her father was wrongly accused of murder. I thought about the injustice of it all. If Darke silenced Trumper before the truth could be told, that injustice would live on for ever. Certainly as long as Mary lived. She would carry the burden of her sorrow to her grave. I couldn't let that happen.

Which meant only one thing.

I had to find Trumper before Darke got to him.

But how?

From his note to Barnet, I now knew that Trumper had been hiding at his sister's house. But my attempts to track her down had failed. The thought that Harriet Sturgess had said something which could help still nagged at my mind. I pushed the cold cheese on toast round my plate in frustration. I closed my eyes. Let my mind drift back to Harriet's sitting room. Heard the clackety-clack of her knitting needles. Tried to recall my questions. And her answers.

What had I asked her?

"When did you last see Dorothy?"

Clackety-clack.

And what had she answered?

"I've not seen her for two years – since her husband died."

Of course. Dorothy's husband had died two years ago. Her husband's death could be the clue I needed to discover where Dorothy lived. And I'd thought of a way I could do it. I wasn't convinced it would work, but I had to try. And to do it, I would need more help from Henrietta and the Clipping Cousins.

I drained my coffee, paid Marcello for my lunch and headed out to the MGB.

Chapter 18

On the way back to the office, I double parked the MGB, sprinted into the bakers and bought a bag of Eccles cakes.

The girl behind the counter was the one with the hazel eyes and mascara.

She said: "You're becoming quite a regular. You must like your cakes, but you don't put on any weight. I like a man who eats hearty but doesn't let it show. Fancy meeting up for some Bakewell tarts after work."

I said: "The cakes are for my housebound wife and the three orphans we've adopted."

She said: "I didn't know. You must be a saint."

I said: "The patron saint of pastries, that's me."

As the conversation was getting out of control, I took the bag with the Eccles and sprinted back to the car.

When I arrived at the *Chronicle*, I took the Cross folder and the bag of cakes and hurried up to the newsroom. Figgis was cruising round the desks chivvying up people for late copy. He spotted me and came over to my desk.

"I was beginning to think that you'd left the paper."

I looked at him sharply. Did he know about my interview with the *Daily Mirror* this evening? I'd not told anybody except Shirley. But Figgis was a crafty old operator. He'd had to be to run the newsroom for twenty-six years. He had contacts on other papers, including the nationals, and I worried that he'd picked up a whisper from one of them.

I said: "Don't know what you're worrying about. I'm a *Chronicle* man to my fingertips."

He said: "What's bothering me is that those fingertips don't seem to have been hitting the keys of your typewriter this morning. When am I going to have some more copy from you?"

I said: "Can we talk in private?"

"Follow me."

I picked up the Cross folder. We threaded our way back across the newsroom and entered Figgis's office. He sat down behind his desk and lit a Woodbine.

I said: "You wanted a front-page splash. I can give you a tidal wave."

"Amaze me."

I said: "Following the Barnet killing, I'm working on two new leads. I'll start with the first."

I told him about my visit to Cross's house earlier that morning and how Cross had confessed to accepting bribes from Septimus Darke. I thought it prudent to leave out the bit about the dustbin rummage. I dropped the Cross file on the desk.

"Cross claims this charts his dealings with Darke. As you can see, there are more than a hundred pages but I haven't had time to study it in detail yet."

Figgis grabbed the file and turned the pages swiftly. "The lawyer will have to look through this before we publish anything. Then we'll have to hand the file to the police."

"That's what I thought. But I want to write the story when the lawyer's decided what we can and can't say."

"Where's Cross now?" Figgis asked.

I couldn't tell Figgis that I'd given Cross twenty-four hours to disappear without involving him in a criminal conspiracy. So I stuck to the literal facts.

"I left him at his home," I said. "I think his wife was on the point of throwing him out."

Figgis said: "You mentioned you had two leads."

I said: "I've got hold of documentary evidence which suggests that Arnold Trumper murdered Robert Barnet. My evidence also suggests that he killed his wife Mildred back in nineteen forty."

I told Figgis about Mildred's letters, Trumper's note and the old copy of the *Chronicle*.

"The lawyer would advise us to hand these documents straight to the police," he said.

"Which would mean that we didn't have time to stand up the story. So what do we do?"

Figgis took a long drag on his cigarette. He exhaled slowly so that the smoke spiralled in a single stream towards the ceiling.

"As it happens, the lawyer isn't here at the moment, so we can't ask him," Figgis said. "But we can't sit on this for more than a day?"

I said: "I believe I can trace Trumper in that time. If he's still alive."

"How?"

I told Figgis about the problems I'd had tracing Trumper's sister Dorothy through her husband John Smith.

I said: "But while I was eating my lunch, I remembered something Harriet Sturgess had told me."

"Sturgess being?"

"Trumper's long-time neighbour. Knew Dorothy before she married. She mentioned that she'd heard Dorothy's husband had died a couple of years ago. I'm going to look through the *Chronicle*'s deaths columns for that period and see if I can find a reference to the funeral of a J Smith. If so, I may be able to trace Dorothy through the undertakers who handled the arrangements."

"Sounds like a long shot to me," Figgis said.

"Not so long as it sounds. Most people announce a loved one's death in the paper. And undertakers will keep records of the addresses of former clients – especially if there is a widow who may eventually become a client too."

"Worth giving it a try," Figgis said.

I rushed back to my desk, grabbed the bag of Eccles cakes and hurried towards the morgue.

As I entered, the Cousins were giggling over some private joke. They looked up expectantly as I marched over and dropped the bag on their table.

I said: "A little late for lunch and a bit early for tea. But you might like a snack in between."

Elsie opened the bag and said: "I can always eat an Eccles cake."

Mabel said: "All those currants are good for you."

Freda said: "I always used to call them flies' graveyards. But they're delicious despite the name."

I said: "Where's Henrietta?"

She said: "Here I am."

I turned as she emerged from the filing-cabinet stacks carrying an armful of buff folders.

I said: "I've got another urgent job. I need to look through all the deaths columns in the bound copies of the paper from nineteen fifty-nine to nineteen sixty-one. I'll be looking for a J Smith who's died."

Henrietta said: "There'll be twelve volumes in those three years and there are five of us. We should be able to do that in an hour."

She led me into the stacks. It seemed darker than usual. The air was dusty. I sneezed.

The bound volumes I was looking for were on a low shelf. I heaved them up two at a time and lugged them into the room. Thumped them down on the Clipping Cousins' table. Each volume created a little cloud of dust as it hit the table. The Cousins fussed around brushing the dust away.

Then we all set to work.

Heads bent over thick volumes. Paper rustled as pages turned. Black-tipped fingers ran down columns. Lips pursued in frustration.

When I'd been sitting in Marcello's, I'd been sure that I'd find John Smith's death in the despatches columns. Now I was not so sure. Briefly, I wondered what I would do if we failed. I couldn't think of another idea.

I pushed it from my mind, closed the volume I'd just finished and reached for another.

Elsie said: "Some of the people choose weird memoriam poems. This one says, 'I wish I could have loved you more/But you went out and shut the door.'"

Mabel said: "This one says, 'With your last breath you made a joke/And had a laugh with one last croak.'"

Freda said: "I've just read one about somebody who was cremated. It says, 'On cigarettes you spent your cash/And now it's you who's simply ash.'"

Henrietta said: "Ladies, this isn't a poetry reading circle. Let's concentrate."

The Cousins fell silent. More pages rustled. More tuts of annoyance. More sighs of frustration. Through the window came the sound of the clock on the Chapel Royal striking two.

Then Henrietta said: "I've found a dead John Smith from nineteen fifty-nine."

I hurried to her side. Looked over her shoulder.

The announcement read: "Smith, John Tunnicliffe. Peacefully at Royal Sussex County Hospital after a long illness. Funeral at Brighton Crematorium, 2.30pm, 17 November. Flowers to Stodges & Hopkins, funeral directors, Lewes Road, Brighton."

I copied down the details.

"We need to keep looking," I said. "I have a feeling dead John Smiths are like buses. You wait ages for one, then two come along together."

And I was right. I found the second John Smith in August nineteen sixty.

The announcement read: "Smith, John. Suddenly at home. Funeral at St Michael and All Angels, Brighton, 11.00am, 19 August. No flowers but donations for cancer research to Arbuckle & Son, funeral directors, Western Road, Brighton."

I copied the details. We continued our search. Twenty minutes later we'd looked at every deaths column from the beginning of nineteen fifty-nine until the end of nineteen sixty-one.

I slammed the heavy board cover of the last volume shut.

"Are you sure your John Smith died during those years," Henrietta asked.

"I'm not sure of anything," I said. "But this is the best lead I've got."

"Good luck," Henrietta said. "You know where we are if you need any more help."

"I couldn't have done it without you," I said. "Enjoy the Eccles cakes"

Elsie said: "They remind me of a man I nearly married."

Mable said: "Was it because he came from Eccles?"

Freda said: "Was it because he liked cakes?"

Elsie said: "No. It was because he was puffed up and very flaky."

I left them laughing and headed back to the newsroom.

I went into a newsroom telephone booth and dialled the first of the funeral directors.

A man's voice answered in sepulchral tones: "Stodges & Hopkins, funeral arrangements with taste and decorum. Mr Hopkins at your personal service."

I said: "This is a very distressing call for me."

Hopkins said: "Please take your time."

"My name is Gareth Llewellyn. I have just returned from Argentina, where I was beef farming in Patagonia, to supervise the funeral arrangements of my great aunt, Lady Arabella Henfield. I am her only surviving relative."

"How may we be of assistance, with taste and decorum, for Lady Arabella?"

I said: "She has a commanding personality, even as she takes those final steps down the lonely corridor that leads to the stairway to heaven. She would like to approve her own funeral arrangements before she reaches the stair and places her foot on the first step. You understand?"

"I quite understand."

"It will be a large funeral. We shall need at least ten cars as well as a horse-drawn hearse and the usual bloke who has a face like a slapped bottom and a top hat."

"That will be me, sir."

"And we shall need pallbearers. And do you still provide mutes?"

"They haven't been in common use for a considerable time."

"I've been out of touch in Patagonia. Point is, could you handle this?"

"We would be honoured to make the arrangements for Lady Arabella with our customary taste and decorum."

"Excellent. I will call at your offices tomorrow to finalise the details. By the way, before I go, I was hoping to look up the wife of an old friend of mine who sadly passed over on the seventeenth of November, nineteen fifty-nine. His name was John Tunnicliffe Smith. You handled the funeral arrangements. I don't suppose you have the address of his widow."

"The addresses of our clients are strictly confidential," he said.

"That's a pity," I said. "I was hoping to ask her whether she would recommend your services for Lady Arabella's large and costly funeral. Never mind, I can always go elsewhere."

There was a discreet cough from the other end of the phone. I imagined Hopkins holding the back of his hand over his mouth in a sort of limp way.

"I think we may make an exception under the circumstances," he said. "If you would hold the line for a moment."

He put the phone down. I heard leather-soled shoes clump across a tiled floor. The drawer of a metal filing-cabinet squealed as it opened and clanged when it banged shut. The shoes clumped back across the tiles. He picked up the phone.

He said: "I am sorry to inform you that Mrs John Smith died last year. We handled the arrangements."

I said: "That would be Dorothy, John's wife."

He said: "I think there must be some mistake. John Smith's wife was not called Dorothy. She was Agnes Rita."

"It's surprising how much you forget in Patagonia," I said.

I rang off. Wrong John Smith.

I dialled Arbuckle & Son. A young man picked up the phone, stopped laughing at something, and said: "Arbuckle & Son. Hold the line, please."

He put his hand part way over the mouthpiece, but not enough to prevent me hear him say: "And the actress said, 'I've heard of three wise men, bishop, but those are not the kind of gifts I had in mind'." Loud male laughter sounded down the line.

The hand was removed from the mouthpiece and the young man said: "Sorry to keep you while I dealt with another client. Son Arbuckle speaking. What can I do for you?"

I said: "Is Daddy Arbuckle in?"

"He's at a cremation."

I said: "Your dad mentioned that you might be able to help me with the address of John Smith, whose funeral you arranged in August nineteen sixty."

"He didn't mention it to me."

I said: "Since when has he remembered to mention important things to you?"

"Too true. Who are you anyway?"

"I'm your dad's drinking oppo from the pub. The one who tells him the dirty jokes."

"You're not that bloke who wears the pork-pie hat and has a whippet?"

"That's me."

"How can I help?"

"John Smith was an old mate of my mine and as the second anniversary of his death is coming round I thought I might take his old missus a few flowers. Trouble is, I've lost her address."

Son Arbuckle said: "Hang on a minute. I'll get it for you."

He put the phone down. I waited. He picked the phone up.

He said: "Dorothy Smith – is that the one?"

I gripped the receiver tighter. I grabbed my pencil.

I took a deep breath and said: "Old Dolly. That's the girl. Do you have her address there?"

"Yes."

He gave me an address in Bevendean. I wrote it down.

I said: "Thanks. Give my regards to your old man."

I put the phone down and stepped out of the box. My hands were hot and sticky. I stared down at the piece of paper with Dorothy's address scribbled on it.

I felt sure that now I was just one step from cracking the most sensational double-murder story the *Chronicle* had ever printed. But it wasn't going to be straightforward. Now I had a double deadline. And a difficult decision to make. I was due for my interview at the *Daily Mirror* at six o'clock. To guarantee reaching the *Mirror* in good time I had to catch the four-thirty express to London from Brighton station.

I glanced at the newsroom clock. Two thirty-five.

Should I head for the interview and postpone my visit to Dorothy's house until tomorrow? I hurried across the newsroom and sat down at my desk. I badly wanted that job on the *Mirror*. But I desperately wanted the Trumper story as well. Could I have both?

I thought I could.

I had less than two hours to drive to Bevendean and confront Trumper. I decided it would be enough time. It had to be enough time. I could drive straight to the railway station afterwards and phone in my copy from a telephone box. Then catch the train.

Figgis would go mad because I hadn't returned to the office. He might even fire me. But, if I landed the *Mirror* job, that would be the least of my worries.

I got up and hurried across the newsroom. Within two minutes, I was in the MGB and cutting up a taxi as I travelled at fifty miles an hour around the Old Steine.

Chapter 19

Eight minutes later, I pulled the MGB into the kerb outside Dorothy's house.

I switched off the engine and looked around. The street was lined with neatly trimmed grass verges and plane trees. Their branches were thrashing in a strengthening south-westerly wind. On the far side of the road, a couple of small boys were playing hopscotch. A middle-aged lady in a mackintosh rode by on a bicycle. She had shopping piled in the basket on the front. She had her head down over the handlebars as she forced the bike into the wind.

Dorothy's house was a modest semi-detached property with pebble-dashed walls. There was a small garden fronted by a privet hedge. A gnome dangled his fishing line hopefully in the water of a small pond. It looked a mundane hideout for a double murderer.

I got out of the car and walked up to the front door. I wondered what I would do if I found Trumper in the house. My day had been crammed with so much activity I hadn't had time to give the questions I wanted to ask him any thought. Perhaps, anyway, he would refuse to answer any questions. That didn't bother me. "No comment" is a damning phrase in most contexts. The thought that he might turn violent briefly flashed through my mind. I dismissed it. He was an old man and I was younger and fitter. But so was Robert Barnet. And he was lying dead in a mortuary.

There was no point worrying about what might happen. The best approach was to take action and see what developed. I pressed the bell and heard it ding-dong in the house. There was a frosted window in the top half of the front door. I saw the shape of a woman come out of a room into the hall and walk towards the door. She opened it.

Dorothy Smith was a slim woman in her middle seventies. She had a kindly face but with eyes that looked into the distance as though she were trying hard to remember something. She was wearing a green blouse with a woollen cardigan which had frayed round the cuffs and elbows.

She said: "Am I expecting you?"

I said: "Your old neighbour Harriet told me about you. She suggested I look you up."

"Harriet? I don't remember a Harriet."

"When you lived in Woodingdean."

"Have I lived in Woodingdean?"

"Yes. Before the war. With your brother Arnold."

The mention of her brother's name brought a hint of recognition into her eyes.

"Arnold – did he know Harriet?"

"Yes," I said. "All three of you were friends."

"We were?" she asked.

"Yes, good friends," I said.

"I don't remember," she said. "There are so many things I don't remember."

Her eyes peered even further into the distance trying to remember things that had happened so long ago in Woodingdean.

I said: "I've come to see Arnold. Is he here?"

She said: "He was here, I think, but not now."

"Will he be coming back?"

"I can't remember what he said. He usually comes back."

"Could I come in and wait for a little while?" I asked.

She looked back down the hall in a gesture that suggested she expected to see somebody. "If you're Arnold's friend I expect it will be all right."

I stepped through the door and she led the way down the hall and into a small sitting room. It was decorated with green wallpaper which had a leaf motif. Three china ducks flew up the wall above the fireplace. There were two winged armchairs covered in a worn fabric. There was a small television set in the corner. Some women's magazines lay on a glass-topped coffee table. There was a photograph of a man on the mantelpiece. He was grinning at the camera and holding a golf club. It had to be Trumper.

Dorothy sunk into her chair with a weary sigh.

I said: "You look exhausted. Can I make you a cup of tea?"

She looked at me as though she didn't understand the question. "Have I already had a cup of tea this afternoon?"

"I don't know," I said. "But I'll make you one anyway."

She said: "That would be nice. You know where the things are, don't you?"

"Leave it to me. I'll find them. Would you like me to turn the television on while I make the tea?"

I moved over and switched the set on before she could answer the question.

She said: "I like watching television."

I waited while the set warmed up and the test card appeared.

I said: "There are no programmes on at the moment, but you can look at the picture of the little girl on the test card."

She said: "I was a little girl once. I do remember that."

I left the sitting room and searched for the kitchen. I found it at the back of the house. The kettle was on the stove. I filled it and put it on a low gas. I wanted the kettle to take its time boiling so that I could have a look around the rest of the house.

I slipped back into the hall and peeked through the sitting-room door. Dorothy's head had lolled back in the winged chair and her eyes were closed. I went quietly up the stairs.

The first room I looked in was Dorothy's bedroom. The bed was neatly made. There was a worn teddy bear with one ear missing on the pillow.

I moved across the landing and opened another door. It was a smaller bedroom. The bed had been slept in but not made. A pair of trousers and two unwashed shirts were tangled among the sheets. The dressing table was strewn with papers. Trumper was evidently not a tidy guest. I went in.

There was a big old-fashioned wardrobe on one wall. I nudged open the door. There was nothing but a few empty clothes hangers. It didn't look to me as though Trumper was coming back. I crossed to the dressing table and stared down at the papers. Some of them seemed to do with the Krazy Kat, others with Trumper's personal affairs. I pulled a pen out of my pocket and moved the papers around so that I could see the ones underneath. I didn't want any of my fingerprints on the papers when the police finally came here.

There was a completion note from a stockbroker. Trumper had been selling his shares. There were two letters from building societies. He'd closed the accounts. There were several letters which looked as though they'd come from Darke's solicitors making formal offers for the Krazy Kat. There was a notelet with a picture of a country church on the front. With the end of my pen, I lifted the front flap and read the message inside. It was dated April, nineteen fifty-one and was from Dorothy with her address in the top left-hand corner. She was inviting her brother to Sunday lunch. I let the front fall back. There were a couple of blobs by the country church that didn't look like part of the design. I got closer so that my nose was almost touching the paper.

They were patches of blood.

So this was how Barnet had discovered Dorothy's address. The notelet would have been among the rubbish in the boxes at the Krazy Kat. He'd have taken it back to his flat. It had been splashed with his blood when Trumper hit him on the forehead. Trumper had had the presence of mind to remove it from Barnet's flat, but he'd left it here. That was a clear sign that he definitely wasn't coming back. And, with that kind of evidence left lying around, he didn't expect to be found either.

So where was he heading?

I pushed the papers around some more with my pen. There was an envelope from a travel agent among them. Using my handkerchief as a kind of glove, I extracted a single sheet of paper – it turned out to be an invoice – and read it. Trumper had booked a one-way passage for himself and his car on the Newhaven ferry. I peered closer to read the small print. And felt my heart beat faster. He was due to catch the afternoon ferry. It sailed at ten past four. I glanced at my watch. It was twenty past three.

Could I reach Newhaven and get on that ferry in fifty minutes? I had to try.

I ran down the stairs and into the kitchen. The kettle was boiling. I took it off the hob and turned off the gas. The tea was in a caddy on the kitchen table. I put some in the pot and poured in the water. I didn't bother to warm the pot. I found a cup and saucer in a cupboard above the sink and milk in the larder. There was also an opened packet of custard creams. I poured the tea and put a few of the biscuits on a plate. Took them into the sitting room.

Dorothy woke up from her doze as I came in. "Why are you here?" she said.

"I'm making you a cup of tea. You remember?"

She took the cup and saucer from me. I put the biscuits on the table beside her chair. Dorothy sipped the tea.

"This is a nice cuppa," she said.

I said: "I have to go. Will you be all right if I leave?"

"Arnold went as well, I think. Was it today?"

"Yes."

She looked up at me. For a moment, her eyes became clearer. It must have been how she used to look before the clouds of confusion started to gather in her mind. She focused her eyes on me. They looked sad but resigned.

"He's not coming back, is he?" she said.

"No," I said.

"I thought so," she said.

She picked up a custard cream, dunked it in her tea and took a bite. She looked at me again but the light behind her eyes had already gone out.

"I've got a nice piece of haddock for later," she said. "I'll save some for Arnold."

"He'll enjoy that," I said.

I went out and closed the door quietly behind me.

It was three twenty-four when I jumped into the MGB, revved up the engine and roared away from the kerb.

I had no choice but to head for Newhaven and hope I reached the ferry before it left. It was clear that Trumper was making his escape. I took the corner into the Lewes Road at thirty and accelerated towards the seafront.

I briefly considered stopping at a telephone box to call the police, but dismissed the idea. By the time I'd found a box that hadn't been vandalised, made the call and orders had been passed, there was no guarantee that the police would reach the ferry in time.

As I reached the seafront, the clock outside the Aquarium ticked onto three thirty-five. I pushed my foot down and the MGB roared up Marine Parade. A road sign said: Newhaven: 9 miles.

Those nine miles flashed by in a nightmare drive. I vaguely recall a couple of pensioners jumping for their lives as I sped across a zebra crossing, a group of Roedean girls scattering as I hurtled passed the school, and the stern faces of the port officials as I rushed through the formalities.

As I drove onto the ferry, the hydraulics in the huge car deck's door hissed and it began to close.

The door of the car hold clanged shut and I was left sitting in the

MGB in the half-light provided by dim overhead bulbs.

Above me a siren sounded. There was some distant shouting. An engine below the deck throbbed rhythmically. Its throttle opened and its beat quickened. The whole ship jolted as it moved away from the quay. It was under way. Next stop: Dieppe.

I clutched my hands to my head and ran them through my hair. They came away sticky and I realised I'd been sweating. For the last half hour, I had been focused on reaching Newhaven before the ferry left. And now that I was on board I wondered whether I'd done the right thing. The implications of my actions began to sink in.

I was going abroad in pursuit of a big story without consulting my news editor. A sacking offence.

I had lost any opportunity of making the *Daily Mirror* interview at six o'clock.

And I would be standing up Shirley again for our night to remember in London. There was no way that I could contact Shirley or the *Mirror* until the ship reached Dieppe.

I sat in the car feeling slightly sick. I closed my eyes and took a few deep breaths. I felt a little better. There was no point in second guessing what I should have done. I'd made my choice – and now I had to justify the decision. I heaved myself out of the car and headed up towards the passenger decks in search of Trumper.

I wondered whether I would be able to recognise him from the photograph I'd seen on Dorothy's mantelpiece. But the ferry was not crowded and most passengers were travelling in pairs or in parties. A single man would stand out. I walked the length of the lower deck scanning faces. Trumper's was not among them.

I climbed a companionway to the upper deck. I clung on to the rails as the ship heaved and rolled in a heavy swell. There was a lounge where most of the passengers had retreated for what was clearly going to be a rough crossing. Some looked gloomily at spume from waves breaking over the deck. Others lay back, clutching stomachs, and moaning. I made a circuit of the lounge but Trumper wasn't there.

I walked back towards the stern where there was a bar and restaurant.

Half a dozen hardy souls were clinging to the bar as their drinks slopped back and forth in the glasses.

I moved on to the restaurant. Few people wanted to eat a meal while the ship pitched and yawed. A young couple at one table seemed to have lost their appetite for shepherd's pie. But a lone diner at a corner table attacked a full plate of fish and chips. He was bent over the table scoffing the food as though it were his last meal. He was in his sixties, but he had thick black hair. He was a big man with broad shoulders. He had a wide face with sagging cheeks and a large nose. He had black eyebrows that met in the middle.

I walked towards him.

He looked up as I came alongside the table and said: "Waiter, bring me some ketchup. These chips are a bit dry."

I said: "That's just become the least of your worries, Arnold."

"That's no way to speak to a paying customer."

I said: "May I join you?"

He said: "No."

I pulled out the chair opposite and sat down.

Trumper slammed down his knife and fork. His face was contorted with fury and, in an instant, I saw how a seemingly harmless golf man could be a two-time killer. Close up, his face seemed powerful. He had sharp eyes and a prominent chin. But the feature that stood out was his teeth. They were huge white gnashers. Like tombstones. Light glinted off them when he opened his large mouth, and they dominated his face.

He said: "Leave my table this instant or I'll call the bosun and have you clapped in the brig." He bared the teeth.

I said: "Hold hard, Hornblower, until you've heard what I've got to say."

"What have you got to say that I could possibly want to hear?"

"You'll want to hear how I know that you killed your wife Mildred twenty-two years ago."

He twitched his neck in an irritable way as if to say "Must I?" He pushed his fish and chips away unfinished. The ship heaved and the plate slid towards the edge of the table.

He said: "That's insulting rubbish. A man was convicted of my dear Mildred's killing."

"Accused, yes. But never convicted."

"Besides, why are you raking all that up after so long?"

I leaned across the table. "Because two days ago, you went to a flat in Sokeham Street in Brighton and killed Robert Barnet, the young man whom you'd hired to help run the Krazy Kat during the summer."

He pushed back his chair and started to rise.

"Sit down," I said. "If you don't, I'll call the bosun and have you clapped in the brig."

He said: "Who are you?"

I took out a card and slid it across the table. He picked it up and peered myopically at it. I guessed he usually wore glasses for reading.

He said: "*Evening Chronicle.*"

He seemed relieved. I wasn't the police. He looked out of the window at the sea heaving and crashing against the stern.

He said: "I reckon we're outside the three-mile limit now. International waters. Nobody can touch me."

I said: "I wouldn't bet on that. But I'm not the police. I'm only interested in writing a story for my paper."

"Why should I want to talk to you?"

"Because sooner or later you'll have to talk to somebody and it looks better from your point of view if you've taken the earliest opportunity to get matters off your chest."

"Where I'm going I won't need to talk to anybody."

"My guess is Spain. Plenty of sunshine. Cheap booze. No

extradition treaty."

"I'll find somewhere quiet. Nobody will ever find me."

I said: "Not the English police, perhaps. Most of them couldn't find the back of their hand even if they had a magnifying glass in the other one. But journalists will track you down and make your life a misery."

He grimaced and the teeth flashed. He looked like a man auditioning for a vampire movie.

"Some hope," he said.

I said: "I found you – and you haven't even got to Spain yet."

"I won't speak to them – and I won't speak to you."

"Makes no difference. When they find you, they'll camp outside your house. They'll doorstep you and you won't be able to come or go without hearing their shouted questions or having your picture taken."

"The local police will see them off."

"You wish. When the local rozzers realise that they're sitting on top of a double murderer they won't want to know you. Neither will the locals who, incidentally, will also find themselves being interviewed at length by the hacks. You'll have no choice but to move on. Until they find you again. How many times can you move, Arnold, before you have to give up."

"It won't be like that. I've got money," he said.

"I suspect the money you've got is small change compared with what national newspapers can throw at this story. I wouldn't mind betting that even the *Chronicle* will finance a trip to the Costas so that I can join the fun in hunting you down."

The ferry yawed and spray splashed against the restaurant windows.

"I need a drink," Trumper said.

"I'll join you."

I signalled for a waiter and ordered the drinks. Trumper had a large whisky. I stuck to my usual gin and tonic. We said nothing while we waited for the drinks to arrive. Trumper's head had sunk on to his chest. He looked like a man in shock. But he didn't look like a man about to give up. What most concerned me was that he didn't look like a man about to talk. And unless he did, I would have no story. I'd have lost everything. Shirley. The *Daily Mirror* job. My place on the *Chronicle*. I had to get Trumper to talk.

Our drinks arrived. Trumper attacked his like a desert traveller who's reached an oasis. He put down his glass. It slid across the table as a huge wave broke over the bows.

He said: "You'll get nothing out of me. So why don't you bugger off?"

The teeth flashed another warning: Go away or I'll bite you.

"Not until I know what happened at the Krazy Kat twenty-two years ago and in Robert Barnet's flat two days ago."

"You'll never know."

I said: "I think I will."

He lounged back in his chair and tossed his head.

"As it happens, I already know most of what happened," I said. "So you're going to sit there and listen while I tell you. And then you're going to fill in the blanks."

He laughed. "This I've got to hear."

Chapter 20

"Twenty-two years of deceit and deception started to unravel when Septimus Darke called on you," I said.

Trumper closed his eyes. But I knew he was listening. He'd bared those teeth. Outside, the storm battered the ferry. Waves smashed over the bows. Rain thrashed at the windows. Wind roared and whistled through rigging. The ship heaved and yawed in the heavy swell.

I said: "Darke made you a very generous offer for the Krazy Kat but you didn't want to sell. I suspect you already knew Darke's reputation and didn't fancy the prospect of doing business with him. So you turned down his offer. But you hadn't realised that when Darke wants to buy, he doesn't care whether the vendor wants to sell. So he returned and made threats – threats which you wisely decided to take seriously."

Trumper opened his eyes. "Darke doesn't frighten me."

"I think he does," I said. "Robert Barnet told me when I visited him at the Krazy Kat, that he'd overheard your argument with Darke. He said you'd seemed cowed by him."

"Nosy little eavesdropper."

I said: "But Darke wasn't only making his usual crude threats of violence, he was also playing a cleverer game. He'd bribed Councillor Derek Cross to tell you that the council might be willing to issue a compulsory purchase order if you failed to sell voluntarily."

"Cross is a bag of wind," Trumper said. "Like you."

I ignored the insult and said: "With Darke and Cross on your case – and Darke presenting a real threat – you decided the days of the Krazy Kat were numbered. You instructed Barnet to throw all the rubbish out of the storeroom and you went into hiding at your sister's house. I've seen your papers there and it looks to me as though you've been in the process of liquidating your assets so that you'd have as much cash as possible for the future."

I had Trumper's attention now. He leant forward snarling. "You've been at Dorothy's house – going through my private things," he said. "I'll have the law on you."

"I think not. And, anyway, how do you think I discovered you were on this ferry? You left the invoice for your ticket behind."

The ship heaved. Furniture slid across the room. Glasses crashed to the floor. I clung onto my G&T.

I said: "But you'd made a mistake leaving Barnet behind at the Krazy Kat. Because instead of throwing all the old boxes out as you'd instructed, he started to rummage through them."

"Interfering little toe-rag."

"Not a nice way to describe a dead employee."

"Wish I'd never hired him."

I said: "Perhaps not. Because, as a law student, Barnet had a sharp mind. He discovered the letters Mildred had written to you all those years ago. I've often wondered why you kept them. But some people are just natural hoarders. And, perhaps, with the pressures of wartime, you'd forgotten you still had them. You'd also kept all those old *Evening Chronicles*. One of them contained a picture of Reggie Farnsworth going off to war – the day before Mildred wrote her last letter to you."

"That was all private," Trumper complained.

"And, no doubt, you hoped it would stay that way. But Barnet worked out for himself that Reggie Farnsworth couldn't have killed Mildred because he'd left for France the day before the date on her last note to you. And he also realised that you had a motive for killing Mildred because she wanted the money for her half share in the Krazy Kat."

"Doesn't mean I did kill her," Trumper said.

"No, it doesn't, but I think you did. And I think Barnet thought you did which is why he blackmailed you. He'd worked out where you were staying from information he'd also found in the boxes. And I'm not saying he played the crude blackmailer.

More likely, he suggested you might like to make a contribution to his student expenses in return for help in retrieving some embarrassing documents. Something like that. Am I right?"

Trumper shrugged.

I said: "So I am right. In any event, you decided that you couldn't afford to pay off Barnet without admitting your guilt. And being a wily business type, you'd also be aware that black-mailers are greedy. They always come back for more. And, in Barnet's case, you were probably right. He'd Xeroxed Mildred's letters. I found the copies at the Krazy Kat. So you told Barnet that you would come to his flat to pay him off. In reality, you intended to kill him. You went to his flat, hit him with something and, probably, while he was unconscious, strangled him."

Trumper relaxed. "Is that it?" he said. "Even your readers will realise that's fantasy. You'll never be able to print that because you can't prove any of it."

"I've got the copies of Mildred's letters and a note from you to Barnet saying that you'll come to his flat."

"A court would laugh at that. The fact is, Crampton, you've got nothing you can use against me. You're finished. You've got no story and, by the time I've finished with you, you'll have no career."

Trumper's eyes shone with triumph. The teeth gleamed malevolently.

He said: "Farnsworth was accused of Mildred's killing and that was good enough for the police then. They never found her body, so there's no way the police now would ever change their mind. And if I didn't kill Mildred, I'd have no reason to kill Barnet."

He was right. The evidence I had was circumstantial. Without new information or the discovery of Mildred's body, it would be impossible to re-open the case. Which meant that I would have no story. And no job. Figgis would fire me for sure when he heard about this.

The ship heaved again and for the first time I felt queasy. My mouth was as dry as old leather. I'd drunk all my G&T but the large wedge of lemon was left in the bottom of the glass. I needed to suck on it to get some moisture. I reached into the glass and pulled out the lemon. The skin of the lemon felt wet and slimy. As it slipped through my fingers, a synapse in my brain triggered a memory. I'd felt the same sensation not long ago.

Wet and slimy.

I'd held something wet and slimy recently. But where?

Another synapse in my brain fired. I knew where.

When playing golf with Barnet at the Krazy Kat. And retrieving the snail from the eighteenth hole. What had Barnet said? "That hole's always getting flooded."

Now my mind was firing like a nuclear power plant. And the clues came flooding back. The surveyor's plan of the Krazy Kat that Barnet had shown me on my second visit. I pictured it in my mind. There was something wrong. On the course, all the holes were in the place they were shown on the surveyor's plan. Except the eighteenth.

Something Mary Farnsworth had said in Palmeira Square: "I recall somebody telling me that after Mr Trumper had fired my father, he had finished the work himself." And then there was the picture in the *Chronicle* which I'd seen when I'd visited the Krazy Kat earlier in the day. The copy that carried the story of Mildred's death. The picture of the Krazy Kat showed the place hidden from public view by the hessian screens for the building work.

I said: "I think I may be keeping my job after all."

Trumper laughed. "You wish."

"Let me tell you another story. It's about the final night Mildred came to see you at the Krazy Kat. After you'd told her in a letter that you were going to give her five hundred pounds for her share of the property."

"I never said that."

"In her letter to you, Mildred claims you did. That's good

enough for me – and I expect for the police. She arrived at the Krazy Kat after it had closed. You were alone there. Mildred had – how shall I put it? – a colourful turn of phrase. She didn't just want the money, she wanted to insult and humiliate you as well. But she went too far and you killed her. For all I know, the same way as you killed Barnet, with a heavy blow to disable her and then by strangling. I'm prepared to believe that it was a flash of temper that went too far. Whatever the explanation, there was Mildred dead on the floor. You had to dispose of her body. You could hardly transport it through the streets of Brighton. So you dug a pit behind the hessian screens and buried her under the eighteenth hole. Mary Farnsworth told me her father had almost finished the work. I'm betting that was the only hole he hadn't completed. And I reckon that you dug that hole in a panic without once consulting the surveyors' plans to find where it should have been."

Trumper's face was as white as his teeth. He grasped his stomach as though in pain. He retched and grey slime appeared at the corner of his mouth. He wiped it away on his sleeve.

"I feel sick," he moaned.

I said: "And then you compounded your crime with another despicable act. You threw suspicion on Reggie Farnsworth as Mildred's murderer."

"He'd been having his way with her. He deserved to pay," Trumper said.

"But his wife and daughter didn't. Mary Farnsworth has had to live with the knowledge that people believe her father was a murderer."

"That was Farnsworth's fault. He should have thought about the consequences before dipping his wick where he shouldn't."

I said: "I know now why Cross's letter about the compulsory purchase order unsettled you so much. You reckoned you might be able to hold off Darke, but if the council made it official, the Krazy Kat would certainly be sold for development. And

Mildred's body would be discovered when the diggers moved in."

Trumper's face sagged.

He said: "It was an accident. I told her I couldn't afford to give her the five hundred pounds. I offered her fifty instead. She screamed abuse and rushed at me with those flashing nails of hers. I picked up one of the golf clubs and hit her. I only meant to defend myself but I caught her on the neck. Much harder than I meant. She was dead as soon as she hit the floor."

"And so, instead of reporting the incident, giving her a decent burial, you dumped her in a hole on the golf course and filled it in."

"What could I do? I risked losing everything."

"And, then, to compound your original crime, you killed Robert Barnet," I said.

"That was self-defence. I swear it. He was blackmailing me. I gave him the money but he wouldn't hand over the letters. He wanted more. He was greedy. I tried to snatch the letters from him. They were rightfully mine. But he punched me. I snatched a beer bottle and hit him. He went down but he was still breathing. I knew then I had to finish him."

"And then you tried to throw suspicion for your crime on Darke by leaving one of his business cards behind."

"I knew I had to make the police think somebody else had done it or I would never live another day in peace."

"But you won't live in peace," I said. "I'm going to see the captain now. When I've told him the story, he will hold you on the ferry and return you to England."

"He can't do that. We're in international waters. British law doesn't apply here."

"That's where you're wrong. You're on a British ship and marine law applies."

Trumper leapt up just as a monster wave hit the side of the ship. He shoved the table towards me and my chair fell backwards. I grabbed at the table, but it was wet and my hands slipped off. The whole ship lurched on one side. I tumbled backwards. The back of my head slammed into the edge of the next table. And blackness closed around me.

When I came to, I was relieved to find that I wasn't waiting outside the Pearly Gates. There was no sign of St Peter ticking off my misdemeanours in the ledger of life. No angel with shiny wings waited to show me to my own cloud.

Instead, a waiter was bending over me breathing garlic breath into my face and asking whether I was all right.

I moved my head. It didn't fall off. I felt behind my neck. It was tender and there would be an ugly bruise later.

The ship yawed as the gale grew stronger and the memories of the last minutes with Trumper flooded back. The waiter helped me to my feet. I swayed a bit at first but didn't fall down again. I scanned the room in a couple of seconds. There was no sign of Trumper.

I said: "Do you know where my friend went?"

The waiter shrugged. "He left in a hurry. When the weather's like this that usually means *mal de mer.*"

I didn't think I'd find Trumper throwing up in the lavatory. He'd have gone into hiding. But there couldn't be many places to hide on a cross-Channel ferry. I had to track him down before the ship docked. Which gave me a little over two hours before we reached Dieppe. I set off in pursuit.

The ship was pitching so heavily now that most passengers were slumped on seats in varying degrees of misery. They sat with glazed eyes or their head in their hands moaning gently. One or two looked up curiously as I loped by.

I found the only way to walk as the ship heaved was to move one side of my body at a time so that there was always one foot planted firmly on the deck. Even so, the ship was tossing so violently I lost my balance every few yards.

I thought about where Trumper would hide. He'd steer clear of the public areas inside the ship because they would be too easy to search. I wondered whether he could have gone down to the car deck. I made my way to the companionway leading to it. The door was locked and there was a sign saying that passengers weren't permitted to enter during the voyage. There was no way that Trumper could get through. He certainly wouldn't be able to enter the crew's quarters without being noticed. One sighting of those teeth would see to that.

Which left only one place he could be. On deck.

Surely, not in this weather.

I staggered over to a companion hatch and looked out of the porthole. Angry waves filled the sea as far as the horizon. The ship rose and fell with them in a deep churning motion. We heaved up to a crest. Plunged down to a trough.

I opened the companion hatch and stepped out on to the deck. I was on the leeward side of the ship, so I was sheltered from the worst of the wind. The wind was driving the rain away from me. The noise was terrible. The howling of the gale competed with the roaring sea. The ship creaked and moaned as the stresses in its plates were tested to the limit.

The rain and spray created a thick mist which cut the distance I could see along the deck. I moved a few yards towards the bow and listened, but all I could hear was the scream of the wind and the thrashing of the sea.

There were plenty of places on deck where Trumper could be hiding. Behind piles of stacked deckchairs. In lifeboats. Behind bollards. Under companionways. I made my way forward, checking possible hiding places as I went. I reached the bows and turned to come back along the starboard side of the ship. I was now on the windward side of the ferry, in the full force of the gale. The wind was so strong I had trouble staying upright. I had to cling on to railings as I inched along the deck, heading towards the stern. The wind-driven rain stung my face like little pins and spray from the waves showered down on me. My hair was plastered to my head. My clothes stuck to my skin. My shoes squelched as I crept along.

Trumper saw me before I spotted him. He was hiding behind a stack of deckchairs which had been lashed to a stairway.

He dashed from behind the stack, slipped and fell heavily on the deck. I moved towards him but the wind forced me back. He scrambled to his feet and loped off in a kind of crab-like sideways shuffle towards the stern. I fought my way into the wind and followed him.

The ship rose out of the water on a wave and seemed to hang suspended in the air. Then it crashed into the trough with a jolt which made the whole vessel shudder. I fell to the deck. Ahead of me, I saw Trumper stumble again. But I was on my feet in seconds and scrambling towards him.

We reached the stern of the ship. There was a small observation area where passengers could sit in fair weather and watch the ship's wake recede towards the horizon. Now it was desolate, lashed by wind, drenched by spray.

I struggled into the area only feet behind Trumper. I positioned myself so that he couldn't get out through the exits on the port or starboard sides of the ship. He turned and faced me. His face had contorted into a snarl. The teeth flashed like an Aldis lamp. He clung to the railings, hunched against the wind. He growled something at me. I moved closer, arms akimbo, keeping balance against the gale. We were feet from one another.

"I'm not going back," he cried. His words carried away on the wind.

"There's nowhere for you to go now," I shouted. "I'm taking you to the captain."

"You and who's crew?"

"You're finished."

"Never," he screamed.

He hoisted himself up onto the railings and swung his legs

over. I moved towards him but the wind forced me to one side. I steadied myself and moved closer.

"It should never have happened," he shouted.

I wanted to grab him. I inched forward until I was two feet away, but he edged himself along outside the railings. The rain was driving straight into my face. I screwed up my eyes.

"You'll die," I shouted.

"But I won't hang," he cried.

I lunged towards him. The ship yawed and a huge wave broke over the stern.

A wall of water hit Trumper and knocked him sideways like a puppet cut from its strings. His head cracked on to a bollard and I saw his body go limp. Somehow his arm had locked round the bollard, but as the ship heaved to one side it slid off and Trumper's body slithered like a lizard's over the stern.

I threw myself at the railings but I was too late to catch him. In any event, he was already dead. I watched helpless as his body plummeted towards the sea. It hit the water with a splash that barely registered among the heaving waves.

Then another huge wave roared over the stern. The water drenched me. It filled my eyes and my ears.

I couldn't see, couldn't hear. I choked, spluttered. For a moment, I thought I was going to drown. Then I pushed the water from my face, opened my eyes. The air was filled with salty spray.

Twenty yards astern, a sodden suit of clothes rose on a wave, then sunk slowly into the trough.

I wouldn't have known it was Trumper, if it hadn't been for the teeth.

I battled my way back inside the ship and pressed the emergency klaxon.

Staff came running. They went on deck and searched the sea, but the ferry was ploughing on to France. It could not turn back in the teeth of the storm.

The captain appeared. He asked me what had happened. It was a straight question. I considered for a moment whether I could give a straight answer. The fact that a man had been lost overboard would be reported to the authorities as soon as we reached France. The French newspapers would soon find out that Trumper was English and the British press wouldn't be far behind. I'd nailed the biggest story the *Chronicle* had had for years and I didn't want Houghton on the *Evening Argus* scooping me. Which he could do if he picked up on the news quickly. After all, he was in England and I would be stuck in France.

So I replied that the man overboard was somebody I'd met for the first time in the restaurant (technically true). I said he'd seemed very troubled about some matters (true). He went out on deck and, as I was worried about him, I followed (true). He climbed over the rail at the stern and a wave washed him overboard (also true).

The captain asked me if I knew the man's name. Another straight question. And an awkward one. If Houghton got hold of the name, and realised that Trumper was the owner of the Krazy Kat, he could well connect it with Robert Barnet's murder. A wily old operator like Houghton would know that Trumper's death at sea, in those circumstances, was no accident and he'd be on the hunt for the full story. But, like George Washington, I could not tell a lie. So I told the captain Trumper's true name, omitting the detail that he owned a miniature golf course in Brighton. The captain seemed satisfied with that information and let me go.

After that, I was taken to the crew's quarters where I took a hot shower and my clothes were dried in front of an electric heater. My jacket ended up wrinkled and creased like an old dog-blanket. And the collar had been singed black by the heater.

We docked in Dieppe two hours late because of the storm.

I took a room in a small dockside hotel and put a call through to the *Chronicle*.

I spoke to the duty reporter and told him to get hold of Figgis at home – or more likely in the pub – and call me back. Forty minutes later Figgis rang. I told him everything that had happened. I said I was already working on the splash for tomorrow's paper.

He said he'd speak to His Holiness about bringing out a morning edition to hit the streets at nine o'clock, three hours ahead of the normal midday paper. It would be the first time since D-day that the paper had produced a "morning special". I said I could phone over copy for it in about an hour. I told him I'd catch the early-morning ferry back to Newhaven, which arrived at eight o'clock, and bring a more detailed background piece that could run in the midday edition.

He agreed and said: "And don't forget we'll need receipts for all these expenses you're running up."

I rang off. Then I called Shirley's home phone number. I let the phone ring for two minutes, but there was no answer. I thought of Shirley in London being stood up again and wondered what revenge she'd take – that's if she spoke to me again.

For the next hour, I worked on my story. After I'd phoned over my copy, I tried Shirley's number again. There was still no answer. Then I went to bed. But I didn't sleep. I lay awake wondering whether I'd ever be able to make it up to Shirley. And I thought about the *Daily Mirror* interview I'd missed. The Trumper story should have been the ace that guaranteed me the job. It had proved to be the joker. By two in the morning, the storm had blown itself out. But, in some kind of weird after-reaction, my stomach had started churning.

When I walked into the newsroom at ten to nine the following morning, work stopped and everyone gave me a rousing cheer. As a modest sort, I naturally blushed becomingly. Newsroom copies of the "morning special" had just come up from the machine room. The headline splashed across all eight columns in one hundred and forty-four point type read:

DOUBLE KILLER DIES AT SEA

Phil Bailey passed me: "Great story," he said. He looked me up and down. "Shame about the jacket."

Susan Wheatcroft gave me one of her winks and said: "All at sea? You can breast my billows any time you like."

Figgis's head appeared from around his office door. "I want to see you now."

I went in and closed the door behind me. Ted Wilson was sitting by Figgis's desk. He was studying the Cross file. Figgis sat down behind his desk and lit up a fresh Woodbine. The smile lines on his face had gone into overtime. He was so happy he'd have smoked two fags and had one up each nostril as well if he could.

He said: "His Holiness has invited me out to lunch. First time I've broken bread with him since Coronation Day."

I said: "Just the single invitation, was it?"

"Oh, and he asked me to pass on to you that he thinks you've done 'quite well'."

"We don't want me getting big-headed," I said.

Wilson said: "I've already got a team at the Krazy Kat investigating the eighteenth hole. I had a call just before I left the office that there is definitely a body there, but it will be some time before we can confirm it is Mildred."

"Not so much a hole in one as one in a hole," I said.

"We can do without your tasteless cracks," Figgis said.

Wilson said: "Before you two get involved in that, can we come to this file." He pointed to the Cross folder.

Figgis put on his serious face.

He said: "Mr Crampton was given this folder by Councillor Cross and passed it to me. I naturally asked the paper's lawyer to look at it and he has advised me to hand it to the police. Hence our meeting."

Wilson said: "I can see that this folder gives me quite sufficient grounds to arrest Septimus Darke on charges of corruption, money laundering, tax evasion, intimidation of public officials, and, for all I know, dropping toffee wrappings under the Litter Act."

"Not bad for a start," I said. "You can get on to the serious stuff like grievous bodily harm and murder later."

Wilson said: "Point is, I'm going to need to get a warrant for his arrest from a magistrate and I don't want the *Chronicle* running a story about the contents of this folder before I've had time to do it."

"How long will it take?" Figgis asked.

"I reckon I can be ready to make an arrest by about two this afternoon," Wilson said. "I need time to study this folder before I move."

Figgis scratched his chin. He drew deeply on his cigarette, blew the smoke at Wilson. Wilson put his hand over his nose. Figgis didn't seem to notice.

"I think we can live with that," Figgis said.

"Excellent," Wilson said.

"Providing I can be present at the arrest," I said.

Figgis grinned: "As I was about to add myself."

Wilson said: "What? That would be highly irregular."

"This whole case is irregular," I said. "You're going to be the hero of the town for nailing Darke. And who's handed you the evidence to do it?" I indicated the Cross file. "All neatly filed, too."

Wilson picked the folder up again. Opened it and flipped through the pages. He nodded thoughtfully.

"Okay," he said. "I suppose I owe you that. But you stay outside the room while I actually feel the collar."

"Agreed," I said. "I'll wait there with the photographer."

"Photographer? By God, you push your luck, Crampton. One day it's going to run out on you on the edge of a cliff."

Figgis stubbed out his cigarette and reached for another.

"That's all agreed, then," he said. "We'll get the Darke arrest into the 'night final' and run with a fuller story including background from the folder tomorrow. Or as much as the lawyer will allow since you'll presumably have laid charges by then."

Wilson stood up. "Well, I've got a racketeer to arrest. Nice to have met you, Mr Figgis."

Figgis extended a nicotine-stained hand.

"I'll come down to the lobby with you," I said to Wilson.

We left Figgis's office and walked down to the reception area in silence.

Wilson pulled me over to a quiet corner. He had a mischievous look on his face which I'd never seen before.

"Consequences," he said.

"Consequences?" I asked.

"Yes, I was just thinking about the consequences of me telling you about Trumper's disappearance at Prinny's Pleasure last Saturday."

"Thanks for the tip," I said. "The stories I'm getting from that are providing me with more splashes than I've had since I joined the paper."

"My pleasure," he said. "As it happens, it's rather served my ends as well. Darke has been paying off at least three officers in the force to my certain knowledge. It's made it very difficult for an honest cop like me to investigate Darke when he's got his own narks on the inside."

"Who are these officers?"

"Can't mention names at the moment. But I have a feeling they're facing their nemesis."

"Will you be able to prove they've been taking pay-offs from Darke?"

"Don't know. Probably not from this file, but when we search Darke's home and office, who knows what we'll find."

I thought about Darke's business card which I'd seen in

Barnet's flat. Wilson had never mentioned it, but it had puzzled me why he'd never questioned Darke about Barnet's murder.

So I asked: "But you never had Darke tagged as Barnet's murderer?"

"Should I?" Wilson gave me a sharp look.

"Just thought he might be a suspect."

Wilson relaxed a little. "We did find one of Darke's business cards at Barnet's flat. But I never had him in my sights as the killer. For a start, murderers don't generally leave their business cards at the scene of the crime. And when we tested it for finger-prints, it was clean. You'd at least have expected the see the prints of the person who gave it and the person who received it. It had been wiped and placed there by someone wearing gloves. That immediately suggested to me it was a blind – intended by the real killer to point us in the wrong direction."

"But you'll arrest Darke now as an unintended consequence of the tip you gave me in Prinny's Pleasure," I said.

"Not entirely unintended," he said.

"What do you mean?"

"When I told you about Trumper, I guessed you'd make the Darke and then the Cross connections. You've blown the case wide open from the outside. Especially as I couldn't do it from the inside because of Darke's stool pigeons."

"You're saying you gave me this tip knowing that I'd make all the connections and you'd get the evidence to arrest Darke?"

"Thought it likely."

"And you never thought to mention that to me?"

"Would have spoilt your fun. Besides, rat up a drainpipe – that's you when it comes to a mystery."

"Not exactly the description I'd have chosen," I said.

"Darke's money has bought a lot of protection in this town," Wilson said.

I said: "Are you saying that when we met in Prinny's Pleasure you were setting me up."

Ted grinned. He held up the Cross folder triumphantly as though he'd just been awarded a school prize on speech day.

"I wouldn't put it exactly like that," he said. "Had interesting consequences, though, didn't it?"

He put on his hat and went out leaving me with my mouth hanging open and feeling rather foolish.

Chapter 21

I was desperate to get in touch with Shirley.

I needed to apologise for standing her up again. To tell her that this time I would make it up to her. To explain that it had all been in a good cause. Although, on reflection, perhaps I wouldn't put it quite like that.

Back in the newsroom, I called her flat from one of the phone booths. I let the number ring for a full minute before replacing the receiver. I called the Happy Tripper restaurant in case Shirley was already at work. Marco answered the phone.

I said: "I'd like to speak to Shirley Goldsmith, please."

Marco said: "She's not supposed to accept personal calls at work."

I said: "This is the consular section of the Australian High Commission. I have an urgent query about the visas on her passport." I thought I made a reasonable job of the Aussie accent.

I heard Marco call out to Shirley: "Some fella with a funny voice says he's the Australian High Commission."

Somewhere in the restaurant I could hear Shirley shouting. "If it's that slimy limey newspaper hack, you can tell him to go bury himself in a pile of kangaroo whoopsies and stay there until he rots. I'd rather spend a night at Ned Kelly's funeral with a dunny bucket on my head than two seconds with him."

Marco came back on the line: "She says she's busy."

I said: "You're the boss. Order her to the phone or I'll run a story saying your chicken escallops are really dead cats from the Home for Distressed Moggies."

"You wouldn't dare."

"Try me."

I heard Marco call: "Shirley, I think you better speak to this man."

There were a couple of minutes of argument, then Shirley

came on the line. "You're a low chiselling little rat. You cheat and lie to get your so-called stories. You make promises you don't keep. You let a person down and then expect them to come running."

"But, be fair," I said. "I also have a few faults."

"Don't start using your wisecracks on me."

"There's nobody else available at the moment."

"I'm not laughing."

"But you're not crying either. I reckon that's a reasonable starting point to see if we can work this out."

"I feel like screaming."

"Don't do that. This phone booth isn't sound-proofed."

"Do you even realise how humiliated I feel?" she said.

There was a catch in her voice and I imagined her eyes welling with tears.

"Yes, I can," I said. "I didn't intend it to happen and I'm very, very sorry."

"You mean it?"

I said: "Of course. I phoned your flat twice last night from France but there was no answer. I tried again from the quayside at Newhaven this morning."

"After you'd stood me up, I decided to spend the night in London," Shirley said.

"In a hotel?"

"No, with an old friend from Oz who's working here. I came straight to work this morning."

I said: "I expect you were able to catch up with all the news from back home with her."

There was a moment's silence. Then Shirley said: "I suppose I have to congratulate you on the story. Marco's just brought in the early edition."

I said: "Thank you. That means a lot. I'd like the opportunity to explain what happened. Why I didn't meet you in London last night. Could we get together after work?"

"I get off at six."

"Shall we have dinner at English's?"

"No, I'll have eaten here. Come to my flat."

"I'd like that."

"But don't bother to bring a toothbrush."

She rang off.

Back at my desk, I spent a couple of minutes thinking about Shirley.

I was pleased that she'd agreed to meet but I'd been unsettled by the conversation. Shirley's anger had blown itself out like a typhoon, as it always did, but she was a determined girl. When she'd made up her mind about something, there was no changing it. I wondered whether we'd still have a relationship by the end of the evening.

But I didn't have long to wonder, because Figgis popped up beside my desk. He was in shirt-sleeves rolled up to the elbows. He was wearing a green visor over his eyes. He'd obviously been watching too many Hollywood newspaper movies.

He said: "I want to splash with Darke's arrest in the night final and relegate the Trumper death to second lead."

I said: "We may have less than half an hour to edition time after the arrest."

"That's why I want you to write the tail of the story now. You know, the usual thing. Notable local businessman, well connected, but controversial developments, attracted criticism, etcetera."

"Three hundred words be enough?"

"Plenty. Phone in the story's peg to the copy takers as soon as you can. I'll alert them to be ready for it."

"What about the Cross file?" I said.

"We'll lead on that tomorrow," he said. "We've naturally made a copy of the contents. Collect it from my office and write the story when you return from the Darke arrest."

He headed back to his office.

Sally Martin pointed at his visor and called out: "Going on holiday, Mr Figgis?"

There was general laughter.

"Everyone, get on with your work," Figgis growled.

The tail of the Darke arrest story would have to be a cuttings job. Which meant another trip to the morgue to seek help from Henrietta and the Clipping Cousins. I glanced at the clock on the newsroom wall. I had just enough time to go to the bakers.

This time, I thought I'd mark my Channel crossing by buying some French fancies.

Freddie Barkworth and I were sitting in his Hillman Minx parked just across the road from the Golden Kiss.

Freddie was the best photographer on the *Chronicle*. He was a small man and he moved like a nimble little gnome. He had a shock of white hair, a bulbous nose and large ears. He'd have been a dead ringer for Bilbo Baggins in *The Hobbit*.

Freddie was a veteran lensman who'd been at the game since the days when he'd put his head under a black cloth. Yet he had the greatest gift a newspaper photographer can possess. He was always in the right place at the right time with his camera pointed in the right direction and his finger on the button.

We were waiting for Wilson and his crew to arrive so that the fun could start. He'd called me ten minutes earlier to say that the arrest team was in place and they were about to move.

Freddie said: "How do we know this Darke is in the club?"

I said: "Ted Wilson has had one of his trusted officers doing a reccie. Besides, that Roller parked near the corner" – I pointed across the street – "belongs to Darke."

As if to confirm what I'd just said, Fat Arthur emerged from the club, and looked up and down the street.

I nudged Freddie and pointed: "And that blob of blubber on two legs goes everywhere with Darke."

"Let's hope he doesn't block out the light when I'm taking my shots."

"Better have your flashgun handy."

"Never go anywhere without it."

I said: "The must-have shot we need is Darke being led out by the police. Make sure you get the handcuffs on Darke's wrists into the shot."

Freddie nodded. And at that moment, two police cars and a black Maria drove silently into the street. Wilson climbed out of the first car with another detective. Eight uniformed officers, one with an Alsatian, emerged from the other car and the black Maria. Freddie and I got out of the Hillman Minx and crossed the road. We reached the entrance to the Golden Kiss at the same time as Wilson and his team.

Wilson turned to his officers: "Right, you know what you've got to do. Let's do it."

He looked at me: "And make sure you keep out of the way."

"Never go where I'm not wanted," I said.

Ted grunted and led the way through the door. We passed through the lobby into the bar. It was empty apart from the singer I'd seen on Sunday evening. He was rehearsing a number with the piano player. It was Roy Orbison's *"Running Scared"*. It was limping badly.

The Alsatian barked and the music stopped.

Wilson said to the dog handler: "Keep Pickles quiet."

The officer patted the animal reassuringly.

Wilson said to the musicians: "For you two, the song has ended. You better leave now."

They rummaged their sheet music together and climbed down from the stage.

At that moment, Fat Arthur emerged from the room behind the bar. He stopped in this tracks. His jaw fell. His eyes glazed with confusion. Messages passed between his brain cells. Both of them. They reached the right conclusion: police raid. He turned on his heels and fled back through the door.

Wilson said: "Turner, Barrett, MacDonald – after him."

Three officers detached themselves from the group and sprinted for the door. They bundled through. And seconds later there were shouts of pain and the sound of furniture splintering.

Pickles barked twice. Wilson scowled at the dog handler. The officer patted the Alsatian.

I said: "Darke is probably in his office through there."

I pointed to the door I'd come out of when I'd entered the club on my previous visit.

Wilson said: "This way."

We headed for the door. The Alsatian was pulling on his leash. We entered the corridor lined with the plush red carpet. Darke's office was the second door on the left. Wilson walked in without knocking. I followed close behind.

Darke's office was huge. There was a walnut desk with brass handles, a padded chair, a red leather Chesterfield, a cocktail cabinet. On the walls, there were a couple of oil paintings of old Victorian types with beards and lofty expressions on their faces. The room smelt of good cigars.

There was no sign of Darke.

The brunette with the voluptuous figure who'd been with Darke on Sunday night was lounging on the Chesterfield. She was reading Harold Robbins' *The Carpetbaggers*. She was pointing at the words and moving her lips.

She looked up as we barged in. Her eyes widened.

She said: "Oh."

Wilson said: "Where's Darke?"

She said: "Oh."

He said: "Was he here?"

"Oh."

I said to Wilson: "That bloody dog barking is better than any warning siren. He's legged it."

Wilson said: "He can't have got far."

I said: "He'll have gone out through the kitchen."

Wilson pointed at two constables. "Dobbs, Young – keep an eye on her."

One of the constables leered into the room. "It'll be a pleasure, guv."

"And watch your behind, not hers," Wilson said. "The rest of you follow me."

The rest of us turned and raced down the corridor towards the kitchen. Piled through the door. And found our way blocked by the kitchen staff.

The chef brandished a meat cleaver.

The sous chef wielded a long carving knife.

The porter held an apple corer.

We stood there and stared at them.

The porter said: "In the hurry, it was the first thing that came out of the drawer." He looked a bit ashamed of himself.

Wilson moved forward.

"No further," the chef said. "The boss says we must give him five minutes to get clear."

Wilson's face was crimson with fury.

"You'll all be charged with obstructing a police officer in the execution of his duty," he yelled.

The porter looked at the chef with worried eyes. "Is that right?" he said.

"Stand by the boss and the boss will stand by you," the chef said.

"We're coming through," Wilson said.

"We've got knives," the chef said.

"And an apple corer," the porter added.

Wilson turned to the dog-handler and gestured him forward.

"We've got an Alsatian," Wilson shouted. "Pickles, go get the bad men!"

The dog-handler unleashed the animal. Pickles leapt forward. The chef reached for a tray on the table behind him.

"And we've got eight pounds of prime fillet steak," he screamed.

He tossed it onto the floor. Pickles slavered, bared his teeth and lunged towards... the steak. An uneasy silence descended on the kitchen. Except for slobbering sounds as Pickles enjoyed the best meal of his life.

I inched towards a set of shelves close to the door. And in one smooth movement grabbed a bag of self-raising flour and hurled it at the chef. It hit him full in the face and exploded. Four pounds of flour filled the room like a snow storm. The place looked like a winter wonderland. The chef staggered and dropped his meat cleaver. Pickles roused himself from his steak dinner. He decided the porter's leg would make a tasty dessert and sunk in his teeth. The porter screamed. He stumbled sideways and knocked the carving knife out of the sous chef's hand.

Wilson hollered: "At 'em."

The constables charged forward and locked fists with the kitchen staff. A knot of struggling bodies surged around the room. Men cursed, screamed, cried out in pain. A plate smashed on the floor. A pile of saucepans overturned with a crash. Cutlery from an upturned drawer slid to the ground with a sound like shrapnel on a slate roof.

Flour dust choked the air. A white mist filled with flailing arms and legs was the last image I saw before I slipped out of the back door into the mews.

Darke was at the far end of the mews.

He was trying to get a car key into the lock of a sporty-looking red Lotus.

I glanced behind me. There was no sign of Freddie Barkworth. I clenched my jaw with frustration – we were going to miss great pictures.

Then I sprinted towards Darke. He was still struggling with

the key.

I was ten yards from him when he opened the door.

Five yards as he slid into the driver's seat.

Two yards as he slammed the door.

I reached the car as he started the engine. I tugged at the door but it was locked. Darke's head turned towards me and he bared his teeth in a triumphant grin. He knew he was going to get away. To escape justice. Then his focus was back on the car controls. He put the Lotus in gear. I moved forward and leapt on to the bonnet. Pressed my body against the windscreen so he had no forward vision. I could feel the engine throbbing smoothly beneath me and the beginnings of warmth as the carburettor glowed hot.

From inside the car Darke screamed something. It was a deep feral roar of fury that echoed off the walls of the mews. I could feel the vibrations come up from the gearbox as Darke shifted back to neutral. He depressed the accelerator until the engine was revving so hard the bonnet was shaking. He was trying to intimidate me with the power of the Lotus.

He shouted: "I'll kill you, Crampton. You won't be the first."

In response, I thumped on the windscreen. The gearbox crashed as Darke thrust the car into first. The engine revs deepened. The exhaust growled like a bear as the car sped forward. The acceleration was frightening. I clung onto the windscreen wipers. Continued to press my body against the windscreen.

Darke slammed his foot on the brake. The Lotus skidded to a halt. I lost my grip and slid from the bonnet. My head thumped into the cobbles as I hit the ground. I lay there dazed. For a moment, the only sensation was the acrid smell of burnt rubber from the tyres. Then my mind refocused and I realised Darke was backing the Lotus up the mews. He stopped and revved the engine, harder than before. He leant forward so that he could see me. He drew his finger across his neck in a cut-throat gesture.

I heard the gearbox squeal angrily as Darke forced the car into first. And then the Lotus was racing towards me as I lay prone on the ground.

I scrambled to my feet. Lost my footing on the slimy cobbles. Regained my balance. Leapt to the side. The Lotus's wing mirror brushed my arm as it raced by.

I watched in dismay as Darke hurtled towards the exit and freedom.

And then the car's brake lights flashed red.

The tyres squealed on the cobbles.

The Lotus's rear-end fishtailed.

The engine stalled.

The car juddered to a stop.

The exit was blocked by Freddie Barkworth's Hillman Minx which had just pulled into view.

Barkworth leapt from his vehicle with his camera already clicking. Seconds later, Wilson and two of the constables rushed from the Golden Kiss kitchen and ran towards me down the mews.

Wilson and the constables sped straight past me. They reached the Lotus and hauled Darke out. He didn't struggle or put up any kind of resistance as they handcuffed him.

As I walked up, Wilson was saying: "...anything you say may be taken down and given in evidence against you."

Darke's eyes had turned a deeper blue and seemed to be drawn closer together than usual. He looked at me with a smouldering hatred.

I said: "Have you any comment on your arrest, Mr Darke?"

He said: "I am completely innocent of any charges brought against me. I am a respectable businessman. It is impossible to bring any charges."

"We'll see about that," said Wilson.

I said: "Will you now be abandoning your casino plans for the Krazy Kat site?"

Darke said: "You'll regret the day you stuck your nose into my business, Crampton."

"I look on it as shining a light into the Darke," I said.

Anger flashed in Darke's eyes. He moved forward and raised his handcuffed hands to strike me. And at that moment, Freddie stepped forward and took his picture.

Two hours later, I was patched up, dusted down and sitting at my desk in the newsroom chatting over a cup of tea with Freddie.

I'd phoned in my copy from a telephone box opposite the Golden Kiss. Now I was looking at the headline in the night final. It read:

TYCOON ARRESTED AFTER CAR DRAMA

Freddie's picture was cut across six columns of the front page.

I said: "When I couldn't see you after I came out into the mews, I thought you'd disappeared."

He said: "As soon as we saw that Darke wasn't in his office, I knew he must have left by the back route. I ran back through the club, jumped in the old Hilly, raced it around the block – and the rest you know."

"So you were in the right place at the right time."

"Can't get the pictures if you're not." He grinned. "Can't spend the rest of the afternoon gossiping with you. I've got prints for tomorrow's paper to develop."

He stood up and loped off to the darkroom.

I pulled open my desk drawer and took out the copy of the Cross file which I'd collected from Figgis's office when I'd got back. I pulled my old Remington towards me and started to bat out the story about the strange disappearance of notable Councillor Derek Cross. It would lead the first edition the following day.

My phone rang and when I lifted the receiver a voice said: "If it isn't salty seadog Colin Crampton. Albert Petrie speaking."

My heartbeat quickened. After missing the interview, I'd

expected my name to be about as popular as *'Daily Express'* with the *Mirror's* news editor.

"I'm very sorry that I wasn't able to get to the interview yesterday – or warn you I wouldn't be coming," I said. The excuse sounded feeble.

"No need to apologise," Petrie said. "The story always comes first. And you landed one of the best crime stories I've seen in many a long year. I've got three of my finest bloodhounds from the newsroom working on our own follow-up even as we speak. But you seemed to have squeezed all the juice out of the story and left nothing for us."

"Does that mean the job offer might still be open?" I asked.

"'Fraid not, bold Colin." Petrie sounded disappointed. "As I mentioned when we first spoke, we needed to fill this post quickly. So we've appointed one of the other candidates – Charlie Youngman from the *Northern Echo*. Great journalist on land. Not sure about the sea."

"Thanks, anyway, for the call. I appreciate it."

"Don't mention it. And if there's anything I can ever do for you, don't hesitate to give me a call."

Could Petrie do anything for me? A little light bulb came on in my brain. I thought he could.

I said: "As you mention it, there is something. And it might also give you that follow-up on the Trumper story that your bloodhounds are hunting. There could be some more juice to squeeze."

"I'm listening."

We talked for another five minutes. After I'd put the phone down, I felt more satisfied than I had done since Ted Wilson had first told me the story of the disappeared golf man in Prinny's Pleasure. I decided I'd write the rest of the Cross copy later. I put on my jacket and went out.

I had an important message to deliver.

Two days earlier, I had left Mary Farnsworth in tears.

Now, she was smiling as she let me into her flat. The smile took years off her. I'd thought she was a young woman turning into an old woman before her time. But it seemed she just needed a fair chance to flourish as the attractive young woman she could be. And, after long years of waiting for her father's name to be cleared, the chance had now come. She led me into her sitting room. A copy of the afternoon's *Chronicle* was on the table. She glanced at it as we walked over to the easy chairs and sat down.

"I'm going to cut out the front page of the paper and frame it," she said.

"And hang it on the wall?" I asked.

"Oh, yes. I'll hang it somewhere I see it every day."

"That won't include the smallest room, I hope. My byline is on that story."

She giggled in a girlish way I would have thought impossible at our previous meeting.

I said: "You may have something else to frame tomorrow."

"You're writing another story?"

"Yes, this is a story that will run for several days. Besides, there are other aspects not involving Reggie that will eventually result in a trial, perhaps more than one. But it's not the *Chronicle* I'm thinking about. An hour ago, I was talking to Albert Petrie, the news editor of the *Daily Mirror*. He was fascinated when I told him about Reggie's heroism in France and how he didn't get the medal he deserved."

"The *Mirror* is interested in father's story?"

"More than interested," I said. "Tomorrow, the *Mirror*'s front page will carry the headline FORGOTTEN HERO. It will be the start of one of the *Mirror*'s famous campaigns to right an injustice."

"That means Reggie will get the medal?"

"Let's not jump to conclusions. The *Mirror* will be running a national campaign which will set out the facts, but it doesn't necessarily mean the War Office will agree to award a medal."

"I understand."

"But let's not forget that the *Daily Mirror* has a circulation of more than five million and its campaigns are highly influential."

Mary's eyes filled with tears and she began to cry.

But this time her tears didn't come from grief. It seemed as though she realised a great shadow had been lifted from her life and that justice was about to be done. She rummaged in the sleeve of her cardigan and found a handkerchief to dab her eyes.

"I'm sorry," she said. "Every time you come, I end up in tears."

"I'll remember to bring some paper tissues with me in future," I said.

"I better stock up if I know you're coming."

A fresh smile broke through the tears.

"I thought I better come to warn you because a journalist from the *Mirror* will be telephoning you in a few minutes. And a reporter will come here to see you tomorrow."

"I'll have plenty to tell them now," she said. "I can't thank you enough."

I grinned. "No need. I get paid for doing this."

I stood up, headed towards the door, turned back.

"But it's at times like this that I realise I'd do it even I weren't."

The telephone rang. Mary looked uncertainly from me to the phone – not sure whether she should see me out or answer it.

I pointed to the phone. "That'll be the *Mirror*. Better get ready to tell them the story of a hero," I said.

I walked back to the front door and let myself out. *That was easy*, I thought. *Now for the difficult bit.* I glanced at my watch.

I was due to meet Shirley in twenty minutes.

Chapter 22

I'd been nearly drowned by Trumper and run down by Darke.

Could what Shirley had in store for me be any worse?

It was half past seven by the time I walked into Clarence Square and made my way towards Shirley's flat. The skies had cleared of cloud and it had become a balmy golden August evening. There were plenty of people out enjoying it. A group of girls skipped with a long rope on the green in the middle of the square. An old man on a pushbike cycled home with a bag of fish and chips in the basket on the handlebars. A young curate with an armful of hymn books hurried towards the church. For them, at least, I thought as I trudged along, life was going on as normal.

But what about mine?

I walked slowly towards Shirley's flat trying to think how I could open the conversation. Should I start with an apology? Or try to explain why I'd acted as I had? Or simply greet her as though nothing had happened? I couldn't think of a thing to say. I formed words into sentences but they just jumbled in my mind. I was supposed to be a hotshot journalist and I was stuck for an intro. Perhaps, after the last few days, I was just too tired.

But I decided to do what I always did when I wasn't sure what to say. I would simply trust to the moment that I'd find the right words. So I strolled up to Shirley's front door and rang the bell. I shuffled from foot to foot while I waited for her to come.

She answered the door looking freshly bathed and without make-up, but more beautiful than ever. She was wearing a tee-shirt and jeans. The tee-shirt had a slogan printed on the front: "The answer's no."

I said: "You don't even know what the question is yet."

She said: "With you, I don't need to. You better come in."

She turned and led me down the hall. The back of her tee-shirt was printed with a single word.

"Probably."

We went into her tiny sitting room. It was temporary accommodation and sparsely furnished. A bit more than four walls and a floor, but not much. It had a couple of worn easy chairs, a small coffee table and a magazine rack. The curtains didn't meet in the middle. A copy of the *Chronicle*'s night final was on the coffee table.

"As instructed, I didn't bring my toothbrush," I said.

"You're learning," Shirley said.

"But I have no rooted objection to waking up in the morning with unscrubbed teeth – if it's in a good cause."

Shirley said: "If you're looking for a good cause, I can recommend Dr Barnardo's."

"Ding ding," I said.

"Becoming a bus conductor, are you?"

"No, just signalling the end of round one," I said. "Shall we retire to our corners and get fanned with towels by our seconds? Then we can come out fighting again."

Shirley shrugged. "I don't want to fight with you."

She sat down in one of the easy chairs. I took that as a signal that I could sit in the other one. Its broken springs pinged and twanged as I lowered myself into it. It felt like sitting on a pile of bicycle parts.

I said: "I see you've read the *Chronicle*."

Shirley glanced down at the paper. "Why do people want to read about such awful things?" she said.

She looked sad.

"Because they happen," I said. "Because they have a right to know. And because, this time at least, it has righted a wrong."

I told Shirley about my visit to Mary Farnsworth and how her father had been cleared of the suspicion of killing Mildred Trumper.

"That's good," she agreed. "But I suppose it's done your career no harm."

"Not exactly. I got the story but missed out on the *Mirror* job because I didn't make the interview."

"Of course. You stood them up before me. Two in one day. Must be some kind of a record for you."

"I'm sorry about that," I said.

"It's the way you are," she said. "That's why I'm moving on."

I paused to absorb that news. The ringing bells of a police car racing down Western Road broke the silence.

"You always said you would," I said at last. "Will it be in a month or two?"

"Sooner than that," Shirley said.

"Next week?"

"Tomorrow."

I stood up, walked over to the window and looked out between the gap in the curtains. I hadn't expected this. I thought there would be time for me to repair our relationship. I turned back to her.

"Does it have to be so soon?" I said. "I planned to take a few days leave next week. I thought we could make that Paris trip we'd been talking about."

"Go to Paris? So you could stand me up again while you're chasing some *fripon* down the *Champs-Elysées*. I don't think so."

"It wouldn't be like that."

"Wouldn't it? I'd rather not take the chance."

She stood up and moved towards the door.

"Now I've got to get on with my packing. I'm planning to catch a morning train to London tomorrow."

She left the sitting room and crossed the hall to a small bedroom. I followed her. A couple of suitcases lay open on the bed. Some clothes were already neatly folded in them. Others lay on the bed or on hangers from the picture rail around the room. Shirley took a pair of red slacks and deftly folded them. She put them in one of the cases.

I said: "It's against my own interests to offer to help with your packing."

"Against mine, too," Shirley said. "I don't want my clothes to end up looking like dish rags."

I sat on the edge of the bed. Faced with Shirley's imminent departure, I felt miserable. She seemed so determined. I couldn't think of anything to say that would be likely to change her mind.

"I'd like to think we'll be keeping in touch," I said.

"You can always write. Shirley Goldsmith, care of The World."

We fell silent while she sorted through some blouses, folded them and put some in one suitcase and some in the other.

I said: "When you've finished packing, could we have a final drink, perhaps even a late supper?"

"I don't think I'll have time," she said.

She picked up a brown jacket and started to fold it.

I said: "Shirley, I know you're angry but we could have more great times together."

She sat on the edge of the bed. On the other side of the bed to me.

"I'm not angry," she said. "Sure, I was spitting like an angry cobra when you stood me up. But when I'd cooled down, I knew you couldn't help it. You had no choice but to follow that story. Trouble is, cobber, you'll always be chasing stories – it's what you live for. And if I stick around, I'll always be waiting for you to return from the hunt. I'm not sure that I want to be the little woman who sits at home. In fact, I know I don't."

I said: "If I wanted a little woman, I'd have dated the midget from the circus."

"It's not a joke," she said. She dropped the jacket on the floor. "Now look what I've done." She picked it up again and started refolding.

I said: "There are two reasons why I want you to stick around. I think you're great company. I admire your adventurous spirit. And, finally, I think I love you."

Shirley stopped folding. She held the jacket half folded in front of her.

"That's three reasons," she said.

"Who's counting?"

Shirley put the jacket on the bed. She leant over her cases and fussed around the clothes she'd already packed. It was two minutes before she spoke. It seemed like half a lifetime.

"I've had a great time with you these past six weeks. Yes, I can't believe I've just said that after you've stood me up twice and got me arrested once. But even great times have to end."

"They don't have to."

"They do if you want to move on."

"And you are sure you want to?"

"That's what my guiding spirit tells me. It's like a voice in my soul which is telling me it's time for walkabout."

She picked up the jacket and started to refold it. I sat on the bed searching my brain for something I could say that would change her mind. But I couldn't think of any argument that would sound convincing. Slowly, I stood up, crossed the room, bent over and kissed Shirley on the cheek.

"Great travelling," I said.

"Thanks."

"Keep in touch."

"Sure."

"And join me for that last drink if you can later this evening. I'll be the only customer in Prinny's Pleasure."

"Have one for me. But you'd do that anyway."

"I'll see myself out," I said.

"See ya!"

I crossed the room and looked back. Shirley was staring at the half-folded jacket as though it held all the secrets of the universe.

I tramped back to the *Chronicle* offices through streets crowded with holidaymakers enjoying the warm evening.

I didn't share their joy. Shirley's news had sent my spirits tumbling. The stories I'd written for the paper in the last few days suddenly didn't seem so great after all. It was as though the adrenalin rush I'd been experiencing had gone into reverse. I thought about giving up my job and going walkabout with Shirley. But I didn't think she'd have me. In the mood she was in, if I decided to go west, she'd head east. It looked as though we had come to a final parting.

But I still had a job to do. I had to write a story about the bent property developer Septimus Darke and the corrupt Councillor Derek Cross. The story, based on the information in the Cross folder, was needed for the first edition tomorrow. So I plodded back to the *Chronicle*, dragged myself up the stairs to the newsroom and slumped down at my desk.

It was a tough story to write as most of the information in the Cross folder would now be evidence in a criminal trial. But I focused on the task and after a couple of hours had only about six pars to write. I was just thinking about how to wrap up the story's conclusion when my phone rang.

I picked up the receiver and an excited woman's voice said: "Mr Crampton, I'm so sorry to call you at work. It's Beatrice Gribble."

The Widow had never called me at the office before.

I said: "Mrs Gribble, is my flat on fire?"

"Mr Crampton, you will have your little jokes. No, your flat is not on fire. But I have just seen the *Evening Chronicle* with the wonderful news that that dreadful Darke man has been arrested."

"Yes, happened this afternoon."

"And this is all your doing, I'm sure. I see your name is on the article."

"Yes, it's my byline."

"I hope this means that the appalling Darke won't be buying Mrs Saunders' house and ruining our lovely square."

"I shouldn't think he'll be buying any houses for quite a time, Mrs Gribble."

She said: "Please call me Beattie. Now that we're such good friends."

I said: "Of course, Mrs Gribble. I have to go now as the crossword compiler wants me to help him with some clues."

"Clues?"

"Yes. One across: Beneficial cricket extra says farewell. Seven letters."

"What's that?" asked the Widow.

"Goodbye."

I rang off, turned back to the Remington and began on the last few pars of my story.

I'd just wound the last folio out of the typewriter when the phone rang again.

Ted Wilson said: "Well, catching the big fish this afternoon has certainly stirred up the hen coop."

I said: "But it hasn't done a lot for the world of mixed metaphors."

"Rogerson, the assistant chief constable has resigned. Official. The chief showed me the letter. And Superintendent Gregson left the office hurriedly after we'd brought in Darke in handcuffs. Word is he won't be coming back."

Ted sounded a little drunk. I could hardly blame him.

"A good result from your end. I'll mention it to Figgis in the morning and we'll run something on it."

"Yes, the place will never be the same again. With Darke out of the way, there are people here wondering where their next backhander is coming from," Wilson said.

I said: "Found anything worth knowing about in the search of Darke's home and office?"

"We've taken possession of three unlicensed handguns. There'll be charges on them and we also think one may have been used in the shooting of Bert 'I Always Pay' Biggins, the bookie who was killed up at the racecourse last year."

"So, Darke is facing a potential capital charge?"

"Yes. Not to mention whatever we find in the stack of books and records we're going through."

"This story will run and run," I said.

Wilson said: "There's more. I took a call from the Portsmouth police forty minutes ago. They've arrested Cross. Apparently, he was Brahms and Liszt and in a highly confused state. He'd boarded the Isle of Wight ferry singing 'Mademoiselle from Armentières'. Seems he thought he was fleeing to France."

"The Cross arrest is official, is it?"

"Yes."

"That means I'll have to rewrite my intro. But thanks for the information. See you soon for a drink."

I replaced the receiver, and rummaged through the completed folios of my story. I found the one with the intro, rolled new copy paper into my typewriter and started on the rewrite.

And was interrupted a third time by the phone. I snatched up the receiver and a familiar voice said: "Here's one in the eye for you." It was Jeff from Prinny's Pleasure.

I said: "What do you want? I'm trying to finish a front-page story here."

He said: "Someone's bought the Scotch egg. Remember you bet me I wouldn't sell it? That's a quid you owe me."

I said: "I'll pay you next time I see you. And, for what it's worth, I pity whoever's eating it."

"As it happens, it's a nice class of customer."

"You don't say?"

"Young lady. Tells me she comes from Australia."

I suddenly felt hot. I loosened my tie. I wiped my sleeve across my forehead.

I said: "Does she have blonde hair that curls round her face and eyes that are as blue as turquoise?"

"Looks a bit like that, I suppose. She's certainly got a healthy appetite for good grub. Talking of having the sausage roll as well."

"Jeff, listen. Tell her that I'm coming round to the pub right away and not to leave until I get there."

"Friend of yours is she?"

"Yes. And tell her something else."

"What's that?"

"Not to eat the sausage roll."

I slammed the phone down, got up and reached for my jacket. I scrambled into it. I was trembling with excitement. I took a few deep breaths to steady myself. This situation called for a calm approach. I needed to be in control.

I sat down again and pulled my Remington towards me. I started typing. Slowly at first, then faster. Rhythmically as the sentences rolled from my mind. The sharp clack of the typewriter keys hitting the carriage filled the silence of the newsroom.

I'd decided I would finish the new intro for my front-page splash before walking round to Prinny's Pleasure.

After all, if Shirley had just eaten Jeff's Scotch egg, she wouldn't be going walkabout for quite some time.

READ MORE CRAMPTON OF THE CHRONICLE STORIES FREE AT:

www.colincrampton.com

ABOUT PETER BARTRAM

Peter Bartram brings years of experience as a journalist to his *Crampton of the Chronicle* series (www.colincrampton.com). His byline has appeared in scores of newspapers and magazines on articles covering many subjects from film-making to finance. His 21 books on biography, current affairs and popular how-to topics have received coverage in newspapers as diverse as *The Daily Telegraph* and *Daily Mirror* – and he's promoted his work on radio and television. Peter's versatile range of work includes a radio play, a comic strip and a magazine serial. He lives in Shoreham-by-sea and is a member of the Society of Authors. His website is www.peterbartram.co.uk.

Acknowledgements

Many people have helped to bring Colin Crampton to life.

First, there is the team of publishers, editors and publicists at John Hunt Publishing. As a veteran of 21 books with other publishers, I am amazed at how efficient they are.

Barney Skinner created the wonderful website (www.colin-crampton.com) which made Colin seem real even before the book had found a publisher. Caroline Duffy realised in fine caricatures on the website the principal characters just as I'd imagined them.

Most important of all, my family has been a constant of source of love and encouragement through the long hours at the laptop.

Peter Bartram

At Roundfire we publish great stories. We lean towards the
spiritual and thought-provoking. But whether it's literary or
popular, a gentle tale or a pulsating thriller, the connecting
theme in all Roundfire fiction titles is that once you pick them
up you won't want to put them down.